Martin Blackbriar *and the* Necronomicon

T.C. Pendragon

Printed in the United States of America
First Edition
ISBN 979-8-7514537-6-3

Cover illustration by B. Jung
Typesetting by Annie Leue
longoverduebooks.com

Martin Blackbriar
and the Necronomicon

To: Brooke English
From: T.C. Pendragon

T.C. Pendragon

For my Mom

1 - THE BLACKBRIAR HOUSE
2 - WOODROW WILSON HIGH SCHOOL
3 - PALMER PARK
4 - BELVEDERE TEA
5 - HENRY FORD MEDICAL CENTER
6 - STRYKER MOTEL
7 - THE SILK SLIPPER MOTEL
8 - DETROIT OPERA HOUSE
9 - CULLEN FAMILY CAROUSEL
10 - PACKARD AUTOMOTIVE PLANT

.ONE.

CAPTIVE

When I woke up, I felt a terrible numbness that followed a bitter cold. I was held in limbo where none of my senses worked. Slowly, my senses returned, one at a time, as I ascended from oblivion to reality.

The first was my sense of hearing, which came back to me with a mechanical *scream*. It was like one of those late-night prison movies where the guard opens a cell with that terrible *ranking* sound, and you discover the TV is far too loud.

The violent sound made my head *ring*, and I wanted to grab onto something to steady myself. Anything to stop my body from vibrating like a tuning fork.

I tried to open my eyes to get a sense of where I was, but I felt fabric pressed hard against them.

A blindfold. Great.

Whoever tied this piece of fabric really knew what they were doing, too. It was latched on so tight, I could feel my pulse running *through* it.

As soon as I tried to move my arms, I felt myself hugging my own body. I wondered why I would do this. Then I felt it. Sleeves of fabric covered my arms. With a few struggles, I tried to free myself from my own embrace.

I heard the *clinking* of buckles just behind me. Metal on metal. With the sudden contraction of leather on metal, it was clear: I was in a straitjacket.

Soon, my attention was pulled toward my temples as they throbbed.

"You're awake," a young woman's voice rang.

It was a somber voice. One I recognized all too well.

The sound of this woman's heels began to *click click click*.

It didn't resonate through the room like a marble floor. But it wasn't a short click like a wooden floor. It was crisp, cold, to the point. Concrete.

"Nobody else has gotten this far," she added, "maybe because they only saw part of the picture."

A metallic *shing* sounded, and I felt the boa constrictor of the blindfold slowly release from my head. I looked around. At first, everything was hazy. All I could see was grey, yellow, red. All of it in a horrendous, nauseating blur.

I looked to the ground and saw concrete. A short victory, as I saw the source of the other two colors follow right after. It scared the hell out of me. My heart started racing.

Beatrice stood before me. I hoped there would be a glimmer of remorse in her welcoming, blue eyes. Remorse was there, but these weren't her eyes anymore. These eyes were a devastating crimson.

She had long hair that went to the middle of her back. Her

skin was white as a sheet, courtesy of spending far too much time inside. Too much time hiding from people that were hunting her.

Spending so much time in the shadows made her look like an eerie porcelain doll. Her dress was red and sleeveless. It was like the dress from *Beetlejuice*, gothic in form and extravagant in its color. I blinked my eyes. I saw blood dripping down her arms. And a splash of blood across her face.

She wore extremely high heels with a point so sharp they could be (and likely already have been) used as murder weapons.

Looking up, there was a large fluorescent bulb burning down on the two of us.

To Beatrice, this was like walking through dawn's first rays. To me, it was like being an ant under a magnifying glass. It seemed to brighten all shades of red. The red of Beatrice's daring dress and the red of her eyes.

I didn't dare look into her demonic eyes. While I knew they couldn't hurt me, it felt like they could stare into my soul.

I tried to say something, but I was stopped by another piece of cloth tied around my mouth.

"What?" she asked. "You gonna say something clever?"

Her eyes held a glimmer of hope as she strode toward me. She reached behind her, and I saw a blade *flash* into view. She made a slight cut. I closed my eyes and flinched.

When I found my courage again, I opened my eyes. I looked harder and saw Beatrice holding a switchblade in her hand. Behind her, there was darkness. The world was reduced to a pale circle of light surrounding us.

"Is that why you approached me early on?" I attempted. "You were hoping I wouldn't see what you were doing?"

"I had no idea who you were back then. I was just trying

to be friendly. But things got...complicated."

"Yeah, they did," I agreed.

"Probably not how you thought this night would end up."

"I might have pictured it differently."

"This was the best I could do on short notice," she offered.

"It could have been a lot worse, given the circumstances."

"Nobody's going to find us here. I think that's a good place to start. Not even you know where this place is."

"Have you been hiding here this whole time?" I asked.

"It's where I got started. Took a lot of trial and error before I could really master the spells. It's hard learning this magic on your own."

"I actually see more than you think," I commented.

"I know," Beatrice smiled weakly. "I still don't know how you do it. Magic?"

"Only the best kind," I answered.

"And what's that?" Beatrice asked.

"Intuition," I whispered.

Beatrice smiled, and a tear fell from her eye.

"I'm going to miss this. The two of us talking like there's nothing else in the world but us."

"Right now, there is nobody else. Beatrice, you can tell me what's really going on."

"I think you have a good grasp on the important pieces. I'm the one killing people. You're the one chasing me. And now we're at a...what would you call it?"

"Crossroads," I offered.

"You know, if I wasn't supposed to kill you now, I'd keep you around just so we could talk every day."

"What would we talk about?"

"Things we don't tell anybody else. Like we always do."

"How did you do it?" I asked.

Silence.

"Kill all those people and not get caught?" she said. "I think you know the answer to that."

"Just saying 'magic' is never a satisfying answer," I clarified.

"Like I said, you're the only one who sees the whole picture. Cops always look for stories they've heard before. Watchmen always look for traces of magic they've seen before. The key is to use something neither of them is expecting."

"From that book? The Necronomicon?"

"Books are where mages put all their dirty little secrets. But this one's special. I'm the only one who can use it."

"And now you're going to use it on me?"

"I wish it didn't have to be this way. But you've forced my hand. If you weren't so clever, we might have had more options."

I heard a phone go off. The ringtone was Marilyn Manson singing *This is Halloween*.

Beatrice looked annoyed.

"I wish I didn't have to do this. Be right back."

She left my small world for a moment and returned with a metal chair and her favorite red and black satchel. It had Jack Skellington's face on it, another haunting homage to *The Nightmare Before Christmas*.

The chair *screeched* into place as she dragged it across the floor. She sat down and met me at eye level.

"I did my best to hide what happened. But somehow, you were able to track us down. How is it a kid knows what to look for when cops and Watchmen don't?" Beatrice asked.

"Like you said, I was looking at the entire picture," I said.

"And I'm not telling you how I tracked you down. Once you know how to cover your tracks properly, you'll kill me and disappear again."

"Maybe. Or there's a chance that you'll be seen as useful once you talk," Beatrice pointed out. "You could help me get away with it."

"You're saying that it's not up to you," I said. "Who was that on the phone?"

"Someone of consequence. Someone who wants the answers a lot more than I do," she warned.

"How do I know you're not going to kill me? Or he won't the minute I tell you how I found you?"

"You don't know. That's what makes it fun. But he expects me to have answers for him the minute he shows up. He's not a patient man."

Silence.

"Just say something. Anything that could help me," Beatrice pleaded.

She looked down after she made the request.

"We knew that demons had something to do with it," I said, "but we were looking at it all from the wrong angle. You were clever enough to steal the drugs so the cops would be looking for the wrong people. And then the Watchmen would be looking for the wrong people."

"I thought I had you for a minute," she smiled.

"You almost did," I admitted. "You almost got me killed. And you would have had an even bigger advantage than you had before. Putting your friend in charge of finding you? That was clever. But it didn't end well for him."

"I would say 'thanks,' but you really fucked it up," Beatrice lamented.

"You get used to it after a while," I smiled.

Beatrice smiled back at me. The crimson cooled in her eyes, if only for a second.

"I just don't understand why you'd go to all this trouble."

"Because I lost something. I lost someone."

"But is it really worth all of the lives you took?"

"Was *Edmond's* revenge worth all the lives he took?" Beatrice asked.

"If I say 'no,' would you let me go?" I attempted.

Beatrice faintly smiled at that.

"'Now the God of Vengeance yields to me his power to punish the wicked,'" Beatrice recited.

"I should have known there was a reason you liked that book so much," I admitted.

"That's because it's the truth. When you survive something so horrible, you are given that duty and power for a reason," she smiled.

"You don't have to do any of this. I know the book belongs to you, but—"

"I'm the only one who can use the book this way. And I want to use it this way. Nobody's going to stop me. Nobody! Especially not you."

The Marilyn Manson phone sang again.

She gave me a look of fake embarrassment and shoved the cloth back into my mouth to keep me quiet. She turned her back, and I struggled as best I could to get out of my restraints. With my arms bound and my mouth gagged, there was no way I could use magic.

After several swift and unsuccessful attempts to break free,

Beatrice held a hand over the phone and looked back at me.

"Hold on, sweetie, I'm on the phone," she insisted in a condescending tone.

She swayed gently, making the slight black lining at the end of her scarlet dress fray from side to side. Whoever was calling had a lot to report.

I struggled again. I searched frantically for anything that could help, but there was nothing inside this circle of white light. But I did see a gleam on the floor. The gleam of wax symbols. I realized I was standing in the middle of a ritual. A big one.

Beatrice gasped.

I looked up. Her back was to me.

"What? Now? But I thought..." she started. Her voice was laced with bitter disappointment.

"That's not fair! You promised I could keep him alive if I..."

It seemed that with every stand Beatrice took, the person on the other end of the call cut her off even quicker. All the while, her posture of stubbornness melted more into defeat. Finally, she just listened for a solid sixty seconds and then turned to me, looking thoroughly upset.

"It looks like we're done. I'm just going to have to kill you now," she whispered.

She had a look of satisfaction that she was finally removing an obstacle from her path. But I also saw tears fall from her eyes.

All I could hear was my own heartbeat, rising to insane heights. What once were steady beats sounded more like the frequency of a hummingbird's wings.

I thought my heart would give out. But the whole time, Beatrice just looked at me with tearful, crimson eyes.

She withdrew the switchblade.

Shick.

My heart rate finally began to slow down to a brutal, steady tempo. Like the *ticking* of a giant clock.

Beatrice reached inside her gothic bag and rummaged through several items. I assumed it was a pile of cosmetics that could be traded for someone's car. Finally, the rummaging stopped. The entire world seemed to hold still.

The result of my investigation was at hand. What I'd been searching for these last months was finally going to be seen. Granted, I'd rather see this instrument of murder put into a plastic evidence bag instead of pulled out of Beatrice's bag. But that hardly mattered now.

Finally, a black leather book protruded from Beatrice's bag. It made no sound as it came into view, but it held an entirely new presence in its own right.

On the front of the book, there was a circle of runes set into human teeth, which surrounded a cracked skull. I looked closely and saw that the teeth and skull were genuine. Normally, I would have discounted this as another one of Beatrice's gothic items, but something about the book sent shivers up my spine.

The book also had a human spine that ran along the binding and seemed to *crack* and *slither*. I wasn't sure if it was really moving or if my mind was playing tricks on me. But whenever those horrible sounds appeared, they were closely followed by the smell of rot. But the worst part of the book was the skull adorning the front.

This wasn't a cartoonish skull; it was a horrifying visage that seemed to pierce through my soul, leaving no trace of anything other than despair as it passed through the air. This was it.

The Necronomicon.

Beatrice offered a very soft *shh.* I couldn't believe she was comfortable holding it, let alone using it for whatever purpose she had in mind.

With that, she bit into her fingertip.

Helch.

Then she smeared her own blood across a corner of the book. A wave of crimson spread from the bloody fingerprint and made the eyes and the runes turn crimson. The circle of human teeth *chattered* as they were met with red light, and an unseen lock opened with an eerie *clatch.* The skull's mandible opened, and the circle of teeth shifted. The eye sockets of the skull were glowing like candles.

She opened the book to the final page, and it was filled with crimson text. The smell of rot circled through the air as she scanned it morosely.

She let a weak smile grow across her face, but soon let it subside. She realized that it would be my name that she was adding to the incantation.

"It's all right. I won't make you suffer," she promised.

With a pinch of hesitation and an extended gaze into my eyes, she started reading.

"Beatrice..." I pleaded.

"*Interficere* Martin Blackbriar."

.TWO.

PUNK

"Martin Blackbriar!" Mrs. Fitzgerald shouted.

The intensity of the outcry was so loud, I heard it through my blaring headphones. A recently divorced and disgruntled chemistry teacher trying to get my attention. You'd think after the same routine for three weeks, she would finally leave me alone.

I lowered my headphones, and AC/DC blared into the room. It was the closest she had ever come to getting my full attention. But, being a seasoned educator, she was careful not to let her anger stay for too long.

"What?" I whispered.

The classic rock blared to the rest of the classroom.

"Are we straining your attention?" she asked.

"Ooooooooooh!" The class chimed in together.

I looked behind and saw everyone had stopped texting, passing notes, and daydreaming to tune into the action.

I looked back at Mrs. Fitzgerald. She regained her composure and was careful not to lose control again. She leaned over my desk, meeting me eye to eye.

"As it happens, yes," I said, unfazed.

Tap.

I turned the music off.

"I'll see myself out," I offered.

"Mr. Blackbriar, I don't think you have the luxury of ignoring my lessons anymore."

There was laughter and a chorus of jeers.

"Is there a problem with my work?"

"No. There's a problem with your attitude," she corrected.

"I didn't realize the state had grading criteria for attitude."

The color flushed from Fitzgerald's face, and her eyes became almost sympathetic.

"How dare you," she responded.

"Point out the obvious? That's exactly what you're doing to me."

"You are stepping on my last nerve," she warned.

"By listening to music and turning in perfect assignments?"

"It doesn't cost me a thing to put you in summer school."

"On what grounds?"

"You've been getting in fights, skipping class, and, when you are present, you manage to blow up the chemistry lab."

My ears went hot with embarrassment.

"I didn't *blow up* the chemistry lab," I corrected. "And I was the one who put the fire out."

"They may not have criteria for attitude, but property damage and assault are two pretty big strikes against you."

"Are we done here?"

"Not by a long shot. Having the right answers isn't enough

to succeed, Martin. You need to treat people with respect. And that is something you know nothing about," she countered.

I felt a hot rush of humiliation come across my face, and I wondered what I looked like for a moment. This dissipated when I realized I had no friends to feel embarrassed for me.

"Every second you spend reprimanding me is taking away from the education of everyone else, you know."

"I think this is a teachable moment. If you treat people like they're not worth your time, then they won't give you their time."

"Are you working a second job as a psychiatrist?" I shot back.

"You're lashing out because you're overwhelmed by..."

I didn't want her to finish.

Accusations of burning school property, starting multiple fights, and having no respect were compounded into a fit of rage. One that made my arm move on its own. I stood up and slammed my heavy backpack onto my desk.

THUD!

"Do you know how easy this class is for me?" I asked.

I unzipped my backpack and dumped all of the homework for the remainder of the semester onto the floor.

The papers and assignments that weren't due for weeks sprawled out across the room in a flood. Nobody said a word.

She reached down to the papers that landed near her feet, and she examined them. It only took a moment, but she seemed, begrudgingly, impressed.

"When did..." Fitzgerald began.

"Looks like having all the answers really *does* mean something," I retorted.

The tension broke when the speaker blared.

SHUH-IIIIIING!

"Martin Blackbriar to the principal's office," the speaker announced.

"Well, guess someone else beat me to it," Mrs. Fitzgerald said. "You're a very popular man this morning, Mr. Blackbriar."

"What? Did ya burn down the band hall, too?" one of my classmates called out.

Everyone laughed.

I looked down at the fruits of my lonely labor, wondering if this would be the last time, at least for a while, that I would be able to come back into this school. I lifted my unburdened backpack, looked around the room, and took a deep breath.

One book that managed to stay on my desk was *The Count of Monte Cristo*. I couldn't bring myself to leave one of my favorite books behind. I returned it to my bag and looked up.

"I'll see myself out," I finalized.

I turned to leave.

I opened the door and shut it harshly.

SLAM!

I turned my eyes toward the hall and closed them. There was a frantic sound of struggling and papers rustling the moment the door had closed.

It wasn't right to reprimand Mrs. Fitzgerald like I did. I replayed the scene in my head, challenging her in front of the class, dumping out all the assignments. I thought all those things would make me feel better, but they only made me feel worse.

I turned to the right and bumped right into someone.

"Oh!" a voice called.

"What the..." I started.

I tried to summon more words, but I was overcome with the intoxicating scent of vanilla. I took a step back and met

Beatrice Hawkins for the first time.

"Oh! Sorry!" she excused.

"It's no problem," I assured.

"I'm still a little lost. I'm trying to find Mrs. Fitzgerald's room."

I took a closer look at her and saw she was wearing a black dress with a silver skull belt. She had a look of wonder in her eyes and a bag with Jack Skellington adorning the front, thrown over her shoulder.

"That's quite a worn bag," I pointed out.

"Oh! Maybe it has seen better days, but it's my favorite. I'm a big fan of Tim Burton."

"So am I."

I put my hands in my pockets and tried to assess her. She looked at me with those blue eyes, and her sweet smile never left her face. I desperately racked my brain, trying to think of something to say.

"Mrs. Fitzgerald's room is right here, by the way," I said. "Tell her I sent you. She'll be thrilled."

I pointed behind me, but she didn't seem to care.

"Thanks. You must be Martin."

"Yes? How'd you know?"

"The intercom just called you to the principal's office."

"Right."

"You're funny," Beatrice smiled.

RUSTLE-RUSTLE.

I turned and realized I was leaving a warzone, and Beatrice was about to walk into it.

"I apologize in advance for the scene I caused in there."

"What happened?"

"A lot of my notes got scattered across the class."

"*Give me that!*" a muffled voice demanded through the door.

"Wow. They must be good notes," Beatrice smiled.

I smiled back at her.

She stared at me with those blue eyes, and I was entranced. For a moment, I forgot all about my destination and wondered what had happened to my world. I was saved by the same intercom that had condemned me.

"Aliena Blackbriar to the principal's office," it ordered.

"Shit," I whispered.

"What?"

"I got to go," I insisted.

"I'm Beatrice Hawkins. It was nice to meet you."

She held out her hand.

I looked at it for a moment and wondered why she was being so forthright.

I extended my hand.

"You have silver eyes," Beatrice smiled.

I felt my hand lingering. And I felt my pulse getting faster. Then I let go.

"Anyway, I really have to go," I insisted.

I walked to the main office without stopping. That was how everyone moved through the halls of this school. And "school" isn't even the right word. Woodrow Wilson was a forge. A cramped, hot, and unforgiving environment where the hardest of Detroit's juvenile offenders were molded into something else. It was up to each student whether they'd turn into something new here or fall apart. There was no place to fall from here.

No matter what the students turned into, the process was always rather violent. You could see it in the dented lockers and the cracked windows. You could hear it in the classrooms that were either quiet as the grave or bursting with some new fight. Finally, there was the smell. Something was always smoking in this place. You were never sure if it was somebody taking a few drags off a cigarette around the corner, or if it was the place getting ready to blow.

Passing by each room, you could see the students on their phones, the teachers taking a smoke break, or you might interrupt a dime bag exchange when nobody thought you were looking. If it were any other time, I would have been stopped somewhere. But nobody stopped me this morning. I was on my way to the one person everyone was still afraid of: Vice Principal Smith.

Normally, I'd feel my heart beating faster, or I'd contemplate what punishment I'd get when I arrived. But no thought was wasted on what was coming. Beatrice Hawkins was all that was on my mind, every step of the way.

THREE

UNUSUAL

"Hello again, Martin," Mrs. Davis offered.

"Hey, Janet," I nodded.

"A trip to the office every day, I think you just broke your own record. Congratulations."

I took a deep breath, savoring the relative lack of filth and cigarette smoke. I knew I was going to have to answer for what I did. Being called to Vice Principal Smith's office meant you were in serious trouble.

It was clean, small, and utterly silent. The only reprieve was the occasional *ringing* of the landline phone or the whispers of delinquents working out their story before they went in for judgment.

I looked at the small divider at the edge of Mrs. Davis's desk. I smiled as I saw a small peak of dark brown hair. Hair that was the same shade as mine. I heard the video games playing and knew only one person could have been insane enough to bring that contraband with them.

Ali.

Beep. Beep. Boom.

When I realized who was waiting on the other side of the divider, Mrs. Davis leaned in closer and lowered her voice.

"I know you've been having a rough year, but try not to let that rub off on your sister. She looks up to you, you know."

I closed my eyes and knew she was right.

"Thanks," I offered.

I rounded the corner of the desk and saw Ali sitting there with a Nintendo DS.

"You brought a DS to Mr. Smith's office?" I asked.

"I stole it fair and square," Ali insisted.

"Is that really the best way to start a meeting with him? By flashing contraband in his face?" I smiled.

"I thought you'd get down here faster."

"I was delayed."

"What could have possibly delayed you? You don't have a lot of redeeming qualities."

"Hey," I started.

"But you're punctual, at least."

"If it's so obvious that something's wrong, maybe you should try guessing."

Ali saved and turned off her game, then looked at me.

Click.

"I've missed these deduction games."

Ali crossed her arms and let a smirk appear on her face. She immediately caught wind of her first clue, and her eyebrows raised.

"Your ears are red," she observed.

"What does that mean?" I inquired.

"You met someone in the hall. I'm assuming she's running for prom queen and was handing out fliers."

"Very funny."

"You lock eyes with her, and she hands over a flier for some boring student organization."

I smiled.

"She's determined to help you, Martin. Get your grades back on track. But deep down, she's taken by your bad boy reputation and thinks, 'maybe, just maybe I could save him.'"

"That's enough," I chuckled.

"But it has to be during her scheduled school activities. 'I have a path going straight to community college, and I want to take him with me to the top.'"

"You're insane. But that is the most convincing argument anyone has given me to start considering college."

"Really?"

"Well, it was entertaining at least."

"So, it *is* a girl."

"Maybe."

Silence.

"You son of a bitch!" Ali celebrated.

She punched my shoulder twice.

WHAP! WHAP!

"Ow! Why is this such a big deal to you?" I grunted.

"You can't get in trouble if you have a girl watching your every move! Not to mention they won't have to lock up the chemistry lab anymore."

"I didn't start that fire."

"Sorry. You *allegedly* started that fire. At least you had the good sense to put it out."

"The fire wasn't that bad," I lied.

"Wasn't that bad? The second floor is melting into the first floor, Martin," Ali added.

"You're one to talk. Why are you sitting here?" I asked.

"I might have *allegedly* gotten into a fight with a few girls in fourth period."

"A few?" I asked.

"I know what you're going to say."

"You're popular."

Ali smoothed her lips to keep herself from laughing.

I looked down at her hands.

There were dabs of crimson on each of her knuckles.

"Jesus, those are some serious bruises."

"None of the girls around here know how to take a punch. They're an utter waste of my boxing talents."

"What could they have possibly done that warrants a left hook?"

"They were picking on that girl with cerebral palsy. Heidi."

"And you stood up for her," I concluded.

"You must think I was stupid for getting in a fight."

"I'm actually proud of you."

"I wish Mom shared your enthusiasm," Ali said. "She's probably going to kill us."

"At least you got a sweet DS out of the deal. And defended a girl from bullies. I lost all my homework and got another strike on my record."

"Okay, Mom is going to kill *you*," Ali rephrased. "But she loves *me*."

"Shut up!" I smiled.

"I haven't seen you smile this much in a long time."

"It helps when you have someone to laugh with you."

We looked at each other and grinned.

Mr. Smith's door opened.

Skeeeewwww.

"Come inside, both of you," he demanded.

Ali and I looked at each other and wondered what could possibly warrant us both going inside at the same time. Mr. Smith led us into his impeccably clean office and gestured to the two seats in front of his desk.

"It's come to my attention that the two of you have been causing problems."

Silence.

"I don't expect either of you to explain yourselves. But between the fighting and the incident at the chemistry lab, I can't help you unless you tell me what happened."

"Do you usually get students to confess with that gambit?" I asked.

Mr. Smith forced a smile.

"Martin, your attitude has already put you on the bad side of every teacher you've had. Don't bat my hand away when I'm trying to help you."

"Maybe he's right, Martin," Ali insisted.

"Fine," I replied.

I crossed my arms and waited for the offer.

"Martin, let's just get the full chemistry lab story on the table. Once and for all. Ms. Swann told me you were deviating from the assigned activity. That you were making some kind of compound?"

"I wasn't interested in what she planned."

"Okay. So what was your compound?"

"It was a combustible powder."

"And why would you want to make combustible powder?"

"Because it was better than drooling over a centrifuge."

"Martin. You were creating an explosive substance. And when you were told to give it up, you dumped it down the drain."

"It wasn't even combustible at that point. And I was caught with it as soon as it formed. I panicked and threw it instantly," I corrected.

"Then why was there a fire? Ms. Swann insists you threw a match down the drain, and blue fire shot out from all of the sinks in the lab."

"I didn't start the fire."

"Ms. Swann is going to assess the damages. But I'm telling you, another incident that causes property damage or risks hurting others will lead to a week's suspension."

My face went hot.

"I wish I could explain it better to you."

"Then try," Mr. Smith encouraged.

"It just didn't make sense. The flames were supposed to be orange with green bursts. Not blue."

"So, you *did* start the fire?"

I looked through the window behind Mr. Smith's chair, hoping to find something to take my mind off of this interrogation.

As he began to ask Ali similar questions, I saw a man dressed in black smoking a cigarette. He was staring directly through the window at me. He was far off. Across the street. But something made him stand out.

"What the..." I whispered.

I tried to get a better look at him, but I heard Mr. Smith

raise his voice.

I took my eyes off the man on the street, and just as soon as my eyes fluttered back a moment later, the man was gone.

"Ali, you were fighting with Ms. Taylor. Again. And there are claims that you've stolen some items of personal property from her," Mr. Smith insisted.

"There must have been a dozen other girls in that room. And they were picking on Heidi. I don't know anything about stuff getting taken," Ali pointed out.

"I appreciate you looking out for another student, but there are alternatives to violence. If you had restrained yourself and come to me first, there wouldn't be any need to have you come here."

"Alternatives. Like what? Sitting back and watching?"

"No. Not sitting back and watching," Mr. Smith insisted.

"I don't know what you want from me, sir," Ali concluded.

Mr. Smith curled his lips inward and gave a defeated sigh through his nose.

Ali leaned to the side and tapped my arm.

"Can you believe this guy?" Ali asked.

I smiled.

Mr. Smith's eyes shut, and his eyebrows shot up in resignation.

"You two have had a chance to say your piece, and I'll just have to make peace with that."

"Are we excused?" I asked.

"No, you are not," Mr. Smith answered. "It breaks my heart as an educator to see you two throwing your gifts away. I expect Martin to do something like this, but *you*?"

Ali looked at me and then back at Mr. Smith.

"We're doing our best to give you the best education we can, but we can't help you if you refuse to cooperate."

"Then what do we do?" Ali asked.

"I've already spoken with your parents. We've talked about giving you an educational experience that would be better suited to your needs."

Silence.

"It seems you two need to weigh your options. But the decision is yours, and I want to give you as much time to reflect on the last couple of weeks as you need. But keep in mind, if this behavior continues, you may no longer have a choice in the matter."

"Are we done here?" I asked.

Silence.

"Yes, we are," Mr. Smith concluded.

"Thank you for your time," Ali nodded.

We got our bags and left the office.

"Want to walk to fifth period?" Ali asked.

"Sure."

"You seemed really upset about the chemistry lab."

"It just doesn't make any sense," I explained.

"How so?" Ali asked.

"I was in the middle of making the compound, and it was basically just sand. You couldn't make it catch fire if you put a match to it."

"Then do you have any idea how the whole lab burst into flames?"

"Who knows what kind of gunk they have lingering in the bottom of those sinks? I've seen people throw dime bags in there before."

Ali gave a slight laugh through her nose.

"Funny how they never seem to notice that, but they have eagle eyes when we screw up. But why are you so hung up on this?"

"It just doesn't make any sense."

"That you were called to the office?"

"No. It's what happened right before I dumped it down the sink."

"What happened?"

"I was getting some salt ready for an experiment, and it turned blue without touching anything else."

"Blue? Are you sure?"

"Yeah. It was electric blue. I thought it was just the glare coming from the window, but I held it up by the light, and it somehow got even brighter."

"That's... odd."

Ali began to slow down. The hallways were still empty, and the faint echo of our footsteps made me realize we still had some time before the bell rang.

"Then what happened?" Ali asked.

"Ms. Swann demanded to know what I was doing, and the compound got even more blue."

"And then it blew up?"

"I dumped it in the sink without thinking. Then I realized how bad it would look, so I turned the sink on and let it wash away. I thought it was gone. But then Regina lit a match for the Bunsen burner and threw it into the sink right after whatever it was I flushed."

"Then every sink shot up a column of blue fire?"

"Yeah. It caught on the ceiling, and everybody ran out. I was next to the fire extinguisher, so I tried putting the fire out."

"And?" Ali asked.

"It took a few tries to get the thing to work, and I told myself, 'dear God, just let this work.' The foam that came out was blue and rubbery. And the flame was drawn to it. Like a magnet."

Ali held still for a moment like she heard of this before.

"You're thinking of something," I observed.

"That sounds kind of like what happened to me."

"Please tell me you didn't light Liz Taylor on fire. Or put her out with blue sludge."

"No, but something like that happened to me."

"What happened?" I insisted.

"Well, Liz was harassing Heidi, and I just wanted to shut her up. Then she starts going off on this rant, only I don't hear her anymore. I just want to throw one good punch and shut her up for good. Then I made a fist, and my hand felt...strange."

"How so?"

"Like it was fuzzy and boiling. If that makes any sense."

"Fuzzy *and* boiling?"

"Yeah. And I looked down and saw that it was starting to turn red."

"And that's when you threw a punch?"

"No. I turned to Liz, and it was like someone else punched her. But I could feel it."

"I bet everyone went quiet after that."

"They did. Then I grabbed my stuff and left."

"That is strange."

"What do you make of all this?"

"How should I know? I'm just as freaked out by this as you are."

"Martin, something weird is happening to us, and you

know it."

"Should we bring this up with Mom and Dad?"

"They're going to hear about it anyway."

"That we got in fights and started lighting up chemistry labs? That's not what happened!"

"We don't know what happened."

"Well, we better figure this out. Because those girls aren't going to stop pissing me off, and you're not going to stop irritating your teachers."

"How do you know that?"

"Because that's how cliques and teachers work."

"How dare you point out the truth?" I smiled.

Ali smiled.

"Maybe they'll take us away to Xavier's School for Gifted Youngsters."

"Who'll do it? That random guy in black outside the office?" I asked.

Ali looked at me, bewildered. I must have returned the same look. I wasn't even sure I saw him. It was like admitting to a hallucination without thinking it through. But we both saw the same thing. And now we had proof of it through each other's reactions.

"Wait. You see him?" Ali asked.

"Yeah. Tall guy. Black trench coat. Edward Van Sloan vibe."

"Did he smoke a cigarette?" Ali asked.

My mind flashed back to him, and I remembered the faint gleam of orange at the end of his face when he stared back at us. That image of a stern face illuminated by orange light had appeared many times the last few weeks. Only now did he come into the forefront of my thinking.

"Yeah. Come to think of it, he's been around for a while, hasn't he?" I contemplated.

"Whew. I thought I was going crazy. He's been hanging around the bus for the last couple of weeks," Ali explained.

"When did you first see him?" I asked.

Ali took a deep breath and tried to remember.

"Remember when we both had those nightmares? I dreamed I was being chased through the woods. Then there were a few flashes of light. And when I woke up, there were scratch marks all over my room," Ali recounted. "It was the next day. He was standing about ten yards away from the bus."

"And I had a dream that same night. I was in a house I didn't recognize. There were three flashes of light, and when I woke up, I found burn marks all over my room. I think I heard a baby crying, too. And I smelled...ether."

"That was the first time I saw this guy. Right after we had those nightmares. I'm sure of it," Ali nodded.

I contemplated the timeline.

"Was he there for the other weird things that have happened?" I asked.

"Well, I saw him when I was walking into school, and I heard some *cracking* noises behind me."

"Cracking?"

"I saw him behind me, and I was freaking out. I ran into the building, and the weeds were growing like crazy all through the concrete behind me. It was like I was watching years of weeds growing in a matter of seconds!"

"You sure they weren't like that before? Woodrow Wilson High isn't exactly known for the quality of its grounds."

"There were maybe just a few patches of weeds when I saw

him. And when I turned back, it was a jungle."

"All right. Look. We just need to get home and try to work this out."

"Should we take the bus?"

"We'll be safer together. How about we duck out early from both of our classes and meet up behind the gym? Then we'll head home from there on foot."

"All right. I'll duck out and meet you there."

.FOUR.

ALIGNMENT

"At least no one followed us home," Ali pointed out.

"But I was expecting Mom to get back at 7:00. She didn't say anything about a double shift at the hospital. Plus, she's never late for *Wheel of Fortune.*"

"And I've been sending her and Dad texts every hour since we got home."

"It's almost midnight! What the hell is going on?" I demanded.

We tried to get some semblance of normalcy back. But with every passing hour with our parents gone, nothing worked. We kept a watchful eye on the street to see if the Dark Man was outside. We took shifts to eat and lay on the couch. But that didn't work, either. We were even more high-strung than when the day began. With no recourse, Ali said it first.

"Let's talk about this," Ali started.

I threw myself into the family's aged leather couch. The

insulation of my cushion began to spill out onto the floor.

"The Dark Man. He isn't a cop, but he knows where to find us," I started.

Ali's fingers formed a steeple. She leaned forward, trying to work with the data I'd supplied her.

"He may work for a boot camp," Ali suggested.

"A boot camp?" I asked.

"Yeah. Some people transport troubled teens to the nearest boot camp. Kind of like kidnapping, only it's sanctioned by the government."

"I can always count on you to cheer things up, can't I?"

"Hey, you wanted my opinion, and I'm giving it to you."

"How about a scenario that doesn't involve kidnapping?"

"Fine," Ali conceded.

I rubbed my forehead with my thumb and forefinger to collect myself.

"Look, things are just intense right now. We don't know where Mom and Dad are, but we don't have to worry. Just because they aren't here, that doesn't mean something bad happened."

"Then what could have happened?"

"Maybe they're running late."

"Them? Running late?" Ali doubted.

"It's possible," I offered. "Who is this guy anyway? What could you see on him?"

"Tall, lean, and dressed like Van Helsing," Ali reiterated.

I looked at Ali, realizing she was right.

"The 1931 version," she clarified.

"That's not enough. We need a name."

"It sounds like the kind of thing you would go for, with your Dungeons & Dragons books and all."

"If Mom and Dad don't come through the door in the next five minutes, I'm calling the cops."

Silence.

"What are we going to do if they don't come back, like, ever?" Ali asked.

For a dreadful moment, we looked at each other and wondered if we were on our own. And there was no way of knowing if this would be permanent or not.

VROOM!

Ali and I shot for the window and looked through the blinds. The Dark Man was in our driveway. A heavily damaged Ford F-150 rolled up, and he made his way to the other side of his truck. For a moment, our hearts sank. Then our parents came out of the passenger seats, and we felt relief flood back into us.

Mom ran to the house. I rushed to the door in response, deactivating the brass lock.

Krun!

Our front door screamed open as the rust was forced off the hinges. Mom came charging in first. She had her arms outstretched and tears welling in her eyes.

"I'm so sorry! I was told to stay away until it was over, but I just couldn't wait anymore!"

Mom's tight hold made us feel safe again. When we stopped shaking and let out the last of our shuddered breaths, we realized what she said.

"You were going to let us stay here alone until he showed up?!" Ali demanded.

"It's not what you think," Mom insisted, "it's really complicated."

"A guy in a dark suit has been stalking us, and weird stuff

has been happening all day. I think we deserve an explanation!"

Mom looked at both of us with sympathy.

"This is a complicated time," Mom explained. "Believe me. I know what you're going through. The only reason we stayed away was because we were required to by law."

"This guy is with the cops?" Ali asked.

"His name is Dorian. And he's a Watchman. Not the kind of policeman you're used to. He works for people who look after kids like you. Parents can't be present for his arrival."

"For his arrival? For kids like us? What are you talking about?"

Mom looked to the ground, like she was hiding something.

"Not everyone is as lucky as you are, Martin. You have to trust me when I say that Dorian, your father, and I all have your best interest at heart."

She embraced us in a hug that was so intense around the neck I was sure I'd lose consciousness if she kept it up.

"Mom! Please!" I grunted.

"I'm sorry!" she repeated.

She let us go.

"What the hell is going on?" Ali gasped.

The door opened again, and our dad came into the room. His cane was *thumping* on the ground like it always did. I had never been happier to hear it.

"I couldn't stay away, either," Dad chimed.

He looked at us with a compassionate smile and made his way to his favorite armchair. He had sweat beading down his forehead. He clearly exerted himself significantly, just to be here.

After he eased himself onto his heavily padded seat, he let out a sigh of relief. Then he looked at the two of us and gave a faint smile behind that silver briar patch of a beard.

I looked outside and saw Dorian rummaging in his truck.

"You mean you know what's going on?!" Ali shouted.

"Well, Christ, you could have told us something ahead of time!" I insisted.

Under normal circumstances, Mom would reprimand me for using the Lord's name that way. But it looked like she was going to make an exception.

"We're sorry we couldn't tell you anything sooner. But we didn't even know this would be needed until these last few weeks. We needed to be sure, and so we called him," she explained.

She sat down in her armchair across from Dad. She removed her favorite fairy earrings, placed them in the bowl next to her, and interlocked her fingers. This was her way of telling us something hard.

"Mom, what is going on?" Ali asked.

"Dorian is an old friend," Mom explained.

"Then why didn't you ever mention him?" I asked. "I've never met him, never seen a picture of him. I never even heard his name until now."

I looked out the window and saw Dorian closely examining every house on our block and both ends of the street.

"Because we never thought you'd have to meet him," Mom admitted.

"We could tell that something was going on with you two," Dad explained. "And so we called him to get a consultation. He said he could help. But when we explained everything, it got... complicated."

"We have to tell you the truth now," Mom concluded.

"What truth?" I asked.

"Martin. Ali. Everything that's been happening to you two

is happening for a reason. We're not sure what the reason is, but you two are being carefully watched because we want to protect you," Mom explained.

"What are you saying?" Ali asked.

Mom and Dad looked at each other.

"We honestly never expected this would be a problem. It normally happens when you're an infant. But we saw that nothing was happening, and you were living a normal life. But now that it's happening as teenagers, we had to get some extra help. So we could tell you the truth. Now that we know what we're dealing with."

"Okay. What *are* we dealing with?" I asked.

Mom took a deep breath and centered herself.

"You two are the Witch and Wizard," Mom answered.

Silence.

"What is this? Some kind of scare tactic?" I attempted.

"Martin. We know that things must be very scary right now. And we know you've both gotten into a lot of trouble lately. But we're serious," Mom concluded.

"If you know what's going on, why the hell weren't you here?" Ali asked.

Silence.

"We weren't supposed to be here. The law says that the guardians of children like you can't be present during the Alignment."

"But you came anyway," I observed. "And what law?"

Mom had tears forming in her eyes.

"I couldn't let you two be alone," Mom whispered. "I had to be here."

"We had to be here," Dad added. "No matter how much

we trust Dorian."

"If you trust him so much, why haven't we even seen or heard of him before?" Ali asked.

"Because, when you were born, you didn't show any potential for magic. And Dorian didn't want to risk exposing you to that. We all agreed it was better if you didn't know about magic at all," Dad continued.

"But something changed," Ali pointed out.

"In most cases, power like yours takes years to develop. But this isn't a normal case."

"This is why everything has been so strange lately?" I asked.

"Yes," Dad answered.

Mom raised her hand and her eyes focused intently on her palm. Ali clutched the couch as the room began to shake lightly. The smallest of tremors made our furniture shake, the picture frames sway, and dust creeped out from the cracks of the floor above us.

Mom's eyes transformed from warm brown to a calculated blue. In the same moment, we watched as the veins on her hand and wrist began to illuminate in the same brilliant shade, and a small light emerged from the palm of her hand.

It was like an infant star, floating gently and innocently in our home. It radiated an azure light that made everyone in the house feel more at ease.

"How did you do that?" Ali asked.

Mom made the light retreat back into her hand, and all of her familiar features returned.

"You asked me a long time ago what it was that I did in the hospital. I told you the truth, but I omitted certain details," Mom admitted.

"You mean you've been healing people with *that*?" Ali said.

"Yes. It may not be perfect, but it does buy cancer patients a couple of months. With continued exposure."

"Kids, we know this is a lot to take in, but you can trust Dorian," Dad said. "He's here to help you."

Ali and I looked at one another.

"We warned him that you two were very observant, but he didn't seem to take my advice. We're sorry he scared you."

"There's also a lot to decide in the next couple of months, but there's no right or wrong answer. You just have to choose what's right for you," Mom added.

I took a deep breath. I wasn't sure if I was ready to hear another piece of advice.

Knock-knock-knock.

We all looked at each other, and Mom got up to answer. She opened the door, and I could feel a familiar presence come into the house. Each steel-toed footstep made me feel as though my warmth was being stolen from my body. I looked up to see Dorian.

He was wearing the same dark suit, had a five o'clock shadow, and had his hair combed back carefully across the top. The sides of his head were cut shorter and held the first inklings of silver. Despite all the earlier smoking, he didn't have a cigarette between his lips now.

His amber eyes pierced through me. They were stern at first, but they softened the moment I maintained eye contact. He looked exhausted. Like he came on a long journey to get here. He smiled and closed his eyes.

He finally let out a shuddered sigh as though he had been waiting for this moment for a long time. Then he turned to

Mom and Dad.

"Eva. Robert. I hope you were able to get them off to a good start," Dorian smiled. "It looks like we have everything we need. And we weren't followed."

"Good. And thank you for allowing us to be here," Mom nodded.

"What the hell is going on?" I demanded.

Everyone looked at me.

"There's a lot to work out," Dorian said. "But tonight, we're going to focus on the essentials."

Dorian turned to Ali and me.

"I do apologize for causing you any anxiety these last few weeks. But as soon as the signs started appearing, I had to keep as close an eye on you two as possible."

"That's why you were stalking us?" Ali asked. "Because weird stuff has been happening?"

"I had to keep a close eye on you. For your own protection."

"We don't need protection," I insisted.

"You've both gotten into fights, and it's a tough school to begin with," Dorian said. "And then I heard about the chemistry lab."

Normally, I might've laughed or at least rolled my eyes, but I kept quiet after Dorian's last point.

"How much have your parents told you?" Dorian asked.

"Well, apparently, we're the Witch and Wizard. Whatever that means," I said.

"That's normally how we begin these conversations. But this is a special occasion," Dorian said.

"Should I order a cake?" Ali asked. "And did our parents really have to be out of the house for this?"

"Not everyone is as lucky as you two," Dorian said. "Some parents have done horrible things when they find out their children have these kinds of abilities. We prefer to keep the secret of magic with people who actually practice it, especially among families."

"So the law is to keep abusive parents away?" I asked.

"Not everyone takes the news that their children are magical very well," Mom said.

"Okay. Now that we're all together in the same room, violating the magical laws, or whatever, what are we going to do?" Ali asked.

The tension in the room lessened, and we were all thankful for it.

"I came here to assess you two and to ensure that your parents' reports were accurate," Dorian insisted.

"The reports about us and what's been happening to us?" Ali asked.

"That's right. There's been a lot of strange occurrences plaguing your lives lately. And since you two have a track record of getting into trouble, it was bound to happen soon," Dorian expanded.

"What's that got to do with anything?" I asked.

"Magic can form when you are in places of great stress. Unfortunately, your high school is teeming with stressors that cause your powers to activate and lash out in ways they're not meant to," Dorian elaborated.

My mind flashed to the chemistry lab.

"It's a lot to take in. But there has to be something that's happened that you can't explain," Dorian prodded.

"I don't know," I resisted.

My mind flashed to the powder and how it changed color.

"You're thinking of something," Dorian pointed out.

I looked into Dorian's eyes and realized I might finally get some answers.

"I was in the chemistry lab, and some powder turned blue in front of me. I couldn't explain it. I even threw it down the sink. The entire lab caught fire. Then I put it out with a fire extinguisher, but with a weird blue substance."

"I thought this would happen," Dorian said. "We've reached the perfect time to perform the test."

"What test?" Ali loathed.

"It's called Alignment. I've done hundreds of these tests, but none of them had circumstances quite like this one. And special circumstances warrant special exceptions."

Dorian looked to my parents.

I turned to Mom and asked a burning question.

"Why did you come back if it was against the law?" I began. "If it's as risky to break as you're saying..."

"Fuck the law," Mom swore.

Nobody said a word in response.

"Mom!" Ali exasperated.

"It's a stupid law," Mom insisted. "It should have been done away with years ago. But now that we're here, let's let Dorian conduct the test."

Dorian took off his black gloves and revealed that his hands were riddled with tattoos. Archaic tattoos that looked nothing like pictorial symbols or gangland ink. If anything, they looked like ancient runes.

He reached into his coat and produced an aged pewter goblet. It had small nodes on the sides, where gems would generally go. But in place of treasure, there were symbols. None of them were familiar to me.

"You're kidding, right?" I asked. "You stalk us for weeks, and now you expect that a cup is going to solve our problems?"

"It won't solve all your problems. But it is a place to start," Dorian clarified.

"I'll bite," Ali conceded. "What's with the cup?"

"This goblet may look like an ordinary cup to you, but it's going to answer a lot of questions," Dorian explained.

"How?" I asked.

"I used magic to turn it into a filter. It's a method to find Alignments. We've been using this method for centuries."

I examined the goblet carefully.

"The only thing you changed were the symbols?" I asked.

"That's right," Dorian smiled.

"What kind of writing is that?" I asked.

"It's an ancient language. Druids used it for some of the oldest symbols we can find. Of any magic. But we've modernized it and made it into a generally accepted form of magical language."

"And we're supposed to do *what* exactly?" Ali asked.

"You don't have to do anything dangerous," Dorian explained. "Just offer some of your magic to the goblet, and the runes will make it take on a form we can assess. Then I can find out how best to help you both."

"Seems complicated," Ali resisted.

"You've been doing it by accident for some time now. Martin did it in the chemistry lab. And you did it at the front entrance to your school. The plants you grew into a jungle."

Ali smiled and bit her lip in embarrassment.

"I know you're skeptical. But there's nothing to be afraid of here. You've both done this before. And this is the safest place you could possibly do it now."

"You first, Martin," Dad insisted.

"Place your hands on the goblet and focus," Dorian instructed.

"What exactly am I focusing on?" I asked.

"Imagine the goblet is filling up," Dorian added.

I extended my hands, touched the goblet, and closed my eyes. The image of the goblet was in my mind, and I saw it filling with water. A light flare of deep blue emerged.

Wharf.

I looked down and saw a blue flame at the center of the goblet. It held still for a moment, then swirled inside the cup. I feared that the flame would grow, but it transformed into a swirling liquid of the same color. I gasped but kept the image of filling the cup in my mind, and, in mere seconds, it was filled. As the liquid kissed the brim of the goblet, an unexpected draining sensation emerged from deep within the center of my chest.

Schwooooo.

I gazed into the deep blue substance, transfixed. But I saw there was a light coming from the bottom. A starlight glow gleamed onto the ceiling.

"Whoa," I whispered.

"Taste it," Dorian insisted.

I didn't know what would come of it, but my parents didn't show any sign of embarrassment or concern. If anything, they looked like they already had an answer and wanted me to confirm it.

"Okay," I said.

I took the cup and took a cautious sip.

"Alcohol," I reported.

"This means you're a Magician," Dorian said.

"I thought I was the Wizard?"

"A Magician is someone who derives their power in magic from practice, determination, and persistence. The main component of any training you will engage in is time. The longer you focus on a spell, the sooner it will come to you."

"And a Wizard?"

"That's someone who has more than just magic. They can access magic that nobody else can. You're also a sort of paragon. That is represented by the light at the bottom of the cup. Out of all the practitioners of real magic, you've been blessed with incredible potential, someone who can learn any magic. No matter how difficult, ancient, or dangerous. The kind of magic that the other Alignments can only dream of."

"What other Alignments are there?"

"In total, there are six types of practitioners that you can be: Magician, Alchemist, Evoker, Thaumaturge, Sorcerer, or Warlock. It's a time-honored approach to learning about magic, so we know the approach best suited to teach you. And it shows a lot of what you can learn along the way. Clearly, you fall within the Alignment of Magicians. And the light at the bottom of the cup means you're the Wizard. There may be thousands of Magicians, but you are the only Wizard in the world. There's only one Wizard and one Witch in the world at a time. That's what makes them so distinctive."

"And what does that mean, exactly?" I asked.

"Magicians are determined and have a great affinity for transmutation. You'll learn through a great deal of practice, and you will be able to learn a great deal of magic if you apply yourself. Illusions are especially intuitive for your Alignment."

"A cup of booze doesn't make a whole chemistry lab burst into flames," I pointed out.

"True, but a Magician has the ability to transmute a substance," Dorian explained. "Your manna must have altered the properties of whatever you were working on in the lab. My guess: your manna fused with it, made it waterproof, and made it twice as flammable."

"Wait. What do you mean by 'manna?'" I asked.

"It's pure energy that comes from every living thing. It's the source of all magic. Where there is magic, there is manna. No exceptions."

"Let's say I believe you for a minute," I said. "How can it do all of that? Make powder glow? Catch fire?"

"It's a common issue. If you don't tell your manna what to do, it's desperate to find a function. So, it latches onto whatever it can and mimics the magical properties of everything it touches, no matter how small."

"I literally just held it up to the sunlight and threw it down the drain."

"The sunlight made it react to heat. Maybe it became illuminated or combustible. And the reaction with water made it buoyant or waterproof. Maybe both."

I remembered how the powder turned electric blue, how I held it up to the sunlight, and how a match chased it down the drain.

"Does that mean using magic will be more...manageable?" I asked. "Will I be able to go to class without burning the school down?"

"You'll be fine as long as you keep your emotions in check

and don't get overwhelmed. Your manna will take on whatever form you command it to. And it will get a lot easier with training. You just have to relax. Besides, it sounds like you put the fire out just fine by yourself."

"Just have to relax? You do realize I'm in high school, right?"

Dorian smiled.

He raised an open hand above the cup and clenched his fingers into a fist. In a flash, the liquid and starlight vanished.

"Now that you know what you're dealing with, I'm sure it'll become less frightening. But we should really focus on Ali right now."

I took my leave and leaned back on the couch. Ali shot up from the edge of her seat.

"Arms out. Focus on filling the goblet," Ali recited.

She extended her hands, touched the goblet, and closed her eyes. A light flare of crimson emerged.

Wharf.

I looked inside the cup and saw a red flame at the center. It held still for a moment, then swirled inside the cup. As it began to fill, more colors emerged. Green, blue, pink, and yellow. In seconds, it filled again. As the liquid kissed the brim of the goblet, the same glow emerged from the bottom and cast beams of light onto the ceiling. Ali immediately took the cup and drank from it.

Schwooooo.

"It's so sweet!" Ali gasped.

"You're a Sorceress," Dorian announced.

"Details, please," Ali insisted.

"It means that you already have a couple of skills under your belt, and you learn magic best by watching others perform it. It will be fairly straightforward if you stay within your comfort zone, but trying anything outside of that will prove to be a challenge."

Dorian looked directly at Ali.

"Sorcerers are intuitive and usually have a great affinity for natural magic, or Green Magic. You'll learn by following example, and you will be able to learn a great deal of magic, in your specialties, if you apply yourself. Elemental magic comes especially easy for your Alignment."

"Is there any reason you're having us try these wacky cocktails?" Ali asked.

"Simple. Now that we know how best to approach this for both of you, you're going to start training with me tomorrow."

"Training?"

"It's for everyone's benefit," Dad insisted.

"If you train with Dorian, he'll be able to keep an eye on you two. And you'll have less incidents with your magic," Mom added.

"How do we know this 'training' is going to work?" I demanded.

"You're not the first Witch or Wizard," Mom explained. "And you're certainly not the first person to take the Alignment test."

"And this is the next step?" Ali asked.

"That's right. If you just follow my instructions, we'll be able to carve out a path for the two of you that's safe and discrete," Dorian promised.

"Why is our safety an issue?" I asked.

All the adults in the room looked at each other warily.

"Magic is a dangerous force," Dorian said. "If you don't know how to control it, it'll be the same as giving you a firearm that can go off at any time."

"Fair point," Ali conceded.

"After school, I'll take you to Palmer Park. You'll get a better sense of what magic is all about. I'll pick you up after class."

"Ok, so we know our categories. What is everyone else in this room?" I asked.

"I'm an Evoker," Dorian started.

I took a moment to remember the whole list he gave me.

"Evokers are volatile and have a great affinity for necromancy. We learn best through rigorous instruction, and we achieve mastery of many spells quickly. But the rest of magic outside our specialties is a real uphill climb. We're one of the few Alignments that can handle demonic magic without suffering the worst of its damaging effects, as our Alignment puts us through a great deal to begin with."

Dorian held his hand over the glass and made a fist. Ali's colorful drink was gone, and the light show had disappeared. He waved his hand over the glass, letting out the slightest dust of purple dance along the rim. A purple flare emerged, and it turned into a midnight black liquid. The drink was reflective, like dark glass.

"And Mom?" Ali asked.

Mom leaned forward and made a fist. The cup emptied, and she opened her hand once again. A flare of azure appeared, and as it swirled, the liquid produced tiny plant seeds. They turned into a golden color and began to grow along the edges of the cup.

Greeeeeeelch.

Small, luminous spores floated out of the glass and gently cascaded across the room. We all enjoyed the lights for a moment, but I saw a pained look on my mother's face. She took a shuddered breath and clenched her fist again. The lights disappeared from the room almost as soon as they appeared.

"This means I'm a Warlock," Mom said. "We rely on emotions to fuel our magic and have a great affinity for empathic spells. We learn through addressing our emotions and gaining strength from them all. Good and bad. Healing is a specialty we share. Almost universally."

"Wow," Ali whispered.

"This is always a lot to take in. But remember, the only person who sets your limits is you. Don't let yourself set a limit just because someone else has done it for you. Not only are you talented kids, but you've been dealt a hand most people never will," Dad said.

"What was your Alignment test like?" Ali asked.

"Your grandparents didn't even want me staying in the house when they found out what I was," Mom said.

"They didn't want you to accept magic?" Ali asked.

"None of us knew I even had it in me," Mom said. "It was the first case of magic we'd ever seen in the family. And they thought I was some kind of monster."

"That's horrible," I grimaced.

So there was a reason I'd never heard of my grandparents outside of their first names. And that's the reason why Mom never wanted us to try and contact them. I had only ever seen one picture of them, and this explained why it was locked away in the basement.

"They found out and tried to...get rid of me. Multiple times. And that's because I was sure they'd understand if I explained it to them. But I broke the law multiple times to try and tell them the truth. But they wouldn't see me again. Then a Watchman came and made them stop hurting me."

I wanted to ask more questions, but the pain in my mother's eyes made me pause. Ali must have seen the same thing because she decided to change the subject.

"Does Dad have an Alignment?" Ali asked.

"I'm not blessed with the same gifts you are," Dad said. "I never had any magic."

"Then how did you find out about Mom?"

"Before we got married, she was given a choice to either tell me the truth or keep it a secret. She chose to trust me."

My parents reached out to each other. They clasped hands and smiled. The pain in my mother's eyes and the warmth in my father's made it clear that I had a secret to keep. I had to be careful who to share it with, if I ever did.

"Who offered you that choice?" I asked.

"The Order," Dorian explained.

"Who are they, exactly?" Ali asked.

"They're responsible for keeping order between mages and ordinary humans."

"The Order is responsible for order," Ali said with a nod. "That checks out."

"They're also responsible for my presence here tonight," Dorian explained.

"Dorian works for the Order," Dad explained. "They run things. They're the government."

"And Dorian is a High Watchman," Mom added. "It's kind of like the FBI."

"Why all the secrecy then?" I asked. "If Mom and Dad were trusted with keeping the secret, then why did Dorian have to stay out of our lives?"

"It was a choice I made a long time ago," Dorian said. "But now that you are the Witch and Wizard, it's forced my hand. There's no avoiding the truth for you two anymore, and so I'm here to help you in any way I can."

"But how did you know that we were the Witch and Wizard?" Ali asked.

"Anyone who is born with magic can cast magic later in life. It's very often that infants exhibit some form of magic without meaning to. But if we don't see magic within the first year of a child's life, then it will not appear."

"And two kids casting spells when they previously couldn't, that probably gave us away," Ali deduced.

"We also knew that a new Witch and Wizard would appear at some point around this time because, when a Witch or Wizard enters adolescence, that's when the transition becomes apparent," Dorian said. "The Order has been looking everywhere to find the Witch and Wizard. And now we have."

"Why have they been looking everywhere recently?" Ali asked.

"Because everyone who practices real magic knows that the Witch and Wizard would be appearing soon. There's only one of each of them in the world at a time. And it takes longer for their magic to come to the surface. Usually, in adolescence, their powers appear. Everyone else, of every Alignment, gets their powers at birth, if they get them at all. And we've waited fifteen years."

"But what are you basing this on?" Ali asked. "You had to wait fifteen years since when, exactly?"

Dorian's face went hard, and his eyes were soft for a moment.

"The Witch and Wizard are reincarnated," Dorian explained.

"Reincarnated?" Ali asked.

"How'd the last Witch and Wizard die?" I asked.

Dorian clenched his fists as he recounted the horrible events.

"They were both assassinated. The last Wizard died fifteen years ago, on December 30th, 1994. The Witch went into hiding. And then she was killed one year later, on October 31st, 1995."

"Our birthdays," Ali whispered, meeting my gaze.

Ali and I looked at our parents, and their heads were hung low. I could tell that recounting the loss was opening some old wounds.

"Who'd want to kill them?" Ali asked.

"We have our suspicions. Whoever it was had incredible skill with magic. They'd never be able to kill them otherwise," Dorian recounted.

"Are you sure we're safe?" I asked.

"Until we know who is after you, I can't promise anything. I have no doubt that whoever killed the Witch and Wizard last time is after you now. And the sooner we hone your abilities, the sooner we can find out who it is," Dorian elaborated.

"Does anyone else know about us?" I asked.

"The only people who know about you are myself, your parents, and a few select members of the Order."

"But if the signs were that obvious to you, someone else might know what we are," I objected.

"Luckily, the incidents surrounding your most recent magic can be chalked up to conventional answers."

"But they may have seen us? How do we know your presence here is safe at all?" I asked.

"I'm here as a precaution. There are people who use magic for terrible things. Every creature you've heard about in movies, books, and urban legends is real. Demons, necromancers, vampires. All of it. Since you two are the Witch and Wizard, they will come after you if they find out who you really are. And they'll do everything in their power to stop you from reaching your potential."

Silence.

"I know this is hard to hear, but I have been charged with guiding you in how to use your magic and to keep you both safe. I will not fail."

"Hence the stalking," Ali said. "Can't wait for that to continue."

"If you two think that accidentally lighting a lab on fire is scary, then I hesitate even to tell you the dangers that are waiting out there," Dorian said.

"We are very grateful that you've come here, Dorian," Dad interjected. "And we're also grateful you've agreed to look after our children. But perhaps now is a good time to leave."

Dorian looked at my father and nodded.

"Thank you for coming by, Dorian," Mom said.

"It's not like he's going to be very far away from us," I pointed out.

"You're right. He will stay near this house to ensure we don't have to worry about unwanted guests. In the meantime, you can expect to see him closer to your school, and he will conduct your lessons in magic from here on out," Mom explained.

"Thank you for your time, Blackbriars. We'll be in touch."

Dorian saw himself out.

Mom shut the door behind him.

BAM.

"It's going to be fine," Mom assured. She placed one hand on my shoulder and the other on Ali's.

"I just don't know what to make of it all," I said. "Neither of us do."

"Get some sleep, if you can," Dad insisted. He pulled himself up and made his way to the kitchen.

I looked at Ali and we both went upstairs to our rooms. I looked out and saw that Dorian was walking along Marlowe Street.

I half-expected him to disappear the moment he moved behind a tree or when a car drove in front of him. But it was darkness that carried him out of sight.

·FIVE·

CHANGE

"You're a hard man to reach," Beatrice said.

It was the end of the final period. Beatrice was leaning against the locker next to mine. She smiled at me, and I couldn't help but get lost in her soft blue eyes. I think I was running on three, *maybe* four and a half hours of sleep. All night and all morning long, I replayed Dorian's warnings in my head. Everything he explained to us. It was only now that they finally stopped. All it took was a smile from the new girl.

"How did you find me?" I asked.

Beatrice pointed to her locker: 246.

"Mine's right next to yours."

"Small world."

"It sure is! I was hoping you could show me around."

I smiled.

"I've got some stuff going on, otherwise I would."

"It doesn't have to be *right* this second. We could always

do it some other time."

I felt my ears turning red.

"Look, I had a rough night. And I have a lot on my mind."

I reached for my last book and saw a small, blue mist come off of my hand. I quickly put on one of my gloves to keep it from view.

"I just came by to give this to you," Beatrice said.

She produced a bundle of papers from her Jack Skellington bag. Some of my upcoming assignments for later this week. Including my book report on *The Count of Monte Cristo*.

"Thanks," I smiled and took them from her.

"I don't think the others will be giving them back to you."

"Well, it's really considerate of you to give this back."

"And I was also hoping I could get some help from you directly."

"Really?" I asked.

A sudden flash of light behind Beatrice drew my attention to the end of the hall. I looked past her shoulder. There was a crowd of kids with iPhones, eagerly observing the situation.

"How so?" I asked, eyes still on the scene.

"Tutoring. Fitzgerald said I should contact you, since you probably don't have anything to do. You know, with the homework being done."

"I'm no tutor," I objected.

"You know, for someone who understands multivariable and destroys school property, you're surprisingly funny."

"I can't tell you what's on the test. I'm not a mind reader," I responded. At least I was pretty sure that wasn't true.

"I just want some extra help. Want to meet up in study hall?" she asked.

She sounded eager. As though I couldn't possibly refuse. I closed my eyes, trying to find a way out of this.

"I got someplace to be after school, but we'll talk about it later."

"Or we can text."

Beatrice produced an iPhone of her own. The case was adorned with Tim Burton characters. She handed me the phone, and I punched in my number.

"There," I said.

I smiled and handed the phone back to her.

Beatrice bit the corner of her lip and sent a text.

BUZZ.

I looked down at my flip phone. I rarely received any texts.

"Hey! This is Beatrice."

"We'll be in touch," I promised.

BUZZ.

I looked down and saw a number I didn't recognize.

"It's Dorian. I'm out front."

I looked up at Beatrice.

"I got to go."

"Text me?"

I made the long journey to the north entrance several minutes before any bell told me that school was out.

Dorian was sitting in a clunker of a truck. It would have been a decent vehicle had it not been ripped to shreds in multiple spots. The fender was missing, claw marks covered most of the doors, and the windshield was cracked diagonally across the center.

Looking inside, I saw that there was smoke swirling around Dorian. He was wearing the same dark suit. It was hard to catch the greying hair amid the cloud of smoke. But the lines under his eyes got darker and heavier. He clearly didn't get any sleep after our last meeting.

"Are you trying to hide your grey hair behind that cloud of nicotine?" I asked.

"Don't be a smartass," Dorian said, "we have a lot of ground to cover. Let's get going."

I threw my backpack onto the backseat and rode shotgun.

My phone went off.

Buzz.

"You need to get that?" Dorian asked.

I flipped my phone open and saw Beatrice had already responded.

"Thanks for agreeing to help out! I'll see you real soon!"

"No, it's fine," I dismissed.

"Okay," Dorian answered.

"Nice truck by the way," I said. "Can't beat the 2009 Ford F-150. Tough as nails."

"You know a lot about cars?"

"I live in Detroit. It's a prerequisite."

"Fair point."

"Aren't we going to pick up Ali?"

"I'd rather work with one of you at a time. Your mom is picking her up today. We're headed to Palmer Park."

"Palmer Park? Wasn't the whole point of you being around to be sure no one saw us using magic?"

"The first lesson is to make sure you can keep your powers concealed," Dorian explained. "Casting blue vapor isn't exactly subtle."

I opened my glove to find that it was still releasing an

azure mist.

"Your magic is going to want to find new ways of expressing itself. It's making up for lost time."

The drive to Palmer Park was brief, and in no time, we were pulling into the lot.

"We're here," Dorian announced.

He parked the truck, slammed the door behind him, and began walking to the nearest park bench.

"We're not going to be feeding birds, are we?" I asked.

"No. We're just going to take a seat."

"Fair enough."

Dorian took a seat on a bench that had a dozen crushed cigarettes lying around the front. A series of old autumn leaves scattered among them, and the lightest touches of frost encrusted their edges.

Had this been any other time, I would have liked to get a sketch of the leaves in a book or stick around for a while. Maybe contribute to the pile of smokes. But this wasn't the time to take it easy.

"I'd hate for us to be in the wrong place and the cops arrest us for a drug deal," I said.

"They're not going to arrest us," Dorian replied.

"How else would you explain a grown man sitting with a teenager and both staring straight ahead on a park bench?"

"Just say I'm your uncle."

"Fine," I smiled.

I took a seat beside Dorian.

"Look out there and tell me what you see," Dorian offered.

Silence.

I stared ahead and took in the scenery.

"A tree. An old man reading a book. And what appears to be a Border Collie and Australian Shepherd mix."

"You know a lot about dogs?"

"Sure. Dad's side of the family used to breed hunting dogs," I said with a smirk.

"He told you that?"

"It's my family history. Not sure why you think that's so surprising."

"I just find it interesting what he tells you and what he doesn't tell you," Dorian explained. "They're closer than I thought."

"You were his hunting buddy? I suppose it's possible. It must have been before you took up smoking."

Dorian smiled.

"This isn't the time for jokes, Martin," Dorian said. "A tree. An old man. A dog. That's what everyone else is going to see, but there's a whole part of the world that only people like us are going to be able to experience."

"Magic," I said.

"It's more than just pulling rabbits out of hats or sawing women in half. At its center, magic is the control of energy."

"Energy?"

"Most people look at one part of magic, but fail to see the whole. But all magic, big and small, concerns energy taking a variety of forms. Energy has a base form that runs through everything. And I do mean *everything*. The energy that makes electricity zap, fire burn, and people live is all derived from the same source. It is all magic. But as mages, we have the ability to take that power and to morph it into any form we want."

"I thought I was a Magician? And you were an Evoker."

"Mage is a general term for someone who practices magic. The Alignment test just goes a long way in showing what kind of a mage you are. And the best methods for casting spells and teaching you how to hone your abilities. Not to mention it proves beyond a shadow of a doubt that you are, indeed, someone who can practice real magic."

"Spells," I whispered.

"If you're going to really understand what I'm talking about, I'm going to have to show you in greater detail."

"If this is anything like your cup trick...."

"It's not a trick," Dorian corrected, "it's *Awakening*."

"Fine. *Awakening*."

"All right," Dorian began.

He held up his hand, and I felt a warm wave course its way inside my body.

"What are you—"

"Don't be afraid, this is a skill called *amplification*. It's the next step in developing your powers."

"What just happened to me?" I breathed.

"I sent a pulse of my own manna to you. If you're going to understand how magic works, you need to know the parts that make magic function. It's the same with chemistry. You can't fully understand the reactions without knowing the function of each particle. The pulse you just felt is to help you see everything in motion."

"Okay, that actually makes it easier to understand," I admitted.

"Martin, every living thing has some kind of magical center. We've been trying to unlock the mysteries behind this force for as far back as history can record. But the only universal term we can apply to it is the essence."

"Essence," I repeated.

"Yes. You have already felt it function many times before. You felt it when you were in danger, you felt it when you needed strength the most, and you felt it when you saw your sister for the first time."

"And you know this because...."

"The essence calls out to us in moments of heightened emotional excitement. When we feel like we're in danger, or we're on the verge of performing a grand feat, or feeling powerful emotions, we can't help but feel the warmth of the essence."

"That sounds a lot like a soul."

"The soul is the collection of all you are and will be. It's the part of you that remains when your body is dead. The essence dies with the body. It's the fountain that creates all magical energy and the heart of your magical circuitry."

"But where does magic really come from?" I asked. "The blending of the soul and essence?"

Dorian's jaw hardened, and his eyes softened for a moment, as he tried to think of a way to explain it.

"Every living thing has an essence. And your soul is the sum of everything you have done in your life. Good and bad. There are some mages who believe the soul directly affects your magic, and it is a reflection of who you are as a person. Depending on what choices you make every day, you eventually determine what kind of a mage you are because there are only six possible Alignments. And if you're lucky enough to be the Witch or Wizard, you will experience the seventh Alignment. Having the power to use magic can bring out the good or the bad in people."

I looked down and saw that the whole world had gone

darker. My body's nervous system seemed to be illuminated, and I saw blue bursting through it all. And at the center was a small marble that was brighter than the rest of my body put together. It was then that Dorian put his hand down and looked ahead as he did before.

A myriad of people soon began to pass in front of us. Moms with their children. Lovers clutching each other's arms. Working men rushing to their jobs. All of them had the circuitry running through them, all had a different color, and all had that same brilliant center. But none of them had the brightness that Dorian and I had.

"Wait. If the essence lives inside of every living thing, why can't every living thing use magic?" I asked.

"Not everyone is aware of magic, to begin with," Dorian replied. "Not to mention that without a proper Awakening, like the one I just gave you, most people would only feel it at erratic intervals. Moments like an adrenaline rush or out-of-body experiences."

I looked at Dorian with careful eyes. He was clearly a man who had dedicated a great deal of his life to understanding this system. If I was going to have a shot at making this bizarre power work inside of me, he had the answers.

"How do I find it?"

"Just take a few deep breaths and reach out to them. You won't harm them, I promise."

I took three deep breaths, each one dedicated to reaching deep within myself. At first, my breath was bated and only seemed to reach the cerebral portions of my mind.

I became disgruntled but took another deep breath and thought of the loving emotions I had for my family and even the mixed feelings I felt when approached by Beatrice.

Finally, I thought of the essence, the circumstances surrounding my new world, and I felt something buried so deep inside me, I was amazed that I could find it.

I found a tiny cavity in the center of my chest, no larger than a grain of sand, and I could feel its life pulsing through me. It was as though I had been holding my breath and only now came up for air. The entire world was tight around me, and I could see nothing. But like the haze that comes from breaching the water's surface, I opened my eyes to see the world clearer than I had ever seen it. And it was full of more secrets than I could ever imagine.

"Stay with me Martin, stay with me!" Dorian ordered.

His words were like a droning at first, but the repeating of his command saved me from becoming overwhelmed.

He broke through the barrier and pulled me back to reality. The entire world seemed darker, and I could see small glowing lights residing in each person that passed by me.

They came in righteous reds, glorious greens, and I looked down to my hands and saw a bursting blue. From my essence, I felt something akin to joyful sadness at finally being released.

"Don't be afraid, Martin. They can't see anything."

I turned to Dorian and saw that he was enveloped in a tightly focused, yet ferocious shade of purple. And that it was covering me, too.

"Why is mine so different?"

"Everyone has a different wavelength for their manna, but right now, you must give your essence a command. It's time for you to learn your first spell."

"What spell is that?" I asked.

"I'm using a *shroud* to keep any excess manna from flowing off of you that people can see. To anyone else, it'll look like we're just talking."

"Okay."

"Take deep breaths and reach into your essence with your mind. It'll feel like you're dipping a finger in a pond."

The calming image soon put my mind at ease, and I closed my eyes. I saw the essence again. It was growing more vibrant now that the pressure from its neglect had been lifted.

I tried to reach toward it, but it detected my intent. It resisted me.

I focused again on my cerebral self, then the emotional level, and then the mysterious level. I focused more intensely. My essence would yield to me.

It would accept me.

I felt the warmth, and then all of the wisps around me began to retreat until it was as though I became shrink-wrapped in them.

No longer was it a wild blue flame that threw itself around my body, but a tightly controlled hue of azure.

"Do you feel that?" Dorian asked.

I took deep breaths and felt as though a truck hit me for a moment. But after catching my breath, my heart began to slow down, and light, soothing cracks started to radiate through my bones. There was a pleasant pain that made me smile. I felt like I had accomplished something grand.

"Yes," I whispered.

"That is the next part of the Arcane Anatomy."

I gave Dorian a look, and he smiled.

"The parts that make up your magic in your body," Dorian

said before I could ask. "It's a system just like any other. It has components, physiology, and a job to do. Now that you have tamed your essence, it is bending to your will and giving you power."

"Really? That's all it took?" I chuckled.

The process had been difficult to accomplish, as it demanded a deep inner focus. But if this was all it took, I wouldn't be surprised if yoga masters were among the world's most powerful mages.

"No, you've only tapped lightly into the source. Now you need to recognize the part of your magic that extends just beyond its origin, unless you'd rather go home now. This is an intense experience. There's no shame in stopping for now."

"Not yet."

Silence.

"All right. What you're feeling now are magic circuits. The activating of the essence is what separates mages from regular humans. But in the case of these circuits, it's how many of these are active and thriving in the body that separates the amateur mage from the best."

"How many times have I seen magic right in front of me and didn't realize it?"

"I can't say for certain. But anybody who values the Old Law would have kept magic from you your entire life."

"They must have been good at staying hidden. Especially in today's world."

"People can tap into the essence by accident and do amazing things. But people tend to write it off as freak accidents or miracles. But if you're looking for a true practitioner of magic, those are much rarer than you might think. Magic circuits make an actual mage. And they take years of practice to create."

I looked at Dorian and saw something incredible. Every inch of the man was glowing like a Christmas tree. He was riddled with these circuits.

Granted, there were some gaps after my eyes had adjusted, but his hands, head, legs, and torso were alight with all of the same type of circuits that were beginning to awaken in me.

I looked down at my hand and saw the circuits. They were as feeble as the veins in wood from a fire that had long exhausted itself. The faint whispers of blue began to leave my hand as soon as they returned.

"No," I hissed.

"You're not going to get everything accomplished today, but we still have some ground to cover."

"Why is this happening?" I pleaded.

"Because you're a Magician. You always start with a small amount of manna and a lot of magic circuits, and then it'll build with practice and dedication."

"All right," I accepted.

"Now that you have accomplished that, we're going to come to the final part of our training for today. You're gonna learn how to handle a core."

"A core," I repeated.

"The core is similar to the essence in that it is a place where magic can grow and prosper inside of a vessel. However, the core is not a substitution for an essence. It's merely a temporary dwelling place."

"I think I need an example."

"My tattoos."

Dorian held up his hand. There were a series of luminous,

swirling pools of energy forming wherever one of the archaic symbols appeared.

"They're not alive," I said, thinking through his example, "they are not a source of magic. But they guide your magic?"

"You're catching on quick."

"I'm not so sure. I'm spending a lot of time finding out everything I knew about magic was wrong."

"You read a lot of fantasy books, Martin. Surely you've heard the word *enchantment* before," Dorian offered.

"Sure."

"The core is like an enchantment. It's a common law of magic that you can't create something out of thin air. You need to be able to manipulate the manna of the world and yourself if you're going to use magic."

"So, a core is like an artificial essence," I attempted. "It's where the energy can be held, but not created?"

"Exactly!" Dorian answered. "It's not easy work, binding manna to a vessel. You've had the luxury of not knowing what that's like for fifteen years, yet here you are feeling its effect on your body."

"I can do it."

"I'm sure you can. If you're able to find a way to sustain these kinds of anchors in something else, it saves you the trouble of subjecting yourself to more pain."

"That'll be nice," I said.

"And that's where spells come from. Spells are simply cores that come directly from your body and adopt another form. A fireball is merely a core with manna concentrating around the center. Then it takes on the property of extreme heat."

"Just like what Mom did," I whispered.

My mind flashed to Mom's spell and the star that emerged from her hand.

"Your mother had worked for years, decades really, to create that spell. It's done wonderful things for people but, like science, magic can only get you so far. There's so much of it we don't understand."

I looked at the sea of cruising lights. I knew that most, if not all of them, would go their whole lives without knowing what I just learned.

I blinked, and light came back into the world. Natural light returned to the shadows and doused the neon lights inside of everyone that passed by.

"That is the beginning," Dorian announced.

He rose up, and I felt my power beginning to drain and his shroud beginning to seep back into his essence.

"That can't be it!" I protested.

"That's as far as we're going today, Martin. I'm impressed you made it this far, but you'll wear yourself out if we continue beyond that."

"When are we meeting next?" I demanded.

"Two days. I still need to show your sister all of this."

"Bullshit. I can show her everything you just showed me!"

"Really? Go ahead."

I attempted to reach back to find my essence, but I felt a terrible pain radiate through my bones.

"Figured it out yet?" Dorian asked.

I thought about it for a moment and realized the only variable that changed from a few seconds ago was Dorian had substantially reduced his energy output.

"It's you!" I exclaimed.

"The only reason you could do so well is because I was here. Having a seasoned spell caster next to you is like having a battery connected to a light bulb; all of the wiring is there, you just don't have a power source sustainable enough to cast your own spells yet."

I took a deep breath to calm myself.

"All right. I can wait."

"Until then, I better get you home so you can get some sleep," Dorian insisted.

He reached inside his coat and produced a small, black book with a starburst illustrated on the front. When he handed it to me, it had a warm, ethereal texture that made me feel relaxed.

It was an old book, with creases on the front, drops of some unknowable potion dribbled across the bottom. Yet, for all its blemishes, it was wondrous to behold.

"Here's something you won't find at Barnes & Noble," I smiled.

"That'll help you get started," Dorian said. "It's one of my old spellbooks."

I looked up to him, and he almost looked wistful.

"Do you really think this will be safe to keep with me?"

"Books can be dangerous. Entering the mind of someone else can be a harrowing journey, if you're not prepared. But if you use its knowledge effectively, it'll carry you a long way when I'm not there."

"Thanks."

I followed Dorian to his truck and looked down at my hand. Somewhere deep down, there was a force that was just waiting to be unlocked. And this book would help me a long way in understanding what that power was.

"By the way, be careful of unexpected visitors," Dorian warned.

"What?" I asked. "When can I expect that little surprise?"

"In twelve days," Dorian promised.

.SIX.

COMPANIONS

"What did he mean? Twelve days?" I thought to myself.

I looked at Dorian's book. A section on levitation. Another on the laws of magic. But nothing mentioned twelve days. I'd read almost the entire book, looking for answers:

"'Familiars & Companions,'" I reasoned. "Last chance for an answer."

Familiars are allies to a mage that shares their manna in a type of bond. This bond runs even closer in the Witch and Wizard, but their case is an exception. Both the Witch and Wizard will receive a Companion within thirteen days of their first Alignment.

I turned to the clock—11:59 pm.

"Whoever this Companion is," I contemplated, "they're running out of time."

I stared at the clock, wondering if there had been some mistake. I was sure that it had been thirteen days since my Alignment. And this was the very last minute that it was—

Scraaaaaaaape.

12:00 am.

Something was clawing beneath my bed.

"What the hell?" I whispered.

I looked over to my nightstand. The faint green numbers of my alarm clock reminded me that the waiting period was over. There was also an aged lamp and a copy of *Faust.*

I reached for the book, but as soon as I began extending my arm, I heard a low and terrible noise somewhere between a hound's growl and a reptile's hiss.

FROWWWWWWWL!

The hairs on my arm shot up. My shallow breathing halted entirely. Every burn across my room flared up and made everything smell of sulfur.

Only something truly vicious could have made that noise,

and I wanted to be ready for whatever it was. I snatched the book from my nightstand—Faust by Goethe. I might have preferred the book just beneath it, *A History of Old Detroit*. That one was considerably heavier. But, either way, it was better than being unarmed.

"Okay," I attempted.

The entire bed began to *shudder*.

REE-TO! REE-TO!

FROWWWWWWWL!

"Dammit. I can do this!" I whispered.

I felt the cool leather of *Faust*'s binding and saw the soft, blue light of my window streaming down to the floor and the edge of my bed. I raised my book, ready for anything. I slowly eased my way to the front of the bed.

Creak.

When I looked down, I saw something far worse than I imagined.

I saw a tiny crimson man.

His back was turned to me, and I saw that his forked tail was gently swaying from side to side, as though he was waiting for someone to see him. All he wore was a cloth surrounding his waist made of material that was somewhere between snake's scales and raw calfskin.

His pointed, garnet ears twitched with every *creak* my bed produced. He turned around to face me.

I saw the charming yellow eyes of a devil, and my world stopped, right down to the dust particles that danced in the moonlight.

"You're him?" the demon asked.

He dusted his tiny, leather wings. His reptilian grin didn't subside. Not even for a second.

"What the fu—" I started.

He spread his wings and leaped up to the foot of my bed to meet me.

"You must be Martin Blackbriar," he grinned.

"What *are* you?" I demanded.

"My name is Alciel. And please, I'm not used to being interrupted."

"Are you... a demon?" I attempted.

"You really don't know much about magic, do you, kid?" he asked.

I shook my head.

"Let me put it this way," he started.

As he moved from one end of the bed to the other, he left eight talon marks. Four talons on each foot.

"Do you have to claw up my bed?"

"I'm going to be joined at your hip for a long time. One hopes. So you better get used to it."

"No offense, but did you actually come from hell?"

"Demons call it 'Gehenna,' but yeah," Alciel admitted.

He eased himself down, letting his tiny, three-inch legs kick back and forth like a child without a care in the world. I was still tempted to strike him with my book, but he seemed willing to answer my questions.

"How do I know you're not here to kill me?" I asked.

"Oh, please, you're hardly that interesting! Not to mention your soul probably tastes like crap."

"Then why are you here?"

"I'm here to be your Companion."

"I'm not sure I want a demon to be my Companion, Alciel,"

I declined.

"And I'm not sure you get any choice in the matter. That's how this works."

He threw his claws behind his crimson head, and he looked at me like he had to get used to something he hated. He gave me a bewildered look but resigned himself to explain further.

"You still don't know what you're getting into," Alciel said.

"Kind of hard to know when you insist on being so cryptic about it."

"You recently had an Alignment. Presumably, you also had an Awakening. I don't know what poor bastard was responsible for all that, but it looks like the floodgates have opened and put things in motion. This happens every time a Wizard is chosen. They get hooked up with a Companion. And your Companion is me."

"But why is this needed?"

"The Witch and Wizard get put through the wringer, and you have to connect yourself to another magical being that can cover your weaknesses. Especially since you've been walking around with no magical ability except for the last couple of weeks."

Alciel stared off in the distance for a moment.

"Think of me as a lantern you carry around in the dark," Alciel offered.

I contemplated what Alciel said. Still, every instinct told me to take *Faust* and beat him to death with it. But the more he spoke, the more I felt satisfied with his answers.

"You probably don't know this yet, but there's this wonderful thing called a *Familiar*. It's a friend that a mage shares their power with. And it helps them in times of struggle, especially when they first pick up their wands."

"I read that in this book," I interjected and held up Dorian's book.

"Oh, good. You actually have people that want to help you. Now I'm here to help you the rest of the way."

"You're here to help. But what's the difference between a Companion and a Familiar?"

"Witches and Wizards have to get a Companion. Everyone else gets a Familiar. If they want."

"What we have is mandatory?"

"Damn right."

"Who arranged this?" I asked.

"The Spectrum," Alciel answered.

He said it like it was obvious.

"I'm not following."

"I really have to explain everything, don't I?"

"Give me a break," I protested, "I just found out about this whole world two weeks ago."

Alciel chuckled at the last comment and had his hands on his hips. He offered a light chuckle as though tormenting me was a source of amusement.

"Okay," Alciel began. "There are three major entities that deal with magic: the Root, the Spectrum, and the Void."

"Okay."

"The Root is the source of all magical power. Some people even believe that the Root is some kind of god. On the other hand, some people think the Root is the source of everything that exists. Long story short, it's the purest and most singular raw source of magical energy anywhere."

"Interesting. Where is this thing?"

"No one is really sure. But there have been a lot of soothsayers that tried to pin it down. And they have defined it as a massive, glowing 'Root.' So that's what we call it."

"Okay," I accepted.

"The Spectrum is where you and I come in. Since the Root is the source of all magical power, that has to be captured, organized, and packaged in neat little containers. Every living being is formed as a result of the Spectrum. It's also where magic is given the ability to take different forms. Mages, mystical beings, all of it."

"And then the Void?" I asked.

"That's where it all ends. At least as far as we can see. Similar to how you humans believe energy is never destroyed, it just changes form. The Void is where the energy takes its leave. Every time a spell is cast, the raw energy of the Root makes the power, the Spectrum makes sure the body performs the spell correctly. In accordance with the laws of the universe, the Void cleans up after it. The Root. The Spectrum. And the Void. I call 'em the Triplets."

"That explains the setup. But why does the Spectrum think it's necessary for you to get mixed up with me?"

"I wish I had an answer for you, kid. But the truth is, those Triplets have a sick sense of humor. No one really knows how they operate or where they are. All we know is that they exist, and they're interested in how the magic of this world works, that goes double for people like you."

"Like me?"

"You're the Wizard, and you can't even light a candle with your powers right now. I'm here to help you get started. Make sure you don't fall on your face."

"You're the training wheels," I smiled.

"If you're fifteen and don't know how to ride a bike yet, I feel sorry for you. But the Spectrum is insisting you get started."

"How do I know you're not going to kill me in my sleep? I was warned certain people might want to use me and my powers for nefarious purposes."

"Don't get the wrong idea. I might be a demon, and I might be unhappy with this arrangement, but our essences are mingled now. In the 'if you die, I die' variety."

"Does that mean if you get a cut, I get a cut?"

"Our essences are mingled. Not our bodies. It will take some getting used to."

I realized I should text Dorian.

"Hold on," I requested.

Alciel sat still and looked around the room. I pulled out my phone.

"Some demon is here named Alciel. He says he's my Companion," I typed.

Whoosh.

A moment passed. I watched Alciel flap his tail and kick his clawed feet back and forth. He seemed to enjoy cutting up the foot of my bed and slightly annoying me while he waited. He oddly reminded me of a cat as his ears twitched.

Buzz.

"What does it look like?" Dorian inquired.

I examined Alciel for a moment and tried to come up with a succinct description.

"Like a classic little red devil."

Whoosh.

A moment passed.

Buzz.

"All right. Just keep a low profile until tomorrow. He's not going to hurt you."

I took a breath.

"At least you won't try to kill me," I mumbled. "That's worth something."

"Companions always show up thirteen days after a new Witch or Wizard performs their first Alignment. Always."

I shot up like a prairie dog at his last comment.

"That means Ali has one too!" I gasped.

I immediately jumped off my bed, but I was careful not to alert my parents.

"What are you so worried about?" Alciel asked. "This is a good thing. It won't hurt her, no matter what it is."

"It doesn't mean this isn't dangerous," I said. "She's not expecting to be bunking with a demon this evening, either."

"Oh, she should be so lucky!"

I turned left and worked my way down the narrow hall. I saw Ali's door was open.

Crunch. Crunch. Crunch.

I saw Alciel crawling up the wall next to me, like a spider. I looked back and saw that the wall was gouged up wherever Alciel left a trail. Each claw mark gave off a light *hiss* as it trailed behind him, and orange sulfur flared from the freshest tracks, like candlelight.

"Do you *have* to gouge up the wall?" I demanded.

"Oh yeah, sorry about that," he said. He pretended to look sorry until a big grin took over his face. "On second thought, I'm a demon. I'm never sorry."

He stuck his forked tongue out at me. It was soon followed by the scent of sulfur. I felt sick looking at his defiant smile. *If*

I got a denizen of the underworld, who knows what's waiting in my sister's room?

I crept forward. Moonlight shone into my sister's bedroom. I was ready for anything—a demon, a pixie, a giant.

"You really think the best idea is just to go charging in?" Alciel whispered.

"What else am I going to do?" I demanded.

"I think you're forgetting that I'm here to *help* you," Alciel reminded me.

"How would you do that?"

"You do realize there's a way to get the drop on someone who knows magic."

Silence.

I remembered Dorian's lesson in Palmer Park.

"Maybe you're right," I admitted.

I closed my eyes and felt the fear of my sister being in danger. I drew further within myself and felt fury. It was terrifying to feel it so vividly.

Finally, I felt the warm embrace of the essence. I reached down to touch it with my mind. As soon as I made contact, a pulse went outwards that forced my eyes and my mind to open.

I looked to my right, and I saw Alciel wreathed in yellow.

I looked down and saw I was flowing with blue.

"Nice job! Think you can see through walls yet?" Alciel asked.

"I can try," I stated.

I looked at the wall and saw there was a burst of red.

"That's got to be Ali," I reasoned.

"What's that in the corner?" Alciel asked.

"That must be her Companion," I reasoned.

I looked out and saw a small bundle of green.

"Looks like it's about as big as me," Alciel whispered.

The green light grew darker and pounced toward the red.

"ALI!" I called out.

I opened the door and saw a small, purple-backed, white-chested wolf puppy with red eyes.

She wasn't much larger than a loaf of bread. Seeing Ali hold her put my mind at ease.

"Martin!" Ali shouted. "Check it out!"

She raised her new friend in the air, facing me.

I looked around the room and noticed the walls were gouged out significantly with a wolf's claw marks. The same marks that appeared the night we had our nightmares. I had no doubt that our Companions were somehow connected to them. This suspicion was only confirmed when I realized Ali's room smelled like a forest.

I turned and tried to get Alciel's attention.

"You haven't been hanging around my room, have you? Before this?" I asked Alciel.

"No way. I just got here tonight."

"Then why has my room been charred up?"

"Probably because our essences were trying to find each other. Companions tend to leave these little calling cards, even before Alignment."

I looked at Ali and her wolf Companion. The color of its fur and eyes caught me off guard.

"What is it?" I asked.

The small wolf growled and feebly attempted to claw at me.

"Or, *who* is it?" I rephrased.

"Her name is Lyse!" Ali smiled.

"She's... adorable."

"And she is my Companion!"

"She's...adorable," I lamented.

Crunch. Crunch. Crunch.

Alciel skittered into the room like a spider. He twisted his head at an inhuman angle to see Ali.

Ali's eyes flashed with apprehension, but when the seconds passed, she seemed more interested than afraid.

"Did you get bored and break out the old Ouija board?" Ali asked. "What is this? A knockoff of *The Exorcist*?"

Alciel's eyes got wider, and his slit pupils got smaller. He seemed annoyed.

Crunch. Crunch. Crunch.

He skittered across the wall and into our midst.

"Well, now I don't feel bad about clawing up your walls anymore," Alciel spat.

"Seriously, is this your Companion, or did you summon a demon?" Ali asked.

"He's my Companion," I admitted.

I rubbed the back of my head, somewhat embarrassed.

"His name is Alciel," I added.

"Nice to meet you, Witch. I like your boldness, if nothing else," Alciel grinned.

"Does he ever stop smiling?" Ali asked.

"Not yet that I've seen," I concluded.

I let my tongue briefly cross my lips, trying to contemplate what we could do next.

"Did Lyse say anything to you when she showed up?" I asked.

"Of course!" Lyse responded.

She wrestled out of Ali's grasp and immediately converged on my feet.

"And I'll have you know that I've made her magic more powerful already!" Lyse said.

Lyse looked back to Ali, and Ali was smiling back at her.

"Is that true?" I asked.

"Yeah, I was just trying to make my pencil cup float."

"Show me," I insisted.

"With that kind of attitude?" Lyse interjected. "I don't think so."

"It's all right," Ali assured, "Martin's just excited because he wants to see magic in action."

"Fine," Lyse puffed.

I saw Ali focus intently on the pencil cup, an art project she made back in first grade. She held out one hand and clenched her fingers.

Red mist started flowing toward the cup, but it didn't make contact. I felt a cool breeze blow from Lyse. The tips of Lyse's ears began to glow with a lightning-green flame, and I felt a surge of energy pulsate from Lyse's essence. I could feel it delve into my sister. She focused even harder, and I saw the red light reach out and envelop the cup.

Ali clutched her fingers like she was holding the cup in her hand.

"*Volate!*" Ali commanded in a whisper.

I saw Ali's cup hover lightly over her desk. The aura was mingling with the color green, and the cup was overflowing with plants as it approached her. It seemed to make the cup heavier, but that only made Ali more determined.

"Traduc ad *mihi*," Ali whispered.

Then it began to glide gently to her hand.

Lyse's ears were lightly fading as the cup approached Ali.

Ali let out a relaxed smile as the cup reached her hand.

"That was..." I began.

"Amazing?" Ali finished with a pleased grin.

"Well, now we know what we were doing wrong," I said to Ali. "We just needed a little bit of help."

I looked at Alciel. His grin grew even wider.

"What do you want to try first?" Alciel asked. "Conjuring fire? Making an illusion? Giving your sister giant wings and flying her around Detroit?"

"That sounds like fun!" Ali exclaimed.

"Out of the question," I answered simply.

"Martin, these are the kind of skills that could actually be fun to use!" Ali protested.

"Let's start small, Alciel," I said. "How about you show me how to measure someone's powers?"

"I'm willing to teach you how to burn, mesmerize, or give your sister the gift of flight, and you're settling for such a meager first step?"

"These powers aren't going to be of any use to us if we don't know what we're up against!"

"What do you mean?" Alciel asked. "No one is after you. At this moment. I think."

"Nice try. But someone like Dorian doesn't show up for no reason."

"Dorian... Proctor?" Alciel asked.

"Have you heard of him?" I asked.

"Yeah," Lyse nodded.

"Is he supposed to be famous?" Ali asked.

"He's a High Watchman," Alciel explained. "If you practice dark magic, then he's the person who rounds them up."

"That explains why he's sure he can protect us," Ali said. "But shouldn't he have more people?"

"Watchmen have worked this way for a long time. They don't like to draw attention to themselves, and their enemies work the same way. Hell, Dorian was one of *their* enemies back then."

Silence.

"We're learning from a criminal?" I asked.

"Dorian knows how these people think. But he's not going to call a massive team. That would just give your position away. There's a reason he's kept his distance before, and why he's seeing you sparingly now."

Alciel looked out the window.

"There are eyes all over Detroit that are trying to find you two," Alciel added.

"How do you know?" Ali asked. "Didn't you arrive like a minute ago?"

"If you let me explain, you'll get your answers," Alciel started.

"And how the hell did you get in our house?!" Ali asked.

Alciel looked at Ali, waiting for a chance to speak.

"Unlike you two, I grew up with the ability to use magic. And I've had my claws in Detroit for a long time. Have you ever heard of the Nain Rouge?"

I was tempted to call it out as an urban legend, but this was very possible. The Nain Rouge was a demon known as the Red Dwarf that usually caused misfortune, showing up before certain tragic events. He mostly drew the occult crowd in Detroit.

"You're the Nain Rouge?" I asked.

"That's right," Alciel confirmed.

"You went from urban legend to a Wizard's Companion," Ali said. "How does that make you feel?"

"It's actually a lot of fun," Alciel grinned.

"Fun?" Ali asked.

"Being a Wizard's Companion means you get to do incredible feats with magic. Things you'd never be able to do on your own. I don't even know what I'm capable of yet," Alciel cackled. His fingers *clattered* together as he tapped his claws together in contemplation.

"But you're giving us a lot of information," I said. "Won't someone take offense to that? A demon or something?"

"Demons love power and knowledge. I don't expect you to understand, but demons also love being envied by our fellow demons. To us, that's the highest form of praise."

I looked at Ali. She raised her eyebrows.

"You didn't choose this, did you?" I asked.

"No more than you chose to be the Witch and Wizard. I noticed my manna was acting strangely. So, I performed an Alignment. I saw floating starlight flakes in my manna, and I felt something deep inside myself. It almost felt like a magnetic force. It brought me to this house, so I came here."

"When did your manna act strangely?" I asked.

"It was pretty late. Thirteen days or so. I had a lingering suspicion that I was a Companion, and so I took my leave. I told nobody and came here."

"Do you know who these people searching for us are?" Ali asked.

"All I know is that Gehenna is in an uproar," Alciel said. "A new Witch or Wizard has that effect. And we're hitting our busy season with crime, drugs, and all that other stuff. Not to mention demons are going missing."

"We were told things are getting dangerous for us, and we

shouldn't let our guard down," I pointed out.

"As far as I'm concerned, everyone expects a few demons to fall through the cracks," Alciel said. "Nobody is going to think anything of it if I disappear for a while. And by the time this dies down, the Order will protect you."

"But who is out there? Do you know who would want to hurt us?" I asked.

"Demons, humans, werewolves. It's anybody's guess. But it won't matter who's hunting you down if you're not ready to face them. And if you're not ready, Lyse and I are at risk of being killed."

I looked at Ali again.

"Now that we can practice magic properly, let's learn how to detect magic abilities," I insisted.

"It's much easier than you think," Alciel insisted.

He leaped off of the wall and landed on the floor expertly, without making a sound.

"Is it like amplification?" Ali inquired.

"Not that far off. Amplification is radar. This is *dissection*."

Alciel pounced on the bed like a cat and stared intently into Lyse's eyes. Lyse immediately began to snap at Alciel.

SNAP!

"Hey! I'm trying to help Martin out," Alciel insisted.

"Then do it without touching me with that filthy semblance!" Lyse demanded.

"Alciel, don't antagonize her," I ordered.

"I'm just showing you the kind of power she has."

Alciel's piercing yellow eyes turned a deep golden red. My vision was drenched with scarlet, like blood dripping on the surface of water.

"Alciel. What..."

"It's just my manna melding with yours."

There was a cooling sensation. Then there was burning.

"Alciel, what are you doing?!" Ali demanded.

Alciel snickered, but didn't respond.

"I'm looking at Lyse's essence," I insisted.

The burning was slight and forced me to narrow my vision.

I looked down and saw a black canvas behind her. This made her essence and magic circuits so much brighter. Flashes appeared in my vision and eclipsed Lyse.

I could faintly make out the image of a wolf pup being born on a mountain slope, her ears burning with power to levitate stones and laying in the earth to form an array of plants around her. I watched time pass, and the pup was growing with each cycle of the moon. Although, she never grew to be very big. One night, she touched her nose to a hollowed stone with three symbols, and a green flame gave way to emerald liquid and a handful of golden seeds. They grew, and starlight fragments shook loose from the vines that formed.

I felt myself fall backward. Ali caught me in her arms.

"Wow," I whispered.

I blinked my eyes, and my world came back to me slowly. First, it was deep red, then dark shades of purple, and then, finally, I saw blue moonlight returning to the world.

"On second thought, maybe this wasn't such a good idea," Alciel lamented.

As Alciel blinked, his eyes changed color. The red was fearful, the orange was paranoid, the yellow was careful contemplation. But his smile never went away; it only weakened for a moment.

"When you read someone's powers, it'll be like staring into

a shallow pond," Alciel explained. "It won't be perfect, but you'll get a good surface view of what they can do."

"I think that's enough for one night," Lyse cautioned.

"But we've only just touched on the basics," Alciel said. "Telekinesis and power reading are interesting tricks, but that's not going to save us against something stronger."

"And why would those be threats to us? We haven't done anything wrong," Ali insisted.

"Everyone who practices real magic is going to know your name. And it's our job to keep you safe because not all of them are going to be your friends," Alciel expanded.

"Well, we can catch up on sleep later," I insisted. "That can't be the end of our training for tonight."

"Right now, you have us," Lyse promised. "We'll take the first watch."

I looked at Ali.

"Okay, goodnight," I accepted.

Alciel followed close behind.

"You really are going to follow me everywhere," I whispered.

"Until the bitter end," Alciel promised.

His mischievous smile made me wonder just how safe we really were.

SEVEN

MONSTERS

"Martin, we've taken some time to reflect on your *incident* with Mrs. Fitzgerald," Mr. Smith began.

"Is that what we're calling it?" I asked.

"And while there will be *some* disciplinary action, maybe there's a silver lining in all of this."

"Community service?"

"No. You'll apologize to Mrs. Fitzgerald."

I lightly pressed my tongue into my right cheek at the thought.

"I know you two haven't been on the best of terms, but she brought us your impressive pile of homework. Or what was left of it."

"And?" I asked.

"You've done all the work for all of your classes. You clearly need something to keep you occupied."

"Occupied?"

Suddenly, I heard the sharp *clacking* of claws not far from Mr. Smith.

I saw Alciel scurry up Mr. Smith's curtains. I kept my paranoid glances to a minimum in fear that Mr. Smith would turn around.

"This isn't the first time your academic prowess has come to my attention. Mrs. Connors tells me that you read Latin fluently, have a prolific knowledge of literature, and are extremely well-versed in chemistry. Not to mention you've taken an interest in criminal law."

I saw Alciel trying to scamper on top of the windowsill, and he lightly kicked the lamp's cord. Its rhythmic *shaking* caught Mr. Smith's attention for a brief moment, and I saw Alciel was trying to give me a signal.

"How exactly are you going to keep me occupied?" I asked.

"We were planning on pairing you up with a student who could use some help. We'd pair you up, make sure you two make a good team, and then you'd just send back weekly reports cataloging their progress."

Alciel tripped over his forked tail, and I heard a light crack of glass.

Mr. Smith's eyes immediately shot upwards, and Alciel swung behind the fabric of the curtains. I felt my heart race in my chest. If the Baptist Mr. Smith saw a creature from hell slinking up his curtains, my life would be over.

Alciel was still trying to gain my attention from the shadows.

"You know what? Tutoring actually sounds pretty good. I'll talk with my parents. We'll get back to you by the end of the week."

I saw Alciel slide down the curtain, and I felt that I was

about to be saved.

"Great!" Mr. Smith said. "I can have them come by and we can talk this out in my office."

I heard Alciel escape through the back door. *Great, a little red demon loose in the hallway.*

"Sounds like a plan!" I confirmed.

I grabbed my light bag and charged out of the room.

I searched desperately for Alciel. As soon as I made it out into the main hall, I saw a red tail entering the men's room.

"At least you're not charging into the open," I grumbled.

I rushed into the bathroom and made sure that no one else was present. The urinals were unoccupied. The stalls were vacant.

Alciel skittered into the open and looked at me, bewildered.

"What the hell was that all about?!" I demanded.

"I had to tell you that there's something in the school!"

"And you had to tell me in front of the vice principal?"

"Relax, kid. I have Selective Presence. I can choose who sees me and who doesn't."

"How can you do that?"

"Pretty simple. My horns do all the work. Demons use it all the time when they don't want to be seen."

"Okay," I challenged, "if things were getting so bad in the school, wouldn't Ali or I have noticed it?"

"You are perceptive, but you aren't used to seeing magic like I am. You've spent your entire life around people that have either no clue about magic or have actively been trying to keep you from it."

"Fine, then what are we dealing with?" I demanded.

"I'm not sure. Whatever it is, it's of demonic origin. And it's been lurking in the locker room."

"And I have gym after this. Great."

"But you have study hall now. And it's not like you're doing anything. Let's head down there together and cause some trouble."

"Are you sure that's a good idea?"

"Yeah, you're right. Let's leave him in the locker room and, eventually, he'll just torture the entire school," Alciel shot back.

I took a deep breath, feeling my heart racing in my chest.

"You think we can take this thing down?"

"You might be just starting out," Alciel assured, "but you're still the Wizard. You should be able to exorcise it."

"Dorian was supposed to show me how to exorcise demons after school today. Am I ready for something like this?"

"You'll be fine," Alciel insisted. "And I'll be right there with you. Let's go."

I pulled out my backpack, and Alciel jumped inside with ease.

"We've got ten minutes until the room becomes occupied," Alciel said in a muffled voice.

"How do you know that?" I inquired.

"I have to do something to keep out of your classrooms. They're boring as—"

"Hell?"

"Gehenna. But we need to get moving now."

"You're right. Let's go," I confirmed.

I threw my backpack on and was careful not to draw attention to myself along the way.

Traversing down the spiral staircase, I felt my spine begin to tingle and my palms sweat.

"You feel it too?" Alciel asked.

"Yeah. How am I supposed to fight this thing anyway?"

"It doesn't matter what kind of magic you use. You just need to tap into your manna reserves in your magic circuits. Then allow them to form spells."

"Got it."

I let my amplification sound with a faint *whir*. There was nothing in the basement. Not even a janitor's closet.

"Try and reach out with your senses," Alciel said. "You're sure to pinpoint the creature easier. Don't overdo it, and you'll be fine."

I took Alciel's advice to heart. I took three deep breaths as I retreated into my essence. One breath to move beyond the threshold of my cold intellect. One breath to move beyond my burning anxiety of what lay ahead. And one breath to finally reach the essence.

I felt the warm flood of manna move past my limbs as I delved into its bursting contents. My eyes felt so enhanced in their perceptive abilities they seemed almost feline. The burn was still there, but less so than the first time I used this spell. The entire world seemed dark, but there was a deep rouge that slithered in the boy's locker room.

"There it is," I pointed.

Alciel unzipped my backpack and climbed onto my shoulder. I looked at him, and I felt a searing heat come off of his body. It made my magic feel more powerful than before.

"What are you doing?" I asked.

I felt Alciel and the unknown entity begin to move.

"We need to accelerate the pace your magic is building. I'm going to unlock something on the surface."

Alciel gripped his claws deeply into my shoulder.

"AH!" I winced.

For a moment, it felt like I was paralyzed and on fire, but I couldn't scream. I felt empowered, my heartbeat began to slow to a calculated crawl, and when I opened my eyes, I saw a blue aura beginning to envelop me. The sensation was like wearing weightless clothes.

"What was that?" I asked.

I stared into my hands, mesmerized.

"I'll explain it later, kid."

I looked back toward the sickly, crooked presence in the locker room and felt my heart beating faster.

Its joints *cracked* with an orange, volcanic heat, and it turned around swiftly, and met my gaze through the wall. I thought my heart would burst out of my chest. It hovered toward the door like a ghost. The door opened without physical touch.

"We're in for a fight," Alciel whispered.

And just as an aura was surely emitting from my hand, there was a presence erupting from the door. It was a crazed, destructive, and twisted force that came bursting through the creases.

Like a rockstar emerging from the obscuring stage fog, I saw a demon take center stage. The creature that emerged looked like a human being burned by the fires of hell.

Its charcoal limbs and joints *cracked* and *hissed* with each movement. And when it looked in my direction, a final *hiss* revealed its unyielding, white eyes. At the center of its chest was a harrowing symbol of three circles joined together like links in a brimstone chain.

The creature had six nostrils that *flared* red whenever it drew breath. Its body was covered in patches of mirrors that held a dark reflection of everything around it. As it passed beneath the fluorescent bulbs illuminating the hallway, they *popped*, and the glass was drawn into its seared flesh like magnets.

"An Addiction Demon," Alciel said. "These guys like to cling to addicts, making them do terrible things."

"Then why is it burned to a crisp?" I asked.

"This type of demon isn't much more than an animal of my kind. He's just as damaged mentally as he is physically. This'll be easier than I thought. Just take a deep breath and—"

Before I could make a move, the Addiction Demon raised its claw, and a stream of ash surged toward me.

"Defend yourself!" Alciel demanded.

I raised my hands and desperately tried to remember enough Latin to form some kind of shield in front of me.

Time seemed to slow down, and my mind rushed to all the images and words I absorbed from the spellbook.

Chapter 9: Combat Magic. Page 190.

There was a spell. An illustration of a man raising his hands forward and yelling a word in Latin. What was it? The word for shield. What—

"*Clipeum!*" I shouted.

A blue disc formed from my manna. It misted out into the open and solidified into a rounded shape. It gleamed when it finally took the form of a perfect circle.

TUNF!

The azure disc stopped the ash, causing it to spray in all directions. I saw the blue of my manna was quickly dissipating, but Alciel's yellow manna was filling in the gaps. The ashen smog began to rush over the barrier like water off a rock. I turned my open hand into a fist.

"*Sphaera!*" I answered.

The blue disc of energy engulfed the ash and formed a

molten bubble.

"That's it!" Alciel called.

The Addiction Demon took a step back, let its head spin around its right shoulder once, and then let it crack back to its original place.

"Now what?!" I demanded.

"Get creative!" Alciel demanded.

I looked to Alciel and saw his horns were turning a vibrant gold, and that wisps of his energy were funneling into my arm. His energy was my own.

"*Falarica!*" I shouted.

The orb hurtled toward the Addiction Demon like a cannonball and broke upon impact.

BOOM!!!

The creature spiraled back, and I saw the twisted remains of what looked like a ribcage inside. It began collecting itself. The terrible scent of burning skin erupted through the air.

This fight was far from over.

CRA-ACK!

The demon twisted its body until it stopped flying.

"Oh, no," I whispered.

The demon raised its hand, and a set of razors raised from its nail beds, like box cutters. Each of them was laced with white powder and crimson ooze. I saw the sharp tufts of energy surging toward me. Then they crystallized into razors. I raised my hand again and called out another command.

"*Clipeum!*" I shouted.

A blue disc appeared in front of me. The red razors stopped in place when they hit the blue barrier.

WOAM!

The demon twisted its charcoal hand.

SHREEEEEEEP!

The red razors were starting to strain the shield.

"Alciel!" I called out.

I looked forward as the ashen demon began to float toward me, overhead lights shattering in its wake.

POP! POP! POP!

"Martin, you have to exorcise it!" Alciel called.

I raised my hands forward, desperate to remember other Latin words.

"*Exorcismi...*" I began.

I saw a white engraving on the demon's stomach. It stopped for a moment, but it raised its hands forward, and a flurry of blows landed on my face, abdomen, and throat. I fell to my knees. This creature was going to kill me if I didn't act fast.

"Martin! Why is this so hard?! You've done this before!"

"Are you crazy?! No, I haven't!"

I looked up and saw the ashen demon raising its hands again. This time, Alciel raised his claws upwards in response.

"*Impetum subsisto!*" Alciel shouted.

Gold clouds formed and made the razors burst.

POP-POP-POP!

FRELCH!

The final attack landed and cut Alciel. Drops of sickly golden liquid fell to the ground, and I grabbed him to run inside the lockers.

"What are you talking about?! I've never done this before."

"Yes, you have! Every Wizard knows how to fight!"

"I DON'T! NOT LIKE THIS!"

HISSSSS!

"GAH!!!" I shouted.

I looked down and saw that Alciel's blood was dripping onto my hand. It burned worse than acid.

"Sorry," he whispered.

"I swear I'm going to get straight answers from you someday."

DOOM.

The doors flew open, and I could already smell the burning flesh.

"But not right now," I insisted.

I threw Alciel in my backpack and looked at the long rows of lockers.

"How are we going to beat this thing?" I asked.

"Addiction Demons will never give up the hunt. They become just as hooked in the rush as any human junkie. You need to take it down quickly before it can do any more damage. With a demon like this, one without a Court, exorcism works best."

The creature hovered into the room, and its head begin spinning. It was looking for us.

"How do I do that?"

"Just say *exorcizamus daemoni hunc totis viribus*."

I repeated it and let the words roll off my tongue carefully.

"Exorcise this demon with all my strength?" I asked.

"Right. I'll get its attention while you focus. Make sure you have eyes on it as you're exorcising. Eye contact is key. They'll do anything to stay out of your line of sight."

Alciel let his damaged wings unfurl.

Flap. Flap. Flap.

"GAH!" Alciel winced as he charged straight into a row of lockers.

BANG! BANG!

The Addiction Demon turned its head in Alciel's direction. A series of *swoops* were soon met by a chorus of hisses, and I knew they were interlocked in battle. I rushed into the open and called for the demon.

"Hey!" I shouted.

The creature turned its head around to meet me.

I extended my hands.

"*Exorcizamus daemoni hunc totis viribus!*" I shouted.

Blue manna shot out from my hands with yellow bursts. A white circle carved into its chest, and it reared back in pain.

GREEEEEEEEENCH!

I took steps towards it and repeated the command.

"*Exorcizamus daemoni hunc totis viribus!*" I shouted.

The demon flew backward, and I felt my manna launch out. It felt like I was launching buckets full of blood from my own body in its direction.

"*Exorcizamus daemoni hunc totis viribus!*" I shouted a final time.

I stared into its eyes, felt a sharp wave of fear, but the blue of my manna began to take form in every crevice of the demon's body. Even the brimstone symbol on its chest. It reared back in pain. The creature twisted backward and crackled into soot.

Finally, Alciel swooped down, too weak to get up on his own.

"Not a bad exorcism," Alciel chuckled.

"I guess," I wheezed.

I fell to my knees.

BUZZ.

Caller ID: Dorian.

The sound of footsteps thundered down the stairs, and I knew I was about to get caught.

“Crap,” I whispered.

There was no way to hide the mess of ashes on the ground, and there was nothing that could hide me or Alciel in our current state.

Unless...

My eyes fixed on the fire alarm.

“Are you...” Alciel whispered.

I stumbled to the crimson box, and I pulled the handle without hesitation.

BWAAAH! BWAAAH!

I heard footsteps go in the other direction.

“Naughty,” Alciel wheezed.

“Just to activate the sprinklers,” I demanded.

Alciel produced a small flame at the tip of his finger and launched it at the nearest sprinkler.

FWOOSH.

STSTSTSTSTSTSTST!

The water turned the ashes to sludge. Alciel leaped into my backpack.

“That was a good head start, but are they going to come down here?” Alciel asked.

“This is the basement. It’s the last place you want to be if there’s a fire,” I insisted.

“Good point.”

“We just bought ourselves some time,” I said. “Alciel, what was this demon looking for?”

I looked to Alciel, and he pressed his claws to his temples, the grin fading away from his face.

“I can’t believe I’m doing this,” Alciel said.

He looked downwards, and I saw his aura beginning to

move wildly throughout the room. I felt my meager strength beginning to leave me. He barked out an order with that serpentine-hound voice of his.

"*Reclude!*" Alciel shouted.

The lockers burst open.

KER-KLUNG!

A handful of items fell out of each. Watches, bags of sweaty gym clothes, and cell phones all sprawled out on the ground.

"Addiction Demons only show up around life-destroying addictions."

"So, what is it? Booze, cigarettes?" I asked.

"A demon of that size, with that much magic, and with extra *nostrils* and *mirrors* on its body?" Alciel began. "That would typically be seen with..."

"Cocaine," I concluded.

"Very good!" Alciel said.

I looked underneath one of the jackets that fell to the ground, and I saw a dozen dime bags of white powder.

"That'll do it. Now let's grab that shit and get out of here."

"I'm not taking this with me!" I objected.

"You've got two options: leave the evidence and get sent to jail or take the evidence and get it to Dorian!"

I looked down and hurriedly gathered the contents into my bag. Alciel quickly jumped in soon after. I picked up my phone and sent a text as quickly as I could.

"Alciel and I are near the south entrance. Fought an Addiction Demon. Hurry or we will get caught," I typed.

I let my head breach the doorway, and saw no one was present.

Buzz.

I looked down.

"Get a sample of everything in the room. Whatever it was latching onto," Dorian insisted.

I smiled.

"Done."

The next message came as soon as I sent it.

"I'm here."

I ran out through the south entrance and saw that Dorian was waiting for me. He threw the door open and waved for me to get inside.

I dove in with what strength I had left, and he immediately grabbed my hands, and I noticed only then that faint blue bruises were lining my fingertips.

"Please don't tell me you made him exorcise the damn thing," Dorian breathed.

"I made a judgment call," Alciel said.

Dorian hit the gas.

SCREEEE!

The truck barreled down the parking lot and onto Fenkell Avenue. I felt my breath slow down and my muscles ache.

"Where are we headed?" I asked.

"To a hideout of sorts," Dorian said. "Nobody will find it."

"How can you be so sure?" I demanded.

"Just wait and see."

"And where's Ali?!" I asked.

"She's fine. She felt a presence in the school, too. She got herself to the nurse's office and leaped out the window. Now she's making her way to where we're headed. I texted her the address."

"She's clever," Alciel acknowledged.

"She really is," I agreed.

EIGHT

HIDEOUT

Dorian marched across the cracked cement, and it caved in with every step. As the slatey *crunches* of the ground faded away, I watched Dorian vanish into the shadowy doorway of a motel called the *Silk Slipper*.

Looking up, I saw a faded and crooked sign.

"Silk Slipper," I said. "Sounds charming."

"I'm glad it has the Martin stamp of approval," Dorian's voice echoed.

His disappearance was so sudden, I wondered if someone had ambushed him as soon as he faded from view. Wouldn't have surprised me. If it wasn't demons, it would have been drug dealers.

The frigid cold made me shiver as I stood outside, but I didn't know what was safer; should I go with the mean Detroit streets in the dead of winter or whatever was waiting inside? I couldn't even see inside because rotten planks covered the windows.

"You think you could have found a place that has fewer boarded-up windows?" I asked.

"That's part of the appeal," Dorian's voice echoed. "Now get in here. I have some tea for you."

I walked inside.

A bitter chill cut through the air. Even worse than the cold outside. Not only were my teeth *chattering*, it felt like they were vibrating. Only a bit, but it was enough to make me stop for a moment before I responded.

"Is the f-f-freezing cold part of the a-p-p-eal?" I shivered.

"You're safer in here than you are out there," Dorian insisted.

True to his word, there was an end table with a small mug filled with Earl Grey.

I crossed over to the table, picked a cup, and let the drink stop my shivering. When the warmth steadied my body, I continued.

"How did you know I liked Earl Grey?" I asked.

"I had a hunch," Dorian said, "but that's not important. We have work to do."

I took another sip and detected sugar. I wondered how Dorian could have known how I liked my tea, but I didn't question it further.

He pointed up, toward an old display for the motel in the lobby. I looked up and saw a dozen Addiction Demons tied together, swaying from side to side, as though they were listening to a song. They all had faint white threads connecting them and had that same brimstone symbol on their chests.

Each of their bodies told a different story. Some had mouths running up their entire torso like scales. Others had limbs and fingers made of poker chips. And some had hypodermic needles for teeth, contorted into a harsh frown. But all of them had that dark brimstone canvas of a body where everything resembling humanity had burned away.

"How did you..." I began.

"It's a complex ritual called a Binding Circle. Addiction Demons love bars, motels, and strip clubs. I decided to take up residence in an abandoned locale so we'd be able to get to the bottom of this without being detected."

"Won't someone come looking for these things?" I asked.

"Not likely," Alciel said. "Demons of all kinds have Selective Presence. It means that they can use magic to prevent themselves from being seen by certain people. And if you manage to wrangle a couple of them, you can use that to your advantage. Besides, it would be a pretty stupid move to come out here and break cover just to recover them."

"How does that happen?"

"The horns of demons serve a double purpose. Remember? In addition to being used as weapons, most of them can conceal someone's presence with demonic magic called Selective Presence."

"And even if someone does notice them, they'll think this used to be a drug den. That they're desperate and looming around promising territory," I concluded.

"Not a bad idea," Alciel answered.

The little demon unzipped my backpack and made his way to a beaten-up leather couch. He kneaded a cushion and walked around in little circles before finally sitting down.

"You get some rest," Dorian insisted.

Alciel let out a slight *purr*. His eyelids fluttered in and out of sleep. And his ears gave off a slight twitch, as though he picked up a word we were saying now and again.

"You sure he'll be safe out here?" I asked. "We just got him away from one Addiction Demon. And now there's twelve of them."

"I weakened them in the fight to get them here. And I put them under a powerful spell," Dorian assured. "Besides, we know for a fact that these things are connected to something bigger. That's why they have those symbols on their torsos. They must have come from a circle just like this one. I've seen it before."

"Those guys are caked with mud and have pieces missing," I pointed out.

"Sure. Addiction doesn't go down without a fight. The demons attached to them won't, either."

Dorian strode over to the front desk of the motel. It had an old-fashioned set of key boxes filled with herbs, chemicals, and spell cards.

"But the doors were busted down. And what about the police? What spell is keeping them out?" I asked.

"Police raided this place three weeks ago," Dorian said. "They took out all the evidence. It serves as a nice nest for future drug dealers to get busted all over again in about a year or two. But, until then, this is my workspace."

"Wow. You really thought this through."

"Every big city has places like this. Watchmen make use of them all the time."

"Alciel mentioned that before. What exactly does a Watchman do?"

"Watchmen are police for the magical world. We make sure people using magic for nefarious purposes are brought to justice."

"That makes sense."

“You seem a bit shaken by what happened. We have time to talk about things, if you want.”

“Alciel mentioned something about Demon Courts.”

“Nasty business. Demons tend to crawl out of their demonic courts and into this world and take control of people. In the same way people can get stronger with an Awakening, demons get stronger when people submit to their lowest instincts. Every now and again, some foolhardy mage tries to bind them to a circle. It’s a good way to tame them and feed off of their energy.”

“That makes sense. It fuels their magic,” I finalized.

“There’s no way we can get them all, but we prevent the worst from happening. Cutting down on genocide, terrorism, and crime.”

“And one motel is going to help you in that fight?”

“A Watchman is capable of doing a whole lot on their own. I’m going to change things for the better in this place. You and Ali are going to help me.”

“How are we going to do that?”

“See all those cots out there?”

I narrowed my vision and saw there were cots spread throughout the lobby.

“Yeah.”

“They’re spread out in every room. We’re going to turn this place into an exorcism facility.”

I looked out and saw some of the sheets were covered in grotesque stains, while other sheets were extremely clean.

“You’ve been keeping busy here.”

“I managed to exorcise twelve demons. That’s where those bastards up top came from. But that’s just scratching the surface.”

“What else have you gone after?”

"Incubi, vampires, dark mages. As long as they cause harm with their magic, I've hunted them."

"I'm starting to sense a trend. Is that why Alciel was called to me? Because he could be put to good use?"

"I can't speak for the Spectrum, Martin."

"With his help, I was able to fight back."

"Just remember, Alciel is a very rare exception. In fact, he may only be an exception because his life is tied to yours."

"You think he'd kill me if he weren't my Companion?"

"I know he'd turn you over to that Demon Court. But since you are tied to him, he has a lot more to lose. This happens a lot with Wizards and their Companions. You're sharing everything now. Your manna, your lives, your circumstances. And neither of you have a clue what any of those things are anymore."

Silence.

I looked at Alciel curled into a ball, and it seemed impossible that he would do anything to hurt me. I wasn't sure if it was because we had helped each other in a fight, or because he was curled up in a helpless ball.

"I'm not sure I believe that," I said

"You can believe what you want. But my job is to protect you. Even from him."

"And how would you do that?"

"Come here and learn something," Dorian insisted.

I walked over to the front desk.

"If you're going to outsmart a demon, you're going to have to learn to take advantage of the local resources. The first few years of a Watchman's training are dedicated to doing just that."

Dorian held out his hand.

"Your bag," Dorian requested.

"Fine," I allowed.

Dorian undid the rest of the zipper of my bag and looked inside.

"*WHAAAAAAAAAAA!*" The demons bellowed.

I looked up and saw the Addiction Demons contorted themselves with hunger as the bag opened.

"Not a bad haul. Should keep them occupied for a few weeks at least."

Dorian reached for a large bowl, most likely used to hold plastic fruit back when the motel was in its heyday. He dumped the dime bags into the bowl.

Telp.

"The first thing you need to know about Addiction Demons is that they might be strong, but they hate drifting and going out on their own. They like to post their territory and lure people into traps. By holding the drugs here, they think they're going to hit the jackpot."

"And yet they're not attacking us. Why?"

"As part of your training, you'll learn to exorcise demons. This time, with supervision," Dorian explained.

"Anything else?"

"You'll also learn to cast some basic Watchman spells."

"I'm sure we'd all love to learn something like that," a voice called.

I turned to the doorway and saw Ali and Lyse.

I ran to meet her.

"How are you two?" Ali asked.

"Alciel took the worst of it, but we're all right now," I assured.

After throwing her backpack onto a nearby table, Ali rushed over and embraced me. When she let go, I saw she was covered in soot.

"Don't tell me," I started.

"Yep. There was a demon hiding in the track shack. You can imagine what kind of stuff goes on in there when the coaches lose track of students."

I held up my hand.

"No further details," I insisted.

"Although, I'm not sure I'm any safer when there are a dozen demons up there and two chain smokers down here," Ali pointed out.

"Addiction Demons latch onto people and cause life-shattering addictions. Drinking your liver to nothing, gambling away your family and house, or overdosing on drugs. The kind of addictions that make you throw your life away completely until there's nothing left."

"When you get black lungs, don't come crying to me," Ali objected.

"I'm touched by your concern," I smiled.

"I heard you took one down in the boy's locker room. Nice work," Ali commended.

She held up her phone, indicating that she got a message from Dorian with the details.

"You're just in time. We were just talking about training," Dorian added.

"Don't let me stop you," Ali insisted.

She threw herself on the couch opposite Alciel.

"Exorcism, Watchman spells, and Binding Circles," Dorian said. "We have a good arsenal, and it's time you learned how to use it. With any luck, they're going to help us get to our final goal."

"Ah! So there is a point to all this," Ali smiled.

"Anything beats wandering around aimlessly," Lyse smiled.

"You impressed me, I'll admit," Dorian said. "But you need to learn how to stay hidden, investigate, and then you can learn to take down these kinds of people."

"What are they after? What's *their* end goal?" Ali asked.

"Every time Addiction Demons start behaving this way in such big numbers, it's because an artifact is being used. Me and my fellow Watchmen believe someone is controlling the actions of these creatures using a powerful spellbook. One that's been missing for years now. The Necronomicon."

Dorian crossed over to a map of Detroit and crossed his arms. He looked into the interlocking streets and took a deep breath, feeling the gravity of what he was about to say.

"And if we don't hurry, whoever stole it will come for you and kill you," Dorian added.

"Necronomicon?" Ali asked.

"It's a book from H.P. Lovecraft's work," I replied swiftly.

"It's more than that, Martin," Dorian insisted.

"You're telling me the Necronomicon is real?"

"And it's being used to collect Addiction Demons and to hunt you down. The symbols on these demons are classic binding runes. And I've only seen them this powerful when they come from that book. "

"What purpose would that serve?" Ali asked.

"Addiction Demons can become more numerous and more powerful if you have an artifact. Something that guides and strengthens your spells."

"And with a book that powerful, they'll be able to find out who the Witch and Wizard are and capture us," I said.

"That's right," Dorian confirmed. "It was made by a family

of necromancers."

"Seems like a lot of trouble," Ali said. "Why make something so dangerous?"

"The Order commissioned them to make the book. The alternative was to let executioners rot away under the weight of all the magic they used to dark mages. That kind of magic does something to you. To your essence."

"And the book prevents that?"

"It's the ultimate murder weapon. It's learned how to give and take life in every imaginable way. And it acts as the executioner's axe for all dark mages that have been sentenced to death."

"A weapon that powerful, and we can't find it?" I asked.

"It was designed to leave no trace. And that's exactly why it's remained hidden."

"Let's say that is *their* plan," Ali started to reason. "To stay hidden and use the book to kill us? Why not just skim the table of contents to find the spell they need and take us out?"

"The book has special countermeasures built into it. If anyone other than its true owner tries to use it, the book can kill them. But if you have someone to take the pain for you, you might be able to open the book. And then you may be able to unlock the book's spells, one at a time."

"How do you know all this?" I asked.

"I've seen the book work before. And I know the book is very dangerous and untrusting. After all, human and demon magic went into creating the book. Maybe whoever is rounding up these demons has discovered a trick to accelerate the process. To force the book to listen to them. Or to reason with it."

"Okay. But they're cracking open the book one piece at a time with the help of Addiction Demons. How tough can they be?"

"They may not look like much, but Addiction Demons have a high pain tolerance. Or a numbness to it, depending on who you ask."

"They look like they all crawled out of a furnace," I added.

"And they all did. They came straight out of Gehenna. Believe it or not, about ninety percent of Gehenna's population looks just as monstrous. The other ten percent look roughly like Alciel."

"Handsome as hell," Alciel answered.

He was still groggy from the fight.

"A grim fate for anyone," Lyse contemplated.

Alciel blinked his eyes, and stirred from his catnap.

"Hell isn't what your holy books make it out to be," Alciel added. "It's not a giant cesspool of the damned, presided over by Satan. At least not anymore."

"Then what is it like?" I asked.

"It used to be like that, but around the year 1066, five women visited Satan. Five women who had left your Catholic Church in favor of Satan and the power he offered. They did everything to gain his attention. Steal the church's treasures, corrupt the officials, and indoctrinate dozens into service. And they did it all with magic. And with every putrid act, their essence got darker. They became some of the most powerful and wicked mages of the age. When they lived, they were some of his favorite servants. When they died, they became his favorite wives," Alciel recounted.

"After a year into their union, the wives wanted more power, and so they stabbed Satan with holy blades and took his kingdom. They divided it up into five different Courts," Dorian concluded.

"Five mages took out... Satan?"

"That couldn't have been the end of it," Ali pointed out.

"The most powerful demons lusted after a position in these courts, where they would be the torturers instead of the tortured, and only a small fraction of them, ten percent became Court Demons," Alciel confirmed.

"I still prefer *Paradise Lost*," I smirked.

"I can't believe I got paired up with such a smartass for a Wizard," Alciel grumbled.

My little demon closed his eyes again, and entered a deep slumber.

"And I can't believe I got a Red Court demon for a Companion while my sister got a puppy."

"I'll take that as a compliment," Lyse said.

"It sounds like the Spectrum knew this was going to happen and gave you a demon because demons were coming," Ali guessed.

"There are some theories as to why certain Companions are chosen," Dorian said. "A Witch that can't heal is given an angel. A Wizard with transformation trouble gets a werewolf. They appear to be chosen to cover weaknesses."

"But if their essences mingle and give the Witch and Wizard a jumpstart, does that mean Companions can reap other benefits as well?" Ali asked.

"With enough practice, sure," Dorian confirmed. "But magic is a dangerous tool. Especially where mingled essences are concerned. Extending your lifespan is certainly possible. Look at what your mother accomplished. She did what most people thought was impossible, on her own power. But most people can't handle the cost of living for so long. Even vampires undergo some serious deformities once they reach a certain age."

"Is that why the Necronomicon is being used now?" I asked. "To make someone immortal?"

"It's too early to speculate the culprit's true motives," Dorian explained. "It's a collection of highly forbidden magic. Some of it comes from demons, and some of it from humans. But it's a book of pure necromancy."

"What can it do?" Ali asked.

"It can infect demons and humans, can make you no longer feel pain, and keep you alive in situations that should have killed you. It protects your essence from taking the horrible damage that comes with killing someone, with magic or by conventional means. With all these demons running around, someone may be trying to gather demonic power to crack the book open."

"Let's say that someone does have the book," I reasoned. "How can we defend ourselves against it?"

"We'll keep hunting down Addiction Demons," Dorian said. "Clearly, they're getting bigger and more numerous because someone has been gathering them. Only they're aiming to hurt people and gain power. Not save people from their influence. And it's not the usual suspects in Detroit. Which means that someone has been coming here recently to use it. And if they bend the rules of magic enough, they just might unlock the entire book."

"Bend the rules?" Ali asked.

"Wands are popular because they remove a lot of the complex gesture components of magic. But something like the Necronomicon only requires the intent to kill. With an essence as unique as yours, it's only a matter of time before they find you. Every time they kill someone, I bet they're trying to ferret you out."

Silence.

"But the timing is just a little too perfect if you ask me," I said. "Ali and I get our powers and the Necronomicon is being used to kill us around the same time?"

"That's just how powerful the Witch and Wizard are," Dorian said. "They are charged with using their power to protect the magical world and keep magic in balance. So, when one of them dies, there's a gap of time where people can make a move without much interference. Most people that practice magic get their powers activated at infancy, but you two got it during adolescence. Someone has kept their heads low for roughly fifteen years, hoping the Witch and Wizard would end up human and enter adolescence more quickly. Unfortunately, they were right."

"But fifteen years is a long time."

"Not long for people with magic and a grudge," Dorian cautioned.

"Tell us more about this book," Ali demanded.

Dorian stopped for a moment, and his face hardened.

"The book was stolen in a home invasion fifteen years ago from the last Wizard," Dorian said. "Nobody knew for certain where he was living, for his own protection. But someone found out where his home was and killed him for the book."

"But if he's dead, how can you be sure that we'll be safe when we get our hands on it?" Ali asked.

"One of you will be the rightful owner of the book and be able to collect it. The book yields to one master, and that's whoever the book is passed on to, or nobody at all. And the Wizard knew that if he died, he could pass the book onto his next reincarnation because it belongs to the Wizard. It would recognize his successor. His essence. Based on what I've seen from you two, it's likely to be Martin."

"Why me?" I asked.

"You're so similar to the last Wizard," Dorian said, "and Ali is so similar to the last Witch. Like echoes of the ones who came before."

"Who was the last Witch and Wizard?" I asked.

"Adrian Hive was an Alchemist. He was the last Wizard. Mila Hollyheart was a Warlock. She was the last Witch."

NINE.

EXORCISM

"Looks like we get to show you how to remove a demon from a host," Dorian smiled.

"You already have someone in mind?" I asked.

"Sure. He's laying right over there."

I turned and saw that a young man with dark hair and black eyes was lying on one of the makeshift hospital beds.

"How long has he been like this?"

"About a week. The Addiction Demon has been eating away at him one piece at a time."

"Reminds me of the patients Mom treats at the hospital."

"He's sicker than you can imagine right now."

I looked at his pale face and realized he still had acne. He couldn't have been much older than me.

Dorian approached with a black surgeon's bag.

"*GRAAAAAAAAAHL!*" The boy thrashed.

He tried to get up, but the full set of bodily restraints were already applied.

"The restraints are a nice touch," Ali said. "You steal those from Henry Ford Hospital, too?"

"Yes," Dorian admitted.

Dorian turned to me.

"Martin. There's a chemistry set in that bag. Set it up."

I took the handles of the case and threw them to the side, and the set stood on its own. Inside were an array of crucifixes, potion bottles, daggers, guns, and ancient coins. Along the top was a set of syringes broken apart by size, needle, and plunger. All of them seemed intricate, yet dangerous. Like archaic surgical tools you'd find in a medieval doctor's cart. I could feel Dorian's magic brimming from each object.

"Whoa," Ali exasperated.

"GRAAAAAAAAAHL!"

The boy yelled and thrashed. Alciel climbed up to the surgeon's bag and observed the boy.

"There's something inside of him," Alciel reported.

I felt a warm rush come over me.

I looked to my side and saw that Ali had used her amplification.

"It's fuzzy, but there's definitely something," Ali acknowledged.

I looked at the thrashing boy and narrowed my vision. The room darkened significantly. And yet, for all the shadows that came into my view, it was the heat that caught my attention.

The boy had black lines flaring off of him. With each of them came a heat, as though I stood beside a furnace.

Through my squinting eyes, I saw a creature. There was a festering, inky mass at the center of this boy's chest, grasping his essence.

"It's definitely some kind of demon," I answered.

Dorian grasped a tool from his bag. It looked like a syringe, but it was too large for any human. He looked at Ali and I.

"This will kill him if we don't do it properly. You'll have to hold him down. On my mark, say *coerce*."

I raised my hand, and Ali held it and did the same. Dorian near the boy's head. We raised our hands, and Dorian nodded.

"Coerce!"

We all shouted the word in unison. Dorian thrust the needle into the boy's chest and pulled on the syringe's plunger with a disgusting sound.

GER-GELCH!

All of us harnessed our magic around the boy, and the demon inside him began to fight.

SCHLOOP!

The screams were so intense, I nearly broke concentration and tried to cover my ears. But I held on. Ali looked like she was about to do the same.

An inky-black substance was filling the syringe, and it *clawed* at the glass. The faintest red branding was on its chest, and it infected the mist it produced behind the glass.

"Gotcha!" Dorian smiled.

Dorian removed the plunger and the needle of the giant syringe. The detachable parts were left on the table by the chemistry set. Only the barrel remained.

"Martin, think fast," Dorian announced.

He tossed me the creature.

I caught it and half expected the creature to attack me the moment it reached my hands. Sure enough, it twitched and produced mist on the side of the glass from breathing. But it didn't do anything more. Dorian checked the boy's vitals and draped a medical blanket over him.

"Tell me about this boy," Dorian demanded.

Ali reached into the boy's pockets and produced a wallet.

"His name is Tyler. He doesn't even have a driver's license yet. He's just got a student ID for Woodrow Wilson."

"Is it just me, or do you kids come from a tough neighborhood?" Dorian asked.

"You didn't grow up in a tough neighborhood?"

"Hardly," Dorian said. "I grew up in Salem."

"Tough neighborhood or not, we seem to have a real problem on our hands. Did you get all of these demons from Detroit?"

"I did," Dorian said. "But these kinds of numbers are almost unheard of, even in places like Detroit or Chicago. In the worst areas of a big city, you may have three or four."

"And there were two of them in our school," Ali reflected. "Well, that's pretty intense."

I looked down at the disembodied demon, and it continued to scratch. Faint white marks appeared on the glass, but they reformed just as soon as the damage was done.

"But you said they were difficult to spot, and they liked to stay in one place," Ali pointed out.

"That's right," Dorian confirmed.

"Thirteen seems excessive, doesn't it? And drawing them to the school. They'd get caught pulling a stunt like that."

"It's only happened a few times before. When Pablo Escobar got his drug empire off the ground, there were thirteen Addiction Demons hovering around his operations. They flew in with the shipments to Miami. And when they latched onto the violence and addiction there, they couldn't get enough. Watchmen still haven't gotten rid of the flock that made it there."

"And now we're looking at the same thing happening in Detroit," I realized.

"They make the perfect spies," Dorian said. "They can hide in plain sight, demons don't think anything of them, and humans fall under their influence all the time."

"Are we looking at a big organization, a group, or just one person?" I asked.

"With the Necronomicon involved, it's probably just one person," Dorian confirmed.

"Are you sure?" Ali asked.

"If there were any more culprits, we'd already be honing in on them. Unless they have experience in keeping hidden and are very clever," Dorian added.

"Not a bad setup," Alciel smiled.

"You go around, collect Addiction Demons, and then you absorb their power and start the cycle over again," Lyse concluded.

"GRAAAAAAAAAAAAL!" the demons hissed.

"Speaking of demons, we should take care of this one," I interrupted.

Alciel's eyes grew wide.

"Take a few steps back, Alciel," Dorian insisted.

I looked at Alciel and he seemed like a child that was shying away from a stranger. Dorian took a large bowl from behind the counter and placed it on the table. He produced a large Mason jar of purple salts, a small stack of clean towels, and a book of matches with the faded words Silk Slipper on the back.

Dorian lifted the Mason jar and poured the purple salts across the bottom of the bowl. He took a book of matches and struck it with a loud *kwisp*. After throwing the match inside the drum, it made a noise.

HOOOOOOOOONE.

"GRAAAAAAAAAAAAL!"

The scratches inside the detached syringe barrel became faster and more vicious. The gas lamps that kept the lobby alight began to flicker. I gazed into the violet fire, but it barely lost any of its strength. It was roaring and the demon had all of its eyes on it.

"Toss it in, Martin," Dorian ordered.

I looked down at the barrel and the desperate creature inside it. I almost felt guilty, but then I saw Tyler sleeping soundly.

I knew if it wasn't for us and what we were doing right now, this kid would be in a body bag. I threw the glass barrel into the violet flames.

The demon pounded, bit, and scratched at the glass, but the white marks disappeared just after the demon had formed them.

The heat made its body harden and its skin boil. It gave me a pitiful look from inside, and it looked like it was going to retch. Its chin bulged like a diseased frog, and then it vomited green sludge.

It was more waste than I thought the little creature was capable of producing. It heaved back in a flood of its own filth and its eyes burst.

POP!

Its voiceless *gurgling* seemed to slither toward me. Like it was trying to get revenge. By the end, the bubbling had stopped, and the light returned to the room. I saw Tyler resting comfortably.

I looked at Dorian. He took a Marlboro Red cigarette, pressed it between his thin lips, and lit it on fire with magic.

Hoarf.

"And that's how you kill a demon," Dorian concluded.

Dorian raised a Damascus dagger from his hip and stabbed it into the front desk, satisfied. I looked at it for a moment and noticed that it was archaic in form. And it gave off a light gleam of purple.

"Nice dagger," Ali complimented.

"Thanks. All the Watchmen get one," Dorian explained.

Ali looked up for a moment as though this was the last thing she could wrap her head around before she started asking questions.

"Why are we doing this?" Ali asked.

"You're helping people by putting demons into those flames."

"But why are Martin and I involved? Why not just get a task force of Watchmen together?"

"Watchmen tend to work alone or in small groups. And the more that are present, the more risk we run of getting spotted. If we're spotted, the culprit will flee."

"So, that's why you came back," Ali deduced. "Because you need to look after us. And even if you succeed, you won't be around forever."

"I *want* to be here," Dorian corrected. "And if I can't teach you how to defend yourselves, then you won't be able to stand on your own as the Witch and Wizard."

"Well, I don't want to spend the rest of my life hiding in motels doing...this," I rejected.

"And you won't. When all of this is over, and you're a fully realized Witch and Wizard, you can do anything you want. You can use magic to heal like your mother, hunt like me, or not use it at all."

Ali and I looked at each other.

"But until then, you need to learn how to control your magic. And we can't let you walk out there when there's someone, or something, out to get you."

"We have three hours until sundown," Lyse pointed out.

"Then there's no time to waste," Ali insisted.

Dorian closed the shutters and lit all of the candles without so much as moving a finger.

It was time to learn about magic.

.TEN.

TRAINING

Darkness engulfed the inside of the Silk Slipper, and the lights reminded me of seeing people's auras. There was just enough light to see ahead between the runes, candles, and the salts in the room. And squinting made the magic inside them brighter.

Looking down at my hands, I let the slightest amount of blue aura flare up. And even that was enough to make my spine tingle. This was the best place to learn magic, here in the shadows. We were finally going to learn it.

"This training boils down to three rules," Dorian instructed. "Do as I say. Don't challenge me. And don't put what I teach you on display."

Ali and I nodded.

"You did well today, fighting that demon," Dorian continued. "But you need to be ready for anything. It's not about learning hundreds of spells. It's about having a handful and using them well. Tonight, we're going to learn a handful of techniques that will keep you out of trouble."

"Do you really think that a handful of tricks are going to keep us safe?"

"I'm not going to sugarcoat it, Martin. These demons are little insects compared to what's coming. They are mobilizing right now to find you and Ali. But you have something they don't, you have the status of Witch and Wizard."

"How do our titles defend us?" I asked.

"Being the Witch and Wizard is more than just a title. While most mages are stuck with the cards they've been dealt, you have the ability to play this game with all of the aces up your sleeve. It's all a question of how you use them."

"All right. What should we learn first?"

"Let's start with three of the basics: semblance, apprehension, and divination. You may have read about them from my old book."

"Yes, and Alciel gave me a bit of a crash course right before that demon attacked us."

"What we saw at the park was your aura being emitted. Your essence will constantly emit aura from birth until death. Humans feel it all the time. Experiences, mood, and temperament all play a role in how swiftly or slowly it flows."

"Really?"

"If you ever get the feeling that something is off about a person, that's your aura reacting to theirs. That reaction is actually your essence warning you."

"That's just intuition," I objected.

"Did it ever occur to you that intuition is magic as well? It might be the best magic there is. When you know something deep down, without knowing it in your head, your essence is responding to it. The essence wants to survive as much as the mind, and it has reserves of knowledge that the mind simply can't pick up on. It's been around longer and knows what you need to survive."

"What does this have to do with semblance?" I demanded.

"All these instincts are present in people, but you can take them even further. By tapping into the essence, you can utilize the energy and use it to cast spells. Try to find your essence and control your aura."

I closed my eyes. I put myself back in the basement, fighting for my life against the demon. The ash was flying at me like bullets. The smell of sulfur. Barely getting away with my life. It terrified me, but it also made me feel stronger when I finally won.

I held onto that sense of triumph, and I could feel the warm embrace of my aura encase me again.

"That's a deeper blue than before," Dorian observed.

"Is that important?" I asked.

I opened my eyes.

"In your case, you'll just need to focus intensely on the spell you want to cast and block everything else out. Then you can conjure anything."

"Anything?" I asked.

"Anything. As long as you pace yourself," Dorian affirmed.

I focused on my hand and tried to picture a small flame forming at the center of it.

Fik.

I saw a blue spark.

Fik. Fik. Fik.

It was like I was trying to sustain a flame in a lighter that was out of fuel.

"I can't do it," I gasped.

"Not with that attitude," Ali insisted.

"Your determination is strong, but your anxiety is keeping you from pulling it off. Focus and Disparity, as we call them. Not a perfect translation, but those are the two forces that govern your control of magic. A force to give form to your manna and something to keep it from growing too powerful. Something that boosts your magic like a gas pedal, and something that halts it, like a brake."

I looked into my hand again. I thought about what my fear could cost me if I were out in the field. If I were to lose myself to anxious thoughts in combat, I'd put my life, or Ali's life, at risk one day. I wasn't going to let that happen. I had to be strong.

"Please... work," I pleaded.

I closed my eyes and saw the flame clearly in my mind. It started to grow stronger, but I thought about what happened in the fight. Alciel was down and I was vulnerable. Would it always be like this? Being cornered and surrounded by enemies who I couldn't see until it was too late?

Fik. Fik. Fik.

"Dammit!" I shouted.

"You'll get it, Martin," Ali assured.

She held her hand out, and she closed her eyes.

Fik. Fik. Wharf!

A red flame appeared in her hand, burning like the head of a medieval torch. At the top, there were green bursts of manna.

"Well done," Dorian smiled.

Ali closed her fist, and the flame went away.

"I don't understand," I whispered. "We both went through the same thing. What's holding me back?"

"Don't worry, Martin. This is why I brought us here. To make sure that we could practice somewhere that was safe," Dorian assured.

"But I've followed your every word. I know that I need Alciel to do magic. At least for now. And he's here. I was able to stand my ground against a demon, but I can't use magic when I'm in a place that should be safer."

"It's because you're still living in that fight, like it's not over yet. You may have won, but you can't get the image of that creature out of your mind, can you?"

I looked up at Dorian and hesitated.

"There's no shame in being afraid, Martin," Dorian said. "It means you have a good head on your shoulders, and you know what you're up against. But I'm here to tell you that you *can* do this. Don't let yourself live in the moment. Just focus on what's happening now."

Dorian looked into my eyes, and I knew he was right. I straightened myself up and took a deep breath. I was exhausted from the previous fight, the exorcism, and trying to use magic now. But I realized that this was what it was going to be like for a long time. If I was going to make it through this, I had to be strong.

"Here we go," I breathed.

"Think about everything you've learned. I wouldn't have given you that book if it wasn't going to help you."

I held my hand in front of me and steadied my breathing.

"Okay," I nodded.

Chapter 6: Semblance. Page 116.

I remembered that semblance needed no words. There was the image of a man focusing on how fire felt to him. Unforgiving.

Wrathful. Dangerous. I focused on the burns I'd experienced before. Then I felt something form in my hand. Something more substantial than the meager sparks I conjured before.

Heat.

Roaring, warm, and blue.

Fik. Fik. WHARF!

I opened my eyes and saw the image in my mind's eye had been made real, in the palm of my hand. I looked down at my hand, and I saw the flame. It flickered at first and emitted a series of random colors. Then it sustained itself in a blend of three colors.

Blue, green, yellow.

"Nice job, Martin!" Ali celebrated.

"*Ignis*," I whispered.

WHARF!

The flame soon took on new life as it grew to three times its original size. But just as soon as it flared up, it vanished from view and left behind an odor of sulfur.

I hissed and clutched my fingers.

"Why are my hands sore?" I asked.

I looked down at them, and it felt like they had battery acid running through them.

"Your manna is fueling that fire," Dorian explained.

"How do I make the pain stop?"

"Practice," Dorian answered.

"Of course," I lamented.

"I know this might come as a shock to you, Martin, but you're already doing so well. It may not feel like it because you're so used to things just coming naturally to you."

"How do you know that?" I asked.

"Your parents already explained how you spoke Latin from an early age. And it didn't take that long for you to learn. And then they started singing your praises on everything else you learned on your own. Chemistry. Literature in multiple languages. There isn't anything you can't learn when you set your mind to it. Now it's time to set your mind to magic."

"I will," I grinned.

Dorian smiled back.

"Speaking of Latin, it's a good thing you know it as well as you do. Most people have difficulty selecting the proper words for using magic."

"It doesn't have to be Latin?" Ali asked.

"There's no universal language for spells. However, Latin is by far the most popular. It speaks to a strong intent to use magic, and Latin isn't used as commonly as English or Spanish, for example. But language isn't all that important for these exercises."

"For semblance," I breathed.

"Don't worry about exhaustion. It's completely natural. You'll be spending all of your training doing one of two things: building your manna's intensity, or refining your magic circuits."

"Is that really all it is?" I asked.

"That's a universal truth for mages. You could have an ocean of manna, but it doesn't amount to much if it's weak. The same goes the other way. You can have all the magic circuits in the world. But if they're feeble, you're no better than a third-rate mage."

"And how does mine compare?" I asked.

"Honestly? Your magic is like a...water pistol. You have fair capacity and decent output," Dorian explained.

Ali started laughing.

"Sorry, it's just funny," Ali said, "Picturing Martin shooting down a demon with a water pistol."

"You are in a different situation," Dorian said.

"How so?" Ali asked.

"Frankly, you're more of a pool noodle."

"Hey!"

I snickered at the thought.

"You have a decent reserve of manna, but when you use it, it comes out in large bursts."

"Come on, the track shack wasn't *that* banged up," Ali defended.

"What happened?" Dorian allowed.

"She turned it into splinters," Lyse answered.

"There was a demon inside," Ali said. "I wasn't going to close the door and let him keep hurting people."

"It's nothing to be ashamed of," Dorian assured.

"Then what's next?" Ali asked.

"Ali is going to cast a basic spell," Dorian insisted.

"Nothing I can't handle," Ali smiled. "I've been levitating cups all night."

"What Martin just did was semblance, the ability to morph an aura into new shapes. What you're about to attempt is a spell. That means you're filtering the aura into a shape that performs a function independent of your essence," Dorian explained.

"That actually explains a lot," Ali said.

"How so?" I asked.

"When I was levitating cups, I borrowed your Latin book and used the Latin word for *fly*. But my aura felt like it was cut off, and it basically did what I asked, but automatically."

"That's because your manna took on the properties of

weightlessness and it cut itself off, so it did what you asked instead of lifting everything in the room," Dorian concluded

"Gotcha," Ali absorbed.

"And she has a pretty healthy manna reserve," Lyse said with a smile. "She was able to lift three cups, two heavy books, and a couple of pencils all at once just yesterday."

"How much manna do you think that would require?" I asked.

"You've performed an exorcism, plus you're getting the hand of levitating multiple objects," Dorian said. "That places you at around the realm of five percent capacity. Not bad, considering you're just starting out."

"I like the sound of that," I answered.

"You should," Dorian added, "most kids your age can't even make a demon stay back. You managed to kill one."

"And what about me?" Ali asked.

"About the same," Dorian smiled. "You managed to use your manna to take on blasting properties."

Dorian turned to the back door, just behind the bar. A small jet of deep purple shot out from the keyhole, and we heard a swift *krun* of a brass lock activating.

"Unlock it," Dorian insisted.

"You got it," Ali accepted.

She started walking to the door, removing a small leather bag from her pocket.

"What's that?" Dorian asked.

"A lockpick," Ali responded.

"I meant for you to unlock it from a distance. Where did you get a lockpick?"

"A locker at school," Ali answered cautiously.

"I'll rephrase my question. *How* did you get a lockpicking kit?"

"The combination was easy to figure out. She always did the first two numbers ahead of time. I just rolled the dial until I got to the last digit, and the lock went undone."

We all looked at Ali, bewildered.

"I know. Ironically, her security wasn't all that good," Ali pondered.

Dorian looked at the ground, shook his head, and smiled.

"Just try to use your magic to open the door, please," Dorian insisted.

Ali raised her hand. The doorknob immediately started reacting, but she could only push and pull the door despite all of her efforts.

I realized she was using semblance. I narrowed my vision and saw the faint wisps of crimson that connected her hand to the doorknob.

"Dang it!" Ali whispered.

"It's all right," Dorian insisted.

He walked to Ali's side and raised his hand. He seemed intent, and he brushed his hand to the left as though to push the deadbolt back. With a single movement, the door was open.

Krun.

It swung open, gently.

Creaaaaak.

"Cool," Ali breathed.

"It can be done through semblance. But this exercise is to get you to be deliberate with your word choice for spells," Dorian explained.

"Okay," Ali accepted.

"Now you try," Dorian ordered.

The door shut and locked itself instantly.

Krun.

The same jet of purple signaled that Ali was back to square one.

As the radiant colors faded back into the darkness, I had an idea cross my mind. I closed my eyes and focused on seeing Ali's aura. In just a moment, I opened my eyes and the world became darker.

The only light came from within each of us. I saw the Addiction Demons were absorbing energy inside of them like manna vacuums. Then I turned to Ali. She took a deep breath and closed her eyes. She raised her hand upward, only this time, the handle lightly jiggled as she interacted with the door.

The red haze around her body narrowed into an elongated arm that attempted to open the door. The red arm became thin and split off, leaving a small cloud. A small beam of crimson was forming in the keyhole, and Ali brushed her hand to the side.

Ali rolled up her sleeve and examined a word scribbled onto it with black marker. Then she closed her eyes to focus.

"*Reclude,*" Ali whispered.

The manna collapsed into a ball and enveloped the lock. Every brass part of the lock was under her control, and her intent started to turn the lock before she even issued the command. But as the last sound left her mouth, the words floated along the path the arm once took. And it coursed through the entire lock, and the sound came again.

Krun.

The deadbolt unlocked and the door swung open.

Creaaaaak.

Ali smiled but refused to open her eyes. She knew she had done it. She pulled her hand back, and the aura around the doorknob turned and pulled, opening the door. I blinked and marveled at how amazing the feat was.

Ali's breath became shaky.

"You okay?" Alciel asked.

"I-I'm fine," Ali chuckled. "I thought it would be a good idea to write some Latin on my arms for future reference. And it paid off."

She rolled up her sleeves, and there was hardly a section of her arms that wasn't scrawled with Latin phrases in black marker.

Dorian looked at me.

"By the way, good thinking, Martin," Dorian encouraged. "You saw Ali's aura in action. It's a good skill to have if something is suspicious or if you're in a fight."

"Thanks," I answered.

I approached the table at the center of the room.

"What can you tell us about Binding Circles?"

"You're not going to bind Addiction Demons today, Martin," Dorian refused.

"I'm not asking to make one. I just want to know more about it."

"Okay. Come here," Dorian invited.

He approached his Binding Circle, and all of us clustered around it. Lyse jumped onto Ali's shoulder, and Alciel floated onto mine.

"A Binding Circle is a ritual. And rituals give manna a direction and form outside your body. Semblance is all about controlling manna in its basic form. And the closer it is to your body, the easier it is to control. Spells are all about making that manna take new forms."

"How can someone do that?" I asked.

"Runes," Dorian expanded.

He gestured down to the different sections of the circle he had drawn. There were several archaic letters that I couldn't read. I narrowed my vision, and the faint dim returned, as if I put on sunglasses. Each symbol was filled with enough manna to fill an entire person.

"They look... alive," I breathed.

Pulses shot to the center of the ritual, and the dime bags took on a glow. They turned purple and reminded me of the powder I formed in the chemistry lab.

"My manna is mingling with the drugs, and the Addiction Demons are bound to it," Dorian added.

"We still need to learn how to write these runes down? But I thought that magic language could have been anything, so long as the words meant something to you," I pointed out.

"In most cases, you're right. Some mages have their own language for spells, but the most commonly shared version of arcane language is Latin. But rituals are different. Each word in a ritual needs to be outlined by strong convictions. Stronger than your average spell. This is the language that mages have been using for centuries, and so it's ingrained in most people's training."

"I'm sensing something coming from inside, but it's not an essence," I added.

"It's a core. Every living thing has an essence, but not every living thing can use magic. The reason is there's a different number of magic circuits. This is nothing you haven't heard from me or read about before. But a ritual depends on depositing energy into cores continually to allow them to perform these functions."

"But does that mean magic can take on a living form?" I asked.

"What do you mean?" Dorian asked.

"Can a ritual have so much magic inside of it that it becomes a living thing?"

"For a brief period, yes. That's how animation works," he explained.

"Hmm," Ali pondered.

Dorian held up a ring whose gemstone matched his aura. "This is a ritual ring. I can have it siphon some of my aura throughout the day, and then deposit it into the ritual to keep everything going."

Dorian placed his hand on the table, and I watched as a violet steam of manna *slithered* from the ring to the ritual. It illuminated each of the archaic letters. And a pulse ran up through the Addiction Demons overhead.

"How much manna are you giving up?" Ali asked.

"I get pretty winded after I offer it up. Like I just ran a marathon."

Silence.

"It's magic like this that helps produce the most powerful results. It's also how I managed to find your Alignments using a common cup."

My mind flashed to the strange symbols on Dorian's goblet.

"What were those runes you used the night you met us?" I asked.

"*Absorb, filter, and reveal,*" Dorian answered.

"Is there any way you could lend us some books on different runes and how to use them?" I asked.

"I got you covered," Alciel answered.

The little demon curled himself into a swirl on the couch and smiled knowingly.

"You know about this stuff?" I asked.

"Runes were the first form of writing I mastered," Alciel confirmed.

Buzz.

Dorian produced a cell phone from his coat pocket and closed his eyes when he saw the caller ID.

"It's your mother. We need to get you two home."

Ali and I looked at each other. We wanted to keep training.

"I know it can be discouraging," Dorian said, catching wind of our reaction. "But we are going to train more, and you are going to be ready for everything coming your way. I promise."

"Okay," I resigned.

I opened my backpack and saw Alciel didn't want to get inside. He was still nestled on the old leather couch. He had literally burnt a hole with all of the kneading and circling to get comfortable. I looked down and realized I was still wearing my scarf.

"How about this?" I asked.

He opened his eyes faintly and seemed resigned to it. I bundled him in the fabric and gently put him inside my back-pack. Lyse simply got up and nuzzled Ali.

We all walked into the open, and Dorian scanned the street. I suddenly got an idea. I honed my vision, and scanned the street with him. Fortunately, I saw nobody. Darkness as far as I could see. We were truly alone in this corner of the city.

Not that long ago, being alone in the cold and dark would have been harrowing to even think about. But now, it was the safest place we could be. But this wasn't going to last. Dorian made that clear. I wondered what kind of demons were waiting for us out there. I wondered who was holding that book and feeding off of this city's junkies. In the cold and dark.

ELEVEN

REGROUP

Coming back home had never been so welcome. The ripped leather furniture, the rattling sound of our junker furnace, and the smell of homemade Italian food let us know we were right where we belonged. Our parents seemed relieved when we came home, but they didn't say a word about where we had gone.

"There's something I still don't understand," Ali insisted.

"What's that, sweetie?" Mom answered.

"How did Dad handle the news when you told him you were a Warlock?"

"He actually saw me using magic at work, and I decided that was the time to explain everything."

"At the hospital? Isn't that risky?"

"Of course. But people needed my help. I couldn't just sit back and do nothing. I had spent years trying to get the spell to work properly. And I met your dad while I was hitting my stride in the oncology department."

"And Dad was... okay with this?"

"We were still dating at the time, and I was tending to a patient with lung cancer. The condition was spreading to his bones, and I knew that if I didn't do something, he might have just a month to live."

"What was your spell called again?"

"Saving Grace," Mom smiled.

"That must have taken years to perfect," I noted.

"It was a little something I pulled together over a few years while I was in nursing school," Mom recounted.

"But why doesn't everyone learn this spell? Why haven't you taught anyone how to do it?"

Mom paused.

"It's because I gave up a lot of my abilities to be able to do it at all. It's something called *pruning*. A skill that can perform incredible feats in exchange for giving up some of your magic permanently."

"Permanently?" I asked.

"Don't worry. It's not something you can do by accident. It requires so much dedication, very few people are even capable of pulling it off."

"Is it semblance? A spell?" I asked.

"It's a complex ritual that shuts off some of your magic circuits for good and makes others work well beyond their normal capabilities."

"Was it painful?" Ali asked.

"It was awful. But I helped a lot of people after that. It was worth it."

Silence.

"Before I forget, Martin, a girl called the house a few times now. She says you haven't answered your phone."

"Ooh. A girl," Ali smiled.

I opened my phone.

Flip.

Nine missed calls. All from Beatrice. I guess my phone was on silent.

"It's not like that," I insisted.

"Sounds like you found someone special."

"Very funny. I'm heading upstairs."

I got up and headed to my room.

I got my phone out and dialed Beatrice's number.

"Are you going to ask her out?" Alciel asked.

"No. I don't even know why she called me."

"You're not all that bright, are you?"

I hit the call button.

Ring.

"Hey!" Beatrice said.

"Hey," I answered.

"It's Beatrice! I missed you at study hall."

"Oh, sorry about that," I attempted.

"Not at all! The fire alarm went off today. I was just concerned when I didn't see you outside with everyone else."

"Yeah."

"I was called away just before that happened."

"For what?"

"Tell her you were exorcising demons!" Alciel chuckled.

"Never mind," Beatrice said. "I don't mean to pry. But that reminds me. Want to meet up after school?"

"I can't," I refused.

"When are you available? And don't say you have homework. The whole school knows that's not true."

I looked at Alciel.

"Hold on," I insisted.

I covered the receiver.

"What are you doing?" Alciel asked.

"We can't afford another stunt like that Addiction Demon. She's following my every step!"

"You aren't used to having friends, are you? Throw her a bone. Ask her out."

"No. I have training with Dorian."

"And this is maintaining your cover. It's all necessary!"

"That'll go along great until another demon shows up!"

"You can't live your life worrying the worst will happen and miss out on all the good stuff!" Alciel pointed out.

I considered his argument.

"Just ask her out before she hangs up."

"Fine!" I whispered.

I lifted my hand.

"...still there?" Beatrice asked.

"Yeah. I'm here," I answered.

"So, tomorrow after class?"

"Yeah," I accepted.

"Great! I'll see you then!"

The phone cut off, and I felt a whole new wave of problems coming at me.

TWELVE

CATCHUP

"You're worrying too much. Class is over. Go to her."

"I can't believe I'm doing this," I whispered.

"It's not as complicated as it seems. Just be there. Live in the moment. Open up to her. Talk about your hobbies."

"Oh yeah. That'd be great. My hobbies include exorcism, near-death experiences, and breaking the laws of nature."

"She might find that fascinating."

"What makes you such an expert on this anyway? Are Companions supposed to be matchmakers too?"

"I'm 900 years old. I've been around the block a few times."

"The Spectrum set us up for this? That's kind of a letdown."

"You know you get more hurtful when you're nervous?" Alciel spat.

It was then that a new voice entered the conversation. My backpack was finally quiet and I moved forward.

"Hey!" Beatrice smiled.

I looked to my right and saw Beatrice waving to me. Today she was wearing a patchwork dress that reminded me of Sally from *The Nightmare Before Christmas*. And, as always, she carried her same bag.

"I was wondering where you went. I thought you were going to stand me up again."

"I didn't mean to. Work just got the better of me."

"I have some trouble with math and was wondering if you could help me out. Everyone I talk to says they understand, but then they have another piece of your homework."

"Yeah," I whispered.

"It's nothing to be embarrassed about. It's cool! Like you're one of those *Beautiful Mind* types."

"Without all the crazy?"

"I'm not so sure. We're just getting to know each other."

"Very funny," I smiled.

"Look, I just moved here, and I'm not that good at school in general. If you could help me out, I'd appreciate it."

"By tutoring you?"

"We could call it that. It might also be nice to make a friend."

I contemplated this for a moment. No one had ever been so forward with me. It was always just me and my books. Ali was the closest thing I'd had to a friend since we were little kids.

"Sure," I allowed.

"So, how about the library?" she asked.

"We could always work right here."

"On the bleachers?"

"At least we get a good view while we work."

I looked out at all of the jocks as they made their way to the adjacent track room. And that left a handful of band geeks and popular kids. All of them looked up to Beatrice and me at least once.

"What is it you're having trouble with?" I asked.

"Geometry," Beatrice groaned.

She pulled out the papers full of problems.

It was at this moment that I had an idea.

I closed my eyes for a moment and opened them. The world was dark all around, and I saw everyone's essence.

I turned my gaze to Beatrice. She was a radiant pink. I saw a few small magic circuits tightly focused around the center of her, but nothing to the extent that would allow her to cast spells.

"Your work is..." Beatrice began.

"Right here," I finished.

I reached out to the page and started recreating my work. Step-by-step. I couldn't be sure, but there were faint wisps of blue as I wrote out each problem. Like my manna was bleeding onto the page.

"You just have to ask if you want it back," Beatrice laughed.

I blinked and realized that Beatrice couldn't see my manna.

"It's no problem. I'm just surprised," I attempted, "Now what were we working with first?"

"There's this proof that's giving me some grief."

"Let's see," I contemplated.

I let myself write out the problem, and manna continued to flow from my pen. But Beatrice made no remarks.

"And...that's the proof."

"Proof that I'm never going to get this," Beatrice chuckled.

"Don't be so hard on yourself. It's a lot easier with practice."

"I just don't see how the formulas do that."

"I'll do it again," I insisted.

I looked down at my hands and saw that they were starting to give off a slight glow. Nothing that was going to put me in danger of getting caught. I only knew it was there because I was looking for it.

Beatrice looked into my eyes the whole time, and I was suddenly grateful for that. As my aura began to calm down, I heard a slight snickering from inside my backpack. I also heard Dorian's words in the back of my mind.

"Intuition is a type of magic."

That would explain why my manna was behaving this way.

"You've been here your whole life?" Beatrice asked. "In Detroit?"

I turned to her and nodded.

"Must be nice to stay in one place for so long. I never stay anywhere long."

"Why is that?" I asked.

"I never knew my family. They all died when I was little."

"You don't have anyone?" I asked.

"I'm staying with some friends of the family. And they insisted we all stay in Michigan. For my high school years."

"I'm sorry," I offered.

"Don't be. It's nice to be able to talk about it with someone."

"Only if you're sure."

"I'm quite sure."

I smiled.

"We've lived two miles from this school all my life," I explained.

"Is it as rough a neighborhood as they say?"

"We're inner city Detroit. So, it gets a little rough."

"But it looks like you turned out pretty well."

"Barely," I smiled.

"If you turned out okay, maybe you're the kind of person I should keep around. You'll at least know the best places to go out with a minimal chance of getting mugged."

"Sure."

Beatrice's phone sang, and she smiled.

"Give me a minute," she insisted.

Beatrice quickly grabbed her phone and pressed it to her ear.

"Hello? Yeah. Gotcha. I'll be right over."

Beatrice looked at me with a small smile.

"Looks like I'm the one that has to go this time. But I'm glad we had this talk."

"Study hall?" I asked.

"Study hall," she confirmed.

Beatrice kissed me on the cheek and rushed off the bleachers. A warm flood came into my face, and I felt my aura and heart rate spiking out of control.

"You dog!" Alciel cheered.

I looked down and saw the whole of the gymnasium stare up at me with knowing grins.

"Not bad for a first date," Alciel snickered.

"It wasn't a date," I whispered.

I threw my bag over my shoulder.

"Try telling her that."

THIRTEEN

UNEARTH

"You're home late," Ali said.

She turned in her favorite chair to face me.

"You heard."

"About your date? Yeah."

"It wasn't a date. Incidentally, you'd make a great James Bond villain."

"You're usually here three hours earlier, and you spend all of your time reading."

"I was helping her with geometry. So I stayed after school for a bit."

"I bet you helped her out," Ali chuckled.

"Now you're just being ridiculous."

"Hey, you need to put yourself out there!" Ali shouted.

She shot up from the chair and gave me two quick punches in the arm.

"You saying I need to get laid?"

"Put yourself *out there*. Not put out!" Ali laughed.

"I still don't get it."

"I'm saying I'm proud of you. You're really getting to know someone. And this is the first time I've seen you try to make any kind of connection."

"Thanks, I guess."

"I know it's hard for you to make connections with new people, but I'm here for you. I don't care if she's your girlfriend or just a friend. If you're happy, I'm happy."

"God knows we could use some of that right now."

"Which reminds me!" Ali insisted.

My sister grabbed my hand and led me to the door to the basement.

"What are you up to?" I asked.

"Just wait!" Ali smiled.

For the first time, I walked into an illuminated basement. There hadn't been working lights in this basement for fifteen years.

"Ta-da!" Ali beamed.

Our basement had long been home to concrete and cardboard boxes. Baseball cards, trinkets of childhood, and most everything we couldn't bring ourselves to throw away. The last time I was here, I was putting a trunk of Dad's formal attire away. Ali had changed it completely.

In place of a neglected pedal bike, there was a drawing table. Baseball gear was replaced with intricately crafted wands, and the dirt floor was replaced with a carpet of grass that was softer than any greenery I had ever felt. All of it was illuminated with what looked like electric lights.

"*Lumina!*" Ali commanded.

With that, a series of soft, white lights shone from above.

But there were no electric fixtures. All of the bulbs and wiring were replaced by small, white flowers nestled in green foliage wires.

"Wow," I whispered.

"I took over the basement."

"I love it! How did you do all of this?"

"I was experimenting with my powers and made some discoveries."

"Discoveries?"

"Lyse knows a lot of Green Magic. Now that she's my Companion, I suppose I do, too!"

"All of this is powered by your manna?"

"That's right. Even the lights."

"What are they?"

"Lyse formed them. Small lotus flowers. I chose white because it illuminates the room without making it look like a disco."

"And you cleaned the place. That's the real miracle."

"I sold the lights to a friend of mine for some cash. The wiring is worth something."

"And the boxes?"

"Sorted."

"But why did you do all of this?"

"I wanted some good to come out of this. Something for me. Maybe even for all of us."

"You're willing to share this with me?"

"You're my brother. Of course you can use this."

"Either way, I love what you've done with the place."

"Check this out," Ali smiled.

She knelt down and peeled back some of the green grass that draped the floor. I saw an image that was a blend between a sun and an oak tree. It was white and smelled of hot wax.

"A rune," I smiled.

"It may not be trapping demons, but it gets the job done."

"That's brilliant! It helps you grow your plants."

"That's right. And it lets me do all sorts of things. I'm enchanting flowers and saplings like you wouldn't believe!"

Plants filled the room like one giant organism. An unexpected warmth came from the center of the room.

Ali detected my curiosity and pointed to a white circle carved into the ground.

"That's the heart of the operation."

Ali peeled back a last bit of greenery and revealed a strange swirl symbol at its center.

Ali smiled and brought me over to her drawing desk. She was already in the process of sketching the flowers on a massive canvas sketching pad. There was a red rose, a blue lily, a green orchid, and a yellow sunflower. All of them perched on the edge of the desk, with their drawn counterparts just beneath them.

"It all comes from that circle I drew. And each one has a different effect. The rose is like a magic GPS. The lily prevents minor hauntings. The orchid stimulates growth. And the sunflower is a catalyst for healing potions."

"How did you come across all of this?"

Ali held up a green book with a tree drawn on the cover. It was almost identical to mine, save those two features.

"Dorian told me it helped him get through the first few stages when he got his powers. Plus, I borrowed your book for a while."

"And no one is going to ask about this?" Alciel asked.

I unzipped my backpack and Alciel crawled onto my shoulder.

"Hey, if anyone asks, I like collecting books and doing botany on the side."

"It's certainly much more innocent than taking junkies off the street and pulling demons out of their chest cavities," Alciel countered.

"Why did you bring him?" Lyse smiled.

"Thanks for showing me this, Ali."

"Sure. But why are you thanking me?"

"Because I have an idea."

"Yeah?" Ali asked.

"Alciel, how much do you know about potions?" I asked.

Alciel's sharp ears twitched at my question.

"All there is to know," Alciel said.

"Teach me," I said.

"I'll only do this if you keep your requests entertaining."

"How's that?" I asked.

I ascended the stairs to get to my room.

"Pyromancy, transformation, or something just as good."

"I'm not sure I'm ready for something like that."

"Most boys would kill to have your power as the Wizard. But I'm stuck with an old man."

"What?"

"You drink copious amounts of tea, you only read the classics, and you're content to just sit in a rocking chair."

"What's wrong with that?"

"I had some hope for you when I saw that beat-up guitar and the Billy Idol music collection. But I didn't think you'd be so timid when it came to using your magic."

"I've been studying. So I'll know how to use it."

"And you're always writing in those blank books on your

bookshelf. What's that all about?"

We made our way into my room.

"Songs. Stories. Some sketches. Whatever comes to mind, really," I admitted. "And I'm not an old man. Last I checked, old men don't fight demons. Hell, they probably don't even know they're real."

"That's what you think," Alciel whispered. "They are some of our best customers."

"Okay. *This* needs to stop," I chuckled.

"What's that?" Alciel asked.

"Old Christian men in retirement homes don't make deals with the devil."

"Why wouldn't they?" Alciel countered. "People only refuse deals when they have something to lose or moral objections. They are in retirement homes. They aren't going to regret it for long."

"You sound like a vulture," I objected.

"Vultures aren't nearly shady enough," Alciel smiled.

"For a creature who talks as much as you do, you really avoid anything that matters. You keep trying to hide everything. Demons, the Necronomicon, not to mention you said something about me not remembering what it means to be the Wizard."

I went into my closet and pulled out a dusty box. Alciel looked at me, impressed.

"You really are observant," Alciel smiled.

"Thanks," I said. "We have some work to do."

"I guess I don't have a choice, but what's in that box?" Alciel asked.

"I got a chemistry set at a garage sale two years ago. Should be useful for practicing alchemy."

"I seriously doubt a chemistry set for kids is going to..."

Alciel stopped mid-sentence when I opened a box filled with everything from gas masks to boiling flasks.

"You sure the guy you bought this from wasn't trying to get rid of evidence?"

"I'll ask the questions," I insisted.

Alciel chuckled at that.

"First of all, I want you to tell me everything there is to know about this Wizard deal. Because you know a lot, and I know next to nothing."

"Fine."

"Start at the beginning," I insisted.

"No one really knows why the Witch or Wizard came into being, but they go very far back. And the Spectrum chooses them. Some famous people were Witches and Wizards before you. Or they were the ones behind major changes in the last few millennia."

"How many Witches and Wizards have there been?"

"Their history goes further back than we can record."

"'We' being the Demon Courts?"

"The Order," Alciel corrected.

Alciel took a seat at the edge of my writing desk as I finished turning it into a full-blown chemistry lab.

"The Order. What is their role in all of this?" I asked. "I've heard Dorian mention it. But he's always cautious about what he says."

"They're the highest rank of government."

"How does that work?"

"Are you familiar with the concept of technocracy?"

"Sure. It's a government that chooses intellectuals and the strongest minds to be leaders," I answered.

"That's essentially what the Order is. They are the most powerful mages bound together to rule, legislate, and keep order. All the most powerful mages have a spot."

"Hmm. *Where* are they? They have to operate from somewhere."

"Everywhere. There's plenty of people who work on behalf of the Order who operate all throughout the world. Some of them are as overtly mystical as Witchdoctors. And others are like Dorian."

"And he's a Watchman. What is that, exactly? In relation to the Order, I mean."

"The Order is what you might call the executive power in the magical world. Watchmen are supposed to protect and serve. They're basically the FBI. Just like Dorian keeps claiming. If a Count Dracula or Frankenstein Monster comes into the picture, people like Dorian take them down."

"That happens a lot?"

"Dark mages and their creations are treated with the same level of fear as terrorists for humans."

"Is it really so common that someone can become a threat?"

"Magic comes to people very young, in most cases. Lots of people have tried to work out why the Root and Spectrum and Void work the way they do. It would go a long way in keeping people safe. But anyone who tries to get too close to the truth ends up getting hurt."

"Dorian's book mentioned that. Divination?" I asked.

"It's extremely dangerous. It requires more manna than most people have. And very few people can use it effectively."

"If there's a skill like that, why doesn't Dorian just use it to track down who has the book?"

"It's not that simple, Martin. Dorian is an expert on demonic and combat magic. As an Evoker, it could be extremely dangerous to use any skill outside of his preferred arsenal."

"Like he could go crazy?"

"Exactly like that. Divination is letting your mind gain access to all manner of things. Some people try to catch a killer using divination and end up seeing every terrible thing in a given town and go crazy. They experience the sensations of the killer and the victim set on a loop."

"Seriously?" I asked.

"Well, that's what people report. And that's when divination works properly."

I prepped the glassware across my desk.

"The Order runs things, the Watchmen maintain order, and what about the Witch and Wizard. What do they do? Or, I guess, what do *we* do?"

"The Witch and Wizard are special. You can bend, even break the laws of magic," Alciel added.

"Laws?"

"Most people can't go beyond their Alignments, but Witches and Wizards can. This means they can be a great help to the Order, or they can be a big problem."

I stopped setting up the chemistry set.

"You're saying the Order is watching over us like this because we're a problem in their eyes?" I added.

"For all they know, you might have the Necronomicon."

"But we don't."

"They wouldn't risk that."

"No one trusts us, do they?" I asked.

"If it helps, I have no reason to despise you yet."

A smile came across my face.

"Fine. Let's move on to the next big thing. What is this book?"

Silence.

"The Necronomicon is an artifact. An item so powerful, it can retain its own essence and bends the rules of magic."

"Whoever made this book, they killed enough people to give the book its own essence."

"What does this book do, exactly?" I asked.

"The book has the ability to keep people from suffering the ill effects of killing somebody. You know this."

"I'm still not sure I follow."

"Magic plays a major part in everything we do. Magic is what gives us intuition. It can enhance the body's capabilities when we're in danger, and it can bend the laws of the physical world if we have enough magic circuits."

"Killing someone with magic harms our essence?"

"People get their intuition from magic, whether they know it or not. Likewise, killing someone hurts the murderer, whether they know it or not."

"What happens, exactly?"

"When you kill someone, your mind and body become corrupted because you cause an essence to die out. It hurts people in ways they can't imagine. A single murder can drive someone insane or cause them to do more terrible things. And if they already know about magic, they can unlock terrible new powers."

"You seem to be well-versed in how murder affects people's magic."

"It's common for demons to visit death row inmates and give them some level of power. Goethe saw us do it once. After a while, we just conformed to the stereotype."

"So, killing someone leaves a trace on your essence. But how can a book prevent that?"

"The book acts as a kind of magnet. It takes the damage for you. In fact, corruption feeds the book. Some even believe it gives the book new spells as it gets stronger."

"And that would just allow its wielder to hide in plain sight."

"It's a coveted artifact, that's for sure."

"Using your magic to kill someone. I can see why certain mages need to be taken down, but it must weigh heavily on people."

"Dark mages need to be punished somehow. Magic can make you immune to a lot of things. Bullets, poison, even aging."

"You need to fight fire with fire," I reasoned.

"The only way to defeat most dark mages is with magic. And we can't let people's essence get clouded when we know the truth of how corrupting that can be. Every time we appoint an executioner, we could be poisoning their essence until we have to put them down someday. And even that would be a real headache."

"That's awful. And the cycle would never stop. Not to mention, if you have an executioner who knows magic, and they can kill dark mages, you don't want that person turning against you."

"Hardly. The book has more abilities than to ease the burden of killing a man."

Clink.

I finished setting up the chemistry set.

"Dorian seems determined to get it back."

"Probably because he was in charge of guarding Hive and the book," Alciel said. "And when I say Hive, I mean Adrian Hive.

He was the last Wizard. And Mila Hollyheart, she was the last Witch. Did you know that already, or was that one of the things I've been hiding from you?"

"Ha-ha, very funny," I said. "But this does explain a lot."

"The book was stolen right from under his nose. Not only does he have a duty to fulfill, he has a score to settle," Alciel said. "And, between us, I don't think Dorian would be able to live with himself if the book was used to harm you or your sister."

"What did Hive do with the book?"

"Hive was smart enough to put a Spell Lock on it. It's a special function that allows certain magic to still exist on a page, but be unreadable to others."

"Like gibberish?"

"Yes. And that book must have been laced with all manner of other enchantments. Burn immunity. Encrypted script. Maybe even instantly killing thieves."

"You know all of this for a fact?"

"It's an educated guess."

"Okay. Assuming everything you said was true, how are we supposed to get it back with Dorian rounding up Addiction Demons and struggling to teach me and my sister magic?"

"It may seem like he's short-handed, but he's actually making the best move right now. We don't know who has the book, and bringing in any more Watchmen would make whoever has it run away. He's cutting them off at the knees and keeping you and Ali safe."

"They could kill more people if they're scared," I added.

"Right. But that's part of why they must be doing this. There's a lot of power to be gained from Addiction Demons. They linger over people and control so much of their lives, so much of their essence."

"And whoever has the book is binding the demons to their power so they get stronger."

"With enough demonic power, they may be able to force the book open. Then they could use every spell inside. But that won't come without complications."

"That's a lot to take in."

"It looks like you finally got the chemistry set unpacked."

"I guess so," I said. "Now that the 'history of magic' detour is complete, wanna show me how potions work?"

"Simple, really," Alciel said. "The only real separation from fake magic and real potion making is that you pour your manna into the ingredients. Giving them their own core. That opens a very big door into a larger world. But it takes a lot of time to learn."

"We have all night."

FOURTEEN

TRAP

Training had gotten better with more trips to the Silk Slipper. My magic was a darker shade of blue and it gave off more heat. The more intense the flame, the more of the room I was able to see. After a few weeks, I noticed a smile form on Dorian's lips that confirmed I was ready for more.

"You're getting a lot better at handling your semblance, Martin," Dorian observed.

"Do we have to keep coming out here to do this?" Alciel asked. "This motel is colder than it is outside. And Martin's still falling asleep."

"That's what happens when your life is constantly in danger," I said. "Otherwise, this training might be fun."

"Your spells are lasting longer, and your manna reserves have gotten considerably stronger in what, a week?"

"I thought I'd do a bit of self-teaching."

"You've been speaking with Alciel, haven't you?"

"He's my Companion. It's what he's supposed to do."

"You're taking knowledge from wherever you can find it. That'll serve you well in the future."

"Hey, boys," Ali greeted.

Ali appeared with more Mason jars for exorcisms.

My phone vibrated in my pocket.

BUZZ.

"Need to get that?" Ali asked.

"God, no," I answered.

"Good, because we have something in mind."

"What's that?" I asked.

"Dorian has been asking me to write up a spell around the demon Binding Circle," Ali smiled.

I looked over to the bowl where all of the drugs were contained and saw more than a handful of runes around it.

Instead of *contain, bind, and pierce,* I saw many runes woven into every strand of the weblike spell that came from the center.

"*Track, hone,* and what's this last one?" I asked.

"*See,*" Dorian answered.

"What are you hoping to see?" I asked.

"I'm sure Alciel has already told you the details of how a ritual like this works. Well, we're going to change things up. See through their eyes so we can find the book."

"That's insane."

"Not so insane, really. They've been put through the wringer. Drained of all their manna for weeks. Even if we cut them loose, they couldn't get very far."

"But that doesn't mean this is safe. There could be some kind of trap you don't know about."

"I'm counting on it."

I hesitated.

"How could springing the trap be a good thing?" I asked.

"Whoever has the Necronomicon is taking it one page at a time. If we spring the trap and they pull out all the stops, we may be able to see just how far they've gotten. And what they'll do next. After all, I'm one of only a few people left alive who have seen it work," Dorian explained.

"It still seems like a risk we shouldn't be taking. Not with just the five of us."

"All of those Addiction Demons up there were drawn by the Necronomicon and weaponized by it. And that kind of power doesn't come without a price."

"I thought the whole point of the Necronomicon was to absorb the side effects of lethal magic?"

"That's because it was crafted by necromancers. They know those sordid secrets to keep your manna from going darker and turning you into a horrible monster. But demonic magic is a... fiefdom of its own. They're mixing two dangerous magics together, and it will leave a trace on them. Somewhere. I'm hoping it's through these demons we have in captivity."

"What exactly do you expect they'll find, Dorian?" I asked.

"To see what kind of powers the wielder has. And it may just be a theory now, but I'm hoping to see just how far this goes. Who else is involved."

"Who else could be involved?" Ali asked.

"Again. It's just a theory," Dorian said. "But there are certain accidents and overdoses all across Detroit. Some of them are as far apart as Warrendale and East English Village. You could only cover that kind of distance with multiple people."

"How many?" I asked.

“Two. Someone holding the book, and someone helping to wrangle demons,” Dorian theorized.

“There’s no telling what we’re up against. We’ll only know by trying to scare them into a reaction,” Alciel grimly acknowledged.

“If we’re going to stay ahead of this, we need to try and get an edge wherever we can. And with this many Addiction Demons, we may have just found it.”

“How?” Ali asked.

“I’m going to use this ritual to look into the minds of each demon. I’ll see if there are any clues about who holds the book. I expect they did the smart thing and kept their face and essence covered, but that doesn’t mean we’ll come up totally empty-handed. We may find clues as to who the current wielder of the book is. A place, a spell they use in response. Something.”

“But that’s divination. I thought that was dangerous. Even for someone like you,” I pointed out.

“You forget, I’m also an expert in demonic magic,” Dorian said. “And it’s a risk I’m willing to take. Besides, I have you here to support me.”

“And this means that we’ll have to watch Dorian’s back while this is happening,” Lyse concluded. “He’ll have to dedicate himself completely to not be consumed by the demons we have here. And that means we’ll protect his body.”

Ali and I looked at one another and realized we were in for a challenge.

“What do you need?” I asked.

“I’m going to stand at the circle and funnel manna inside, specifically into the new runes. They’ll react and flow into the Binding Circle, making sure the Addiction Demons are the only ones affected,” Dorian explained.

"Okay," I nodded.

"Meanwhile, you two are going to prepare a rune erasure spell. If anything goes awry, I want you two to use that spell and wipe the runes away. Once the connection is severed, the danger is over."

"You got it!" Ali assured. "Also, what's a rune erasure spell?"

I raised my hands. I closed my eyes and concentrated on the spellbook and the incantation I read in Dorian's black spellbook.

Chapter 10: Runes. Page 222.

There was a spell. An illustration of a woman raising her hands forward and washing wax runes in the ground by whispering a phrase in Latin. I could see it clearly. The Latin phrase for *wipe this ritual away*.

An aura of blue surrounded my hands, and golden sparks followed. Alciel's ears perked up and we both started speaking.

"*Extergimus caerimonias istas,*" we whispered.

Ali stepped to my side and repeated the exact motions and phrasing I had just performed.

Her red aura enveloped her hands and emerald sparks followed. Lyse's ears perked up and they both began speaking.

"*Extergimus caerimonias istas,*" they whispered.

Both of our hands were enveloped in a bright blue aura that was similar to a flame. Only this flame was sky blue and had a cooling effect on our hands.

We all looked at Dorian and nodded. We were ready.

I took my Companion and Ali took hers. We watched as Dorian put his hands to the Binding Circle and began chanting.

"*Accipe virtutem meam. Ostende mihi quod vidi.*"

"What's he saying, Martin?" Ali asked.

"Take my power. Show me what you have seen," I answered.

Dorian closed his eyes and whispered the incantation repeatedly. We looked up and saw that the thin, translucent line that bound each of the Addiction Demons together was starting to glow.

SCREEEEEEEE!

They gave off that horrible sound, like a condemned man's dying wail.

Dorian rose into the air.

Each of the demons had a purple light emerge from their eyes. Their contorted and burned bodies had eyes open in all manner of places and shapes on their faces. But, in the end, they all opened wide as Dorian's. They were *forced* open.

I saw the manna flow from Dorian's hands without any need of altering my vision.

"Is he all right?" I asked.

"He's fine," Alciel confirmed. "He's been putting these demons through the wringer by binding them to the circle. Whatever happens, we'll be ready for it."

I took a deep breath, certain Dorian had this under control.

"Martin," Ali whispered.

She pointed directly to the Binding Circle, and I saw a terrible stain of midnight black begin to work its way through the ritual.

I looked up and saw the eyes of the Addiction Demons had a sickly red light corrupting them. The runes on their chest started to change shape and become thicker and denser. They split off from a unified Venn diagram of three circles to three separate, hollow dots in the formation of a triangle. I recognized this rune as the symbol of oppression. I'd seen it in chapter ten of Dorian's spellbook.

“They’re going to attack him,” I cautioned.

Alciel soon rushed to the Binding Circle. But as soon as he started running, it was as though the black stain knew he was about to tamper with it. The dark liquid on the ground festered and lashed out at him, leaving sparks in their wake. Alciel doubled back before he could be hit.

SHREEE.

Another black bolt shot from the circle, and Dorian barely managed to dodge it. As he struggled, I saw the same thin lines that held the demons together were now tied to Dorian. We dove behind some worn-out furniture and didn’t move an inch.

“What is that?” Ali asked.

“Primordial lightning,” Alciel explained. “You see it when someone is paranoid about their ritual circles.”

“Something the demons carried with them?” I asked.

“Got to be. Whoever has the Necronomicon must have wised up and put a virus in them,” Alciel surmised.

“What does that mean for Dorian?” I asked.

CRACK!

I looked up and saw the black energy raging around Dorian. Burns only an Addiction Demon could conjure.

He waved his arms, and his tattoos and manna burned violently. They pierced through the horrible jets of hellfire ash and shined like a terrible dawn.

They got close many times, but they never once reached him. It was like watching a man push aside incoming bullets.

The demons’ crimson eyes were wide open, and they were looking directly at Dorian.

“If we don’t get to him before the fire reaches him, he just might become the worst Addiction Demon I’ve ever seen,” Alciel warned.

"There's got to be something we can do," Ali insisted.

"There is. We can cut off the Binding Circle," I proposed.

I held up my sky blue hand.

"I'm ready when you are," Ali smiled.

"We just need a good shot," I insisted.

We looked at each other, knowing we had no other choice.

"How's your Combat Magic?" I asked.

"*Clipeum,*" Ali replied.

A circle of crimson hovered above her arm and I knew we had the same plan.

"Just get me close," I insisted.

Ali rushed forward and Lyse came close behind. As Ali held up her arm, she blocked every bolt that came her way.

FREW-FREW!

The crimson shield she carried started to crack, but every time it was about to give, Lyse's ears perked up and flared green, repairing it. I heard shots sound off behind me.

I looked up and saw the Addiction Demons were in as much pain as our friend. Wounds of pure white formed on the demons, and they doubled back. They bent at inhuman angles. The terrible heat from the center of the ritual was growing weak.

They were repairing themselves, but they were distracted. I rushed forward and made my way to the black ritual that lay on the table.

"All right, talk me through this, Alciel," I insisted.

"They're trying to take control of the ritual," Alciel said. "The runes for *see* and *pierce* are glowing. Which means they're trying to see what Dorian has seen. They're trying to see where we are, I bet. Or they're trying to get a good shot."

"Then we can just undo them," I responded.

I attempted to wipe away the rune for *pierce*, but it burned my hand fiercely. A small column of black flame threatened to consume my hand.

FOAST!

"AAAH!!!" I shouted.

I looked down, and it was turning pitch-black.

"You can't just scratch out runes like that!" Alciel shouted.

"I'll try something else."

I held my hand up and focused intently on the same rune.

"*Repelle flammae!*" I shouted.

The rune began to wipe itself away, and the table started to radiate a horrible flame. One that was being washed away from my hand.

"With me, Alciel," I insisted.

My Companion reared himself like a cat, and his horns began to glow deep gold.

"*Repelle flammae!*" I shouted.

My blue blast was augmented by a set of gold bursts. It coursed through the entire table in the form of a bubble, and it burst over everything, washing away every rune there was. The screams of the demons above were desperate.

The runes seemed to resist for a moment, and the demons had their *oppression* runes burn in kind.

SCREEEEEEEE!

"*Repelle flammae!*" I shouted.

The runes were scrubbed away to less than half their original shape.

SCREEEEEEEEEEEEEEEEEEEEE!

"*Repelle flammae!*" I roared.

It felt like my eardrums were filled with vibrating glass. Dorian fell to the ground, and every demon along with him. Every *thud* was noiseless to me, but I could feel them.

The demons fell to the ground and shattered into pieces. Some of it was hunks of black flesh, and some of it was caked mud.

I rose up and let my hearing come back to me. I faced the ritual circle, and the entire table had been blown to splinters and ash.

"Nice job," Dorian shuddered.

"Let's get you fixed up, Dorian," Ali insisted.

She knelt down and grabbed Dorian by the arms. I grabbed him by the legs. We lifted Dorian onto one of the makeshift hospital beds we had been using for junkies.

"I'll get some plants grown for healing ointments," Ali announced.

She held her hand to the ground and red radiated from her palm.

"*Cresce alta.*"

Plants took root and grew tall at Ali's feet.

I rushed over to the reception desk, where Dorian kept all of his equipment and began concocting the ingredients.

"You kids are really something else," Alciel smiled.

Ali crushed flower petals over Dorian.

"GAH!" Dorian grunted.

"Quit your whining," I responded, holding back a smile.

"Not sure you noticed, but I just got attacked, Blackbriar," Dorian responded.

I looked into Dorian's eyes. They were still amber, like I remembered. He was not afflicted.

"You look... all right," I observed.

“I was lucky. You two managed to cut the demons off before they could reach my essence.”

“How’s that possible?”

“They were corrupting my manna, but they didn’t get anywhere near my essence. That’s how they work. They possess your spells and turn them into their own power. Then they make you one of them by taking who you were away. Bit by bit.”

“They were really trying to turn you?”

“It takes away who you are and turns you into a demon. One piece at a time.”

“Whoever set this up really knows what they’re doing. I didn’t even catch a glimpse of their face. It felt like old demonic magic.”

“You must have found something useful,” Ali insisted. “This couldn’t have been for nothing.”

Silence.

“That onslaught told me a lot about how powerful the mage is who’s holding the book,” Dorian said. “And they are considerably further along than I thought. It felt like I was being attacked by multiple people. That only proves my theory.”

Dorian looked to Ali with grim acknowledgment. We all did.

“This means they have powerful demonic magic on their side from the book,” I answered. “Not a good sign.”

“But they also overplayed their hand,” Dorian said. “Whoever was taking potshots at me, they looked through the demons’ eyes. And that kind of connection always leaves a trace. Always.”

Ali handed me small bundles of plants. Purple sage, blue roses, and yellow orchids. As she gave them to me, I was getting them ready with a mortar and pestle.

“How do you know so much about this book and what

it's capable of?" Ali asked. "It's about time you told us what's going on."

"The last owner of the book was my mentor," Dorian started. "More than that, really. Hive was like a father to me. He trained me just as I've been training you two. How to use magic, how to defend myself, and how to become a Watchman. Naturally, that book was a constant part of my life. Wherever Adrian was, it was."

"And you saw what magic he was wielding. Every spell that came out of that book," Ali nodded.

"Hive was there for every major execution of a dark mage for fifty years. I was the closest person to that book aside from him."

"And how did he kill his prisoners?" Ali asked.

"There's all manner of spells in that book. Some are basic killing spells. But the vast majority of the spells are used to protect you from harm and to carry out your lethal abilities in ways that can't be traced back to you."

"Makes me wish we had it sooner," Lyse interjected.

"But as Adrian got further along, I knew that the book was capable of doing so much more than being a glorified executioner's axe."

"What was it?" I asked.

"The book can bring people back, prolong the user's life, and perform and protect you against any spell within the domain of necromancy."

Silence.

"You two had taken to your powers so quickly, I had to make sure you were under careful watch," Dorian said. "There's no telling who is hunting you down, and they'd be able to find you very quickly if I didn't show you the way."

"To reign our powers in and make sure they didn't grow

too big to be detected," Alciel finished.

"So, how far along are they in the book, Dorian?" I asked.

"I've seen Hive use an infection spell like that once, and that was at the center of the book. A little more than halfway through. We're in for a real fight if they get much further. The book gets more dangerous as you approach the end."

"Half?!" Ali shouted.

"I know it sounds bad. Being able to infect rituals complicates things enough as it is. But on the plus side, we cut them off at the knees."

"Did you see anything?" I asked. "And, more importantly, did whoever set the trap see us here?"

"I saw lots of people dying. Most of them are in rehab and in drug houses. Which was clever. They really knew how to cover their tracks."

"What did we learn about the victims?" Ali asked. "Maybe that'll help something."

"There were no wounds anywhere," Dorian said. "There were no cuts, shots, or poisons. They looked like they were in the best health possible right up until they were infected with darkness. It leaves no trace. Just like the first spell in Hive's book."

Dorian turned to the map. His eyes were filled with dread; it was like just looking at the map was enough to take him to each of those horrible places where these tragedies happened.

"And it gets worse," Dorian added.

"How does it get worse than *that*?" Alciel asked.

"Dorian brings people in after they've been possessed," I said. "Before long, he'll be bringing in corpses."

"The book took Hive fifty years to get to the end," Dorian said, "but somehow, this book has been out of his hands for fifteen years, and it is *still* causing people to drop like flies. Which means someone is undoing the Spell Lock and may be dangerously close to getting it undone."

"What if they saw us through the demons?" Ali asked.

"I was careful not to let them see us," Dorian said. "I utilized the Selective Presence of the Addiction Demons to make sure the entire place was a blur. Even I wouldn't be able to break through something like that from the outside."

"That tells us a lot," I mumbled.

"How so?" Ali asked.

"They know about magic well enough to use Selective Presence," I continued. "They have access to rehab facilities. And they're smart enough to know what we're going to do next."

"I guess that does tell us something," Ali acknowledged.

"If our attempts at getting a look at them didn't work, how are we supposed to find them?" Lyse asked.

"Instead of us trying to draw them out, we can play the waiting game," Dorian answered.

"You're planning on just letting the book be used to kill people?" I asked.

"Whoever is behind all of this is clearly panicked," Dorian said. "They've been attacked. And they pulled out all the stops trying to end this fight before it started. I think we have the advantage. They'll slip up. And we'll be there when they do."

FIFTEEN.

TUTOR

"Martin?" Beatrice asked.

"Yeah?" I answered.

"You all right? I've been asking you about geometry for the last hour, and you keep staring off into space. Something on your mind?"

"Just the usual stuff," I insisted.

I tried to look at the problem in front of us.

"Don't tell me it's girl trouble."

That sentence arrested me.

"Girl trouble?" I repeated.

"You've got to fill in the hours somehow, and something tells me this is girl trouble."

"I've never even been with a girl aside from you," I admitted.

"*With* a girl?" she said, raising an eyebrow.

I felt my face start to burn in embarrassment.

"Not like that," I quickly insisted. "Hey, don't we have a

problem to work out?"

"I'd say we do. You've been helping me a ton with classwork, but we've never spent any real time together. Which is odd, because I still know nothing about you."

"There's not much to know."

"You're telling me there's nothing to know about a guy who has the brain of Einstein but the track record of Jesse James?"

"You make it sound so much worse than it really is."

"Clearly you don't listen to the teachers coming out of the lounge. They talk about how you have the highest scores they've ever seen, but how you will probably graduate to Wayne County Jail."

"I'm assuming that was Fitzgerald," I deduced.

"But it wasn't bitter like you'd expect. It was like she was afraid. Like she thought you'd waste your potential. And, somehow at the same time, you'd become a super-villain."

I laughed at the prospect.

"You *do* have a sense of humor!" Beatrice chuckled.

"Stop trying to warm up to me."

"No, I'm having too much fun with it now," Beatrice chuckled. "I just realized you know next to nothing about me, either."

"We can make this a game if it'll help pass the time. But the library isn't the best place to strike up a Q&A."

"Agreed. How about the back of the school?"

Beatrice reached inside her Jack Skellington bag and produced a pack of smokes.

"How did you know I smoked?" I asked.

"You usually smoke one of these during your free period, right?"

"Yeah. I just didn't know you were watching me so closely,"

I smirked.

"The smell gave it away. Caught wind of it the first time I met you." Beatrice admitted.

She pulled a Tim Burton lighter from her bag, making me wonder just how deep her obsession with the acclaimed director went.

"Let's head out back," she smiled. "Nobody will bother us there."

I took a moment to contemplate it. Then I nodded. The two of us walked out the back. Beatrice held out my cigarette, and I took it quickly.

Phish.

The flame formed, and the smoke billowed. Beatrice leaned in and lit her own cigarette on mine.

"Where'd you manage to get these?" I asked.

"It was easy. I promised to give some seniors a look at my notes. First time anyone's ever treated my classwork like it was something of value," Beatrice smiled.

"Classy," I returned.

"Just trying to expand my social circle."

"You're in luck," I said, holding my cigarette up. "These are a prerequisite to a conversation around here."

"Really?" Beatrice asked. She looked at her cigarette with interest. Like she found the first part of a grand puzzle.

"But no one wants to talk about T.S. Eliot, so I end up on my own most of the time," I added.

"And the other times?" Beatrice asked.

"There's always the alley cats," I concluded. I pointed to a lone cat that was keeping an eye on us.

"It's funny how you can turn your sad story into a funny

one," Beatrice smiled.

"Now that you know all about my commitment to dead scholars and dead lung cells, how about you? What's something I don't know?" I asked.

"I just got transferred here from Radcliffe Academy," she offered.

"Now we're getting somewhere. And you're here because...."

"I hate the subway," Beatrice laughed.

"Come on, I'm trying to start a conversation here," I said. "Isn't that what you wanted? And I only have so many drags left."

I took a drag of my cigarette like it was making the hands of a clock run faster.

"I'm serious," Beatrice laughed. "The subway's filthy!"

"Why are you here?" I insisted. "Be real with me."

"I needed a fresh start, and a friend of my family made that happen," Beatrice admitted.

"It's good to see you have some people you can count on," I offered.

"Yeah," Beatrice nodded, "it sucked, but I was able to move away from it all."

"I guess that's something. Not everybody gets a chance to start over," I added.

"Your turn," Beatrice insisted. She took a drag from her cigarette. "You have any ex-girlfriends at this school?"

I looked down at both our cigarettes. We still had the better half of them left.

"Always asking about my love life."

"Hardly. I was just checking to make sure you were all... there. You don't seem attracted to anything except books written by dead men."

She took her free hand and made a circle between us like she was casting her own spell. It certainly felt like she was.

"All *there*?" I repeated.

"It's just a little odd. Hearing a freshman who wants to talk about T.S. Eliot. It's like walking up to a dog and having it meow at you."

I chuckled at that.

"That has to be the funniest thing you've said all day."

"I'm serious," Beatrice smiled.

"So, what's your big interest in my love life?"

"Maybe I'm just making conversation," Beatrice dodged.

"Fine. How about the next question?"

Silence.

"Well, what is it?" I asked.

Beatrice looked at her studded punk boots and then up to me.

"You have a girlfriend?"

"No," I answered.

"Some rumors were floating around that you did have one."

"I've only been hanging around with you."

Beatrice stared into my eyes and bit her lip.

"Specifically, the rumors were that *I* was your girlfriend."

Silence.

I was spending more time with Beatrice than anyone else outside of Dorian. It dawned on me that we might be in a relationship.

"Maybe we are."

"So, it's official now?" Beatrice asked.

"Official?" I whispered.

"We got some time before next period."

"This game has been a lot of fun, but I'm going to stop

while I'm ahead," I started.

"Well, come on, do you like hanging out with me?" Beatrice asked.

"Yeah," I smiled.

"Do you have a girlfriend that isn't me?"

"No."

"So, you're available."

"Yes."

"So, you want to do something a little more interesting than studying geometry?"

Silence.

"Yeah, sure."

"There we are! Interested, available, and looking for something to do."

"Okay."

"All right! Then I guess we're dating."

"Yeah," I smiled, "I guess we are."

RING!

Beatrice took her cigarette and put it out on the brick wall behind her.

"I'll make this easy," Beatrice said with a smile.

"Okay," I accepted.

"And since we're dating now...."

Beatrice leaned forward.

KISS.

She separated from me, and I saw her blue eyes were ecstatic.

She walked away jubilant.

I turned to stone.

My ears felt like they were on fire.

What the hell just happened?

SIXTEEN.

HOME

"Martin, that's the fourth time we've tried making a potion, and you didn't get it right," Alciel exasperated.

"Sorry. Let's do it over."

"We both know what's going on," Alciel smiled.

"Please, don't start."

"Oh, but I want to," Alciel ignored. "You're dating someone now! That'll sure take your mind off the junkies and monsters you're dealing with!"

"Really? Because there's this one demon that's still on my nerves."

"Always the smartass. Especially when you feel threatened."

"Just hand me that newt's tail," I insisted.

Alciel reached into the box of ingredients, providing me with a shriveled, grey-green newt tail.

"Why don't you just admit this is a good thing?"

"Because maybe it's not," I answered.

"What are you so worried about? She clearly likes you."

"How about the fact that everyone was gawking at us before when nothing was going on?"

"Now you're giving them a reason. I don't see the problem."

"I'm not used to people being nice to me in school."

"You always find problems in everything. You'd make a terrible demon."

"Hey, this is new to me! I have no idea what's going to happen. I don't know if I'm going to mess this up completely or if I'd be putting her in danger."

"You like her, don't you?" Alciel asked.

"Of course I do," I admitted.

"And she likes you. That's all you need. Quit worrying about getting caught for using magic. Even if you get caught, you can always dream up some excuse. You're practicing close-up magic. I keep forgetting you were a recluse before I showed up. How about you just see this for what it is. You're going out with a girl. Or you will be very soon."

"Okay," I contemplated.

"Just calm down. This can only be good for you," Alciel smiled.

"I guess you're right," I joked, "for once."

"Why don't you just admit that this partnership actually does have its benefits?" Alciel chuckled.

"I suppose it does," I smiled. "She really is—"

"I meant us," Alciel corrected. "Remember? Wizard and Companion."

"Oh, right. That's what I meant, too."

"I'm sure it was. Besides, I could be a good life coach for you."

"I don't need a life coach."

"In the time I've been here, you've killed an Addiction Demon, learned dozens of spells, and you got a hot date. I'm three for three."

"Come on, man," I attempted.

"I'm on fire!" Alciel jabbed. "If we can just get this Necronomicon thing under control, we can build you a new life from the ground up."

I had a sketch of the Necronomicon of what Dorian had described it looked like. A book I'd been hunting for months now. And the more I thought about what was inside of it, the more I realized I was overlooking a major resource. I had a teacher of demonic magic sitting three feet away from me.

"Speaking of which," I said. "What can you tell me about demonic magic?"

"Pretty standard stuff, really. It's infectious by nature. It taps into your essence very strongly whenever it's used. It leaves a trace, like when you kill someone."

"Wow."

"And demonic magic can also alter your physical appearance as well."

"How so?" I asked.

"It varies depending on how you use it. People who ask for strength can sometimes get barbs on their knuckles, or they might get yellow eyes if they want to see the world as a demon does."

"Like a mutation."

"It eats away at your humanity. So, I'd pace yourself. Once you cross that line, there's no coming back. And whoever has the book clearly isn't pacing themselves."

"I'm assuming Dorian has been looking at every victim, making sure they don't own the book or could have used it."

"Yes, he's checked them all. And all of it comes from being affected like a junkie, not a master."

"Do you know a lot of masters?" I asked.

"Sure. It's what demons do. At least, those of us who don't look like they've been burnt to a crisp. We lend people power, and when they overextend themselves, they take the fall, and we get what we came for."

"You're talking about Faustian bargains," I observed. "Deals with the devil."

"It's not that far removed from our arrangement. Familiars can blend their magic with a partner, and both parties get stronger. In a lot of cases, demons partner themselves with people who have no potential for magic. Then they can perform the basics with someone to enhance their essence enough to pull off some parlor tricks."

"And what about those side effects you mentioned?"

"Binding yourself to a demon for a Familiar is always dangerous. But some of them are fairly unrecognizable. Teens might bond themselves to a demon who makes boils appear on their bodies. But that doesn't do much to expose them. What's a little more acne in exchange for pyromancy?"

"Fair point. But I haven't noticed any changes to my body. And you're my Companion."

"It's different for Companions. Our essences are so intertwined that there's practically no difference between them. They coexist in a way that is more...homogeneous than most."

"Is that why my semblance is changing colors?"

"Your blue manna is melding with my gold manna. That's right."

"Well, it's good to know we have that going for us. It'll keep us from getting discovered by people who might be looking for us."

"You won't stick out like a sore thumb, but we're not out of the woods yet. Not with demons attacking us in your school."

"It still bothers me," I said. "How does a mindless demon get into my school without Dorian knowing it was there?"

"It might have to do with you blowing up that chemistry lab."

"For the last time, I didn't—"

"I'm joking. I'm joking. But it might have been all they needed to narrow down their search."

"Come on."

"I'm serious. Most people either have magic when they're born, or they never get it. The fact that a high school had an explosion indicates that some kid probably got magic out of the blue and doesn't know how to handle it."

"So, it's my fault the demon showed up."

"Nobody can blame you for that. You had no idea what was happening. It's just that we've had to be more careful. And it may have even had people chasing their tails."

"Chasing their tails?"

"Even if someone was going to visit the lab, it's a chemistry lab. It's not like it's difficult to create blue fire. Copper chloride is enough to change a flame's color, and it could be that a demon is claiming dominion over the school. Or maybe they bound themselves as a Familiar to somebody. Simply put, it's not a dead giveaway that you're the Wizard."

"I'm not sure if that makes me feel better or worse."

"It is surprising. Spending your whole life thinking there's a simple solution to anything. But now the whole world's gotten more complicated."

"Do you have any idea what kind of demon would be after us? Somebody who would be trying to open the Necronomicon?"

Silence.

"You were on a roll," I insisted. "Don't stop now."

"All we've seen is Addiction Demons. They're like mad dogs."

Alciel's surprisingly short answer made me pause.

"Alciel. The demons we've been fighting. They wouldn't be looking for you would they?"

Silence.

"It's possible," he admitted.

"You ran away from Gehenna. But that was because your Alignment changed. Did you do that because they wouldn't let you leave? If they ever discovered the truth?"

"I did what I had to do. I was never going to survive that place if I wasn't the Companion to a powerful demon. And the odds of that were astronomical."

"That's your defense?"

"It was the only chance I had. And I would do it again if I could."

"You wouldn't change anything about what you did?" I demanded.

"You're a good kid, but I had no idea what I was in for when my Alignment changed. All I knew was people were going to get hurt if I stayed. And I would have gotten the worst of it. And whoever my Wizard was, they would have gotten it, too."

I took a deep breath.

"Martin. I'm sorry for everything I've put you through. This whole situation is insane, even for me. But if we're going to get out of this, we're going to have to work together. And we've done pretty well so far. We beat an Addiction Demon, we've saved dozens of people, and we're getting some of our lives back, despite everything."

"It's hard to know who to trust," I whispered.

"You can trust me," Alciel offered.

"Can I ask you something?"

"Of course."

"Would you still be helping me, even if you didn't have to?"

"I'm not sure if we'd even meet, had it not been for the Spectrum."

"But would you help me? If you had that choice?"

"I honestly don't know."

Silence.

"But for what it's worth, I'm glad that it worked out this way," Alciel finished.

I raised some glassware and placed it on the desk. The glassware was glowing with manna-infused potions.

Clink.

"I don't expect we'll know for sure if we can trust each other unless we commit to proving it," I said.

"I hope we've done pretty well so far," Alciel attempted.

"We have," I answered.

I turned the light out and got ready to sleep, but with the only light in the room being the blue moonlight and Alciel's yellow eyes, I wondered how much I really trusted him.

SEVENTEEN.

OUT

"You're in a good mood," Beatrice observed.

She broke a tea packet and began bobbing the bag in a fancy mug with the words *Belvedere Tea* on it.

"Things have been taking a turn for the better," I answered.

I looked out the window and saw the snow was falling lightly. Even in the grimiest parts of Detroit, the snow could make them beautiful.

"And here I thought the tea was just making things better," Beatrice smiled.

"Tea makes everything better," I answered.

"Including first dates?" Beatrice asked.

I reached a hand to the center of the table.

With her free hand, she reached out to me. And our fingers interlocked.

"Especially first dates," I smiled.

"I like this place," Beatrice smiled. "Although it does seem a little out of character for you to not carry your backpack around."

Beatrice studied me before she sipped her tea.

"Are you hoping to get a look at some assignments for next year?" I jested.

"That would be a trick, but I'm actually glad to see you comfortable," she answered.

"Do I seem out of place at school?" I asked.

"In a way," she admitted.

"How's that?" I insisted.

"You have this look on your face like you belong in another time," Beatrice attempted.

"I like old-fashioned things," I insisted.

"You sure it's not because Woodrow Wilson High is for a different kind of education?" Beatrice queried.

"I'll never fathom why I'm going to that place," I pondered. "It's like a daycare center for the parents in Wayne County jail."

"Yeah," Beatrice added.

"Makes me wonder how you ended up at Woodrow Wilson when Radcliffe Academy is in the next district over. They have some of the best high school accommodations in the state. Maybe the whole Midwest."

"I come here for conversations," Beatrice smiled.

She pulled out another cigarette.

"How has work been?" Beatrice asked.

"It's been busy," I answered.

"You never told me what you do," Beatrice pointed out.

"I help in the ER," I lied.

"Car accidents and bar fights?"

Beatrice seemed excited at the prospect.

"More of a drug problem at the moment," I corrected.

"I bet," she nodded.

Beatrice lit her next cigarette.

Phish.

"You'll have to show me the place sometime."

"The ER?" I asked.

"Sure. I'd like to get to know you better," she insisted.

"You already know plenty about me."

"Taste in movies and books isn't knowing somebody."

"It's basically all there is to me," I lied.

"I think it's time we play another question game," she smiled.

Beatrice's eyes flashed as she made the proposition.

"I don't know what you could possibly ask me at this point," I challenged.

"You got a date to the Winter Dance?" Beatrice asked.

Time stopped. I took a moment to sip my tea, and I realized that she was asking me.

"No," I answered. "At least not yet."

"I think you do," Beatrice added.

"You would be the first to know," I pointed out.

Beatrice laughed.

"Isn't it about time we made this official?"

"One dance doesn't make things official."

"Sure. But a limo, meeting your parents, and one dance just might."

"You're not letting this go," I observed. "Meeting my parents?"

"You're worth fighting for," Beatrice insisted.

I looked into Beatrice's blue eyes and knew she wasn't joking.

"You're serious," I smiled.

"Plus, it would be nice to have something else on my mind aside from geometry and Orson Welles," Beatrice added.

"You actually saw *The Third Man*?"

"Better than I gave it credit for," Beatrice conceded, "I can see why you like it."

"Because it's an amazing movie?" I smiled triumphantly.

"The dialogue is good, and it focuses on a writer," she corrected.

"Is that all it takes?" I asked.

"You're basically a writer with how you talk at the pace of a book a minute," Beatrice pointed out.

"I don't mean to override our conversations," I excused.

"Not at all. I enjoy listening. It's like there's a whole world inside your head," Beatrice admitted.

"Yeah," I offered.

"Granted, it's a black-and-white world where every building is a library," Beatrice continued. "But yeah, a whole world."

I laughed.

"So, it's settled," Beatrice answered.

"What's settled?" I asked.

"We're going to the Winter Dance together."

"How is it you do that?" I asked.

"Do what?"

"Get me to do things before I even agree to them."

"People have a hard time saying 'no' to me."

"I can see why," I smirked.

"What?" Beatrice asked.

"You're so... magnetic."

"Never heard it put that way before," Beatrice smiled. "Look at that, I'm getting closer."

Beatrice leaned forward.

KISS.

"Walk me home after class?"

"Of course."

As Beatrice walked out, I felt my heart pounding out of my chest. I got up to pay for my tea and made my way out in the cold. It was always peaceful this time of year.

The lights coming from shop windows, the smell of gasoline, and the light *honk* of a car some blocks down the road. I let myself feel the weight of the world come off of me. The demon off my back, the responsibilities of being the Wizard distant for the first time in months.

Things appeared to be looking up. And right as that feeling settled in, I rounded the corner and saw a familiar face. Mrs. Fitzgerald. Walking through the biting cold. She made eye contact with me, and I could sense her disappointment.

We both stopped walking, stood there for a moment, and I thought she was going to give some retort about how my tutoring proved I wasn't all talk.

Neither of us got the chance to break the silence. A car horn did that for us. It was rushing straight at Fitzgerald, and it must have been going ninety miles per hour.

I saw headlights gleaming through the falling snow, like a predator rushing toward its prey. I didn't even think. Seeing those lights beset by surrounding darkness made my heart race and my feet move on their own. It was like seeing a hostile essence rushing toward us.

HOOOOOOOOOOONK!

I spotted an alleyway just to the side of us, and I ran to get her pushed to safety. There was no time for words, incantations, or any way to make my semblance pitch in to prevent damage. She looked afraid for a moment, but I couldn't see if she landed safely or not. The blinding flash from headlights made everything go white. I didn't even see the impact. But I sure as hell felt it.

FRAK!

I was hurtled back. My legs were peeled off the ground, my eyes rolled into a haze of colors, and I saw glittering fragments of glass sprawl out into the cold Detroit air.

The whites and greys vanished as a whole spectrum formed at the moment of impact. And I was caught in the center of it.

The smell of gasoline took a strange turn as it began to ignite. I heard a faint *hum* ring in my ears, and it was soon replaced with the terrible screams of people witnessing the accident. The shrill cries made it clear. I was in a lot of trouble.

I rolled onto the grimy floor of a back alley. I could feel the warmth draining out of me. I looked down, and any haze I could see past was bright red.

I tried to pick myself up, but I felt my side shooting with pain, like air igniting the veins of lit timbers. I tasted iron as I winced in pain. My vision came back, and I saw that the damage was worse than I thought. My torso had a massive cut along the front, and it was seeping red.

I saw through the passenger side window, revealing the bloodied face of a man who was either dead or unconscious behind the wheel. A dark presence loomed from inside the door, and a *cracked* face of an Addiction Demon eclipsed the man behind him. One with pour spouts for teeth and reeking of rye whiskey.

I gasped and raised my hand upwards, but any amount of magic was only causing my arm to burn. The demon loomed forward and held its arms wide, ready to embrace me. Its body was riddled with fragments of whiskey bottles of all shapes and colors. A trio of circles interlocked at its center, just like all of the runes that Dorian formed; only these burned deep crimson, not deep purple. I hissed at the creature and gritted my teeth. I didn't care how much it hurt. I was going to fight back.

The way ahead of me was blocked by the crashed car. The demon floated toward me slowly. I had enough time to look back for a moment. I saw a maze of brick and mortar diverting in all directions, with no witnesses.

This was an encounter the demon had probably seen many times before. A victim looking back to see if anybody could help. If anybody could see the monster haunting their steps. But when I turned back, I wouldn't run away. I would face it head-on.

"*Exorcizamus demoni hunc totis virbius,*" I hissed.

The creature reared back, and it burst with a terrible array of blue lights. Every crack and crevice of the creature began to *hiss* with blue light. The damage cascaded across its body, and reached each of the three interlocking circles on its chest, and made it scream. The circles shrank until they became three pinpoints of deep volcanic blue. And when those dots disappeared, it held its head up in agony, and it flared into a cloud of blue sulfur.

I felt my strength fading, and I could barely hold my head up. A low hissing sound emerged, like a tea kettle, and my ears rang with this eerie sound. The car released massive plumes of black smoke. Finally, the engine let out a flare of orange, and the hissing stopped.

BOOM!

A white flash came into the alleyway, and I was knocked onto my back. I heard footsteps approaching me, but I didn't have the strength to get up. And my vision was fading.

Two women came into my vision. Both of them were crying. One was Beatrice, the other was Fitzgerald. Beatrice held my hand and shakily answered her phone. I assumed she was calling for an ambulance. Fitzgerald looked at me with disbelief.

Then everything went black.

EIGHTEEN

RETURNED

I woke up and found I was surrounded by small noises.

Beep. Beep. Beep.

A heart rate monitor.

Outside was the whirring of a landline phone, the rustling of sheets, and serious voices mingled in a cloud. I tried to reach for my aching head, but the pain from my side was so piercing, I collapsed.

A pained inhale made the smell of ether pierce my nostrils. I must have been somewhere familiar. All of this felt like I had been here before. I looked out the window to see if I could find a distinctive landmark. But sitting just beside the window was someone I knew. I saw Beatrice. She was sitting in a chair, facing me.

I looked down and saw she had prepared several books, a sleeping bag, and her Jack Skellington bag. Her constant companion. As soon as I caught her in my sight, I saw she was crying.

"Oh, my God," she whispered. "You're awake."

"Don't they just let family in here?" I asked.

"I told them we were dating," Beatrice said. "And that I was there when it happened."

"That was nice of them."

"Your parents are on their way right now."

"What about Ali?" I asked.

"She's on her way, too. She said she was with a friend. She said you would understand."

"I definitely understand."

I wondered if Dorian would be visiting, too.

"Is Fitzgerald okay?" I asked.

"She's been waiting outside. She hasn't left the lobby since you got here."

"Maybe she'll go easy on me now," I joked.

"The driver died in the crash. Martin, I was terrified. I just wanted to make sure you were okay."

"I'm okay," I insisted, "my ribs and head are killing me, though."

"I don't want to put you on the spot, but what do you *really* do after school?" Beatrice asked.

"What?"

"You said you worked in the ER. But everyone around here says you were just here to see your mother."

Silence.

"I come here with my family because they help people. And I want to be a part of that."

"I just want you to be honest with me. Is there something else going on?"

"No. I'm trying to help people. There's just not much I

can do now. I'm learning everything I can by watching the best people in the field do their job."

That was more truthful than I expected.

"I haven't known you that long, Martin, but I do care what happens to you."

"Thanks."

"Can you just promise me that you'll be more careful? Can you give me that?"

"Sure," I confirmed.

SWING!

With that, the doors burst open, and my family was on the other side. Ali, Mom, Dad, and Dorian. And with my sister carrying my backpack, I was sure our Companions were inside.

"My baby!" Mom cried.

I felt my face go hot, and I thought I would never stop being embarrassed.

"It's good to see you're recovering," Dorian added.

"Dumbass!" Ali shouted.

"The rules are two at a time!" a nurse called.

"Get lost, Helen!" Mom shouted.

They all gathered around me, and I felt like things were going to be okay.

"The doctor says you have some cracked ribs," Dad explained. "You're lucky you got away with only that."

"I checked both ways before crossing," I chuckled.

I felt my rib cage burn and strain under the weight of my own laughter, and I stopped quickly.

"We're going to take things slowly," Mom insisted. "You'll be staying home for a couple of days for recovery."

"That'll be a nice change of pace," Ali added, "you finally

get to relax."

"I'm sure I'll have a lot of work to do," I attempted.

"Don't worry. I played it up for you. I was crying on the phone about how you were mangled and how you wouldn't be able to go to school for at least a month," Ali smiled.

"I wasn't *mangled*," I objected.

"Well, it worked. You got all the time in the world to rest up."

"And I'll come by after school. Every day until you're better," Beatrice promised.

It was comforting to look into Beatrice's eyes.

"Anyone want coffee?" Beatrice offered.

"I'd love some," Dad accepted.

Dorian looked at all of us carefully. I noticed he had a grim expression on his face, despite the good news.

"But I think that'll do for now. We'll take you home tonight," Dad concluded.

"You sure?" I asked.

"Martin, we're medical professionals," Mom said. "We'll give you all the care you need."

After all, Mom could delay cancer. Cracked ribs should be a cakewalk for her.

"I'll pull the car around," Dad announced.

Mom followed him, and Ali took my bag and left. With the bag moving slightly, I was sure that our Companions would offer the same sentiment, if they could.

"I'll see you tomorrow," Beatrice promised.

She leaned forward.

KISS.

She walked out, letting her heeled boots fade into the distance.

Click. Click. Click.

As she left, someone else came into view.

"Martin?" Fitzgerald asked.

"I'm here," I confirmed.

Fitzgerald looked like she hadn't slept in a week.

"Thank God you're alive," she exhaled.

"It's nothing."

"It's not nothing. You saved my life."

"I couldn't let you get hit by a car. Is that worth any extra credit?"

"You didn't have time to think about what happened. You just... did it."

"Is that surprising?"

"You risked your life to save me. Your classmates figured you'd be the first one to push me into oncoming traffic."

"Now you can tell them they're wrong."

Silence.

"By the way," I started, "I'm sorry for the way I've acted before."

"Wow, the surprises continue," Fitzgerald admitted. "I wasn't expecting an apology."

"Neither was I. But I had to say that."

"Because of what happened?"

"Because I don't want to be that guy who thinks one good deed means he doesn't have to apologize. You still deserve an apology. I'm sorry."

Fitzgerald looked into my eyes, and I knew that things were going to be different now. All our resentments toward each other had vanished, and there was nothing we wanted from each other.

"Don't worry about any assignments or tests while you

recover. Knowing you, you probably did them already," Fitzgerald smiled.

"That helps a lot. Take care of yourself out there."

"I will," Fitzgerald nodded.

Looking into her eyes, she didn't have a hint of curiosity or suspicion. She just seemed grateful that everything turned out okay.

She looked at Dorian and left. Dorian was my last visitor.

"You barely said anything," I pointed out.

"That's because things have changed."

"How so?" I asked.

"You were attacked," Dorian said, "and I wasn't there to help you."

"That wasn't your fault. People get into accidents all the time."

"You shouldn't," he pointed out.

"What are you saying?" I demanded.

"You're going to be assigned a new handler," Dorian insisted.

"What? Why? I don't want anybody else."

"That's not for you to decide. It's already been done. Nothing changes outside of that. You'll keep learning, be watched over, and everything else will work out."

"I refuse to accept that," I demanded. "Tell them I won't!"

"The Order has already made up their mind," Dorian lamented, "and they have the final say on the Watchmen assignments."

"They can't just tell you to leave because you made one mistake. And it wasn't even a mistake. It was a freak accident."

"An Addiction Demon infiltrated your school, I overplayed my hand with that ritual, and now you've been hit by a car. Any one of those errors should have gotten me dismissed."

"None of this is right. What happened in the street was a

goddamn accident!" I shouted.

I cringed from the pain in my ribs.

"I let you come to harm," he accepted.

"Where were you, anyway?" I asked.

"I was watching over your family. Your neighborhood had an Addiction Demon. One of your neighbors had been abusing drugs and had gotten infected by their influence."

"Then you did what you were supposed to do."

"I just wanted to say that it meant the world to me, Martin. That you would let me train you. Even after everything that has happened."

Silence.

I had a thought brewing in my mind, but I hesitated to even say it. But I tried to think of anything to keep Dorian around. Even if it meant hurting him.

"This isn't what Adrian would want," I added.

Dorian looked to the ground, his lip hardening in anguish.

"But this is what has to be done."

Dorian rose up and offered to help me to my feet.

"At least let me take you down to your family."

I looked at Dorian, infuriated. I was mad he passively put a timer on our partnership. I looked down and undid the oximeter.

Beeeeeeeep.

"Got some clothes?" I asked.

"Your mother brought them. They're in this bag."

Krink.

Dorian placed them on the bed.

"Call me when you're out of those rags."

Dorian left the room.

I struggled to get my clothes on, but I thought of how far

we had come. It didn't make sense that Dorian had done so well protecting us and that he would be stepping down. He should have been given a medal for everything he did.

Finally, I threw on my jacket.

"Done," I called.

Dorian came back and smiled.

"Hold on," Dorian insisted.

Dorian lifted me up from the hospital bed.

"I gotcha," he promised.

WHARF.

A pulse of purple shot out and made the wheelchair in the corner open up. He gently lowered me into the chair and pushed me out.

"It's still not right," I objected.

"I did my best, and you've come a long way, Martin. Don't think of it as me being cut out. Think of it as me stepping down for your sake."

"I know you don't want to do this. I know how much of a stake you have in this."

Silence.

"And how would you know about that?"

"Alciel told me everything."

"That slippery little reptile."

"I wanted to know what was going on. And it was clear that you weren't going to tell me everything."

"You must think the worst of me, now."

"Not at all. You were just trying to protect us. To protect everyone, really."

"I managed to get my foot in the door because I failed once. But I was warned that failing again would mean I'd be taken off the case."

"One drunk driving accident in Detroit is grounds for that?"

"I admire your passion. But I messed up. There's no excuse for it."

"I don't want this."

"At least you're alive, Martin. And your family is waiting for you."

Dorian rounded the corner, and we made our way to the elevator.

"Do I get to know this guy's name at least? This new handler?" I asked.

Dorian opened the doors to the elevator, and I saw we were going down to the lobby. Once the doors shut, he resumed the conversation.

"A Watchman named Asclepius."

"Like the son of Apollo?" I asked.

"Most people call him Ash."

"Is he Greek?"

"He's a Gorgon. But he's also the Watchman who was entrusted with my position after I had failed to protect Adrian. And he's an expert on necromancy. He's the best man for protecting you now."

"I don't buy it. No one is better than you."

"You give me too much credit."

Dorian reached behind him and produced a blanket. He must have carried it in with him.

He draped it over me.

"It gets cold out there. That'll keep you warm for the car ride home. I know your father's car heater doesn't work for shit."

"Thanks," I offered.

I was touched by the gesture. Even more touched that Dorian wanted to be the one to lead me outside.

Ding.

"Let's get you to the car. Your mother is going to be worried if we don't hurry."

I felt my hands grip onto the arms of the wheelchair. But I felt better, knowing Dorian was still guiding me. Like he had always done.

The doors to the outside world opened.

Sweep.

The bitter cold cut through me, and it was only a few feet until we made it to the car. But it wasn't all bad. Dorian's blanket was warm. And Dad had already brought the car around.

We stepped out of the realm of the hospital's dial tones and ether fumes. We came into the angry traffic and cigarette smoke of downtown Detroit. Among the honking, tire screeches, and *slushing* of rubber on snow, I remembered the moment the car had hit me. In that instant, I could hear almost every honking of a horn like it was warning me to get out of the way.

I looked to my family, knowing they were the ones I wanted to protect the most. They were probably all on their third cup of coffee, staying up and staying by my side until we finally got home.

"This is where we part ways," Dorian said.

"Wait," I insisted.

He activated the brake on the wheelchair and came around to meet me at eye level. I reached around and embraced Dorian with what little strength I had.

"I'm going to make this right," I said. "I'm sorry."

Dorian's arms were open for a moment. He had no idea

how to react. But then I felt him return the embrace. I also felt warm drops hit the top of my head. I looked up and saw that Dorian had shed a few tears.

"Go on, now," he insisted.

Sniff.

Ali took my wheelchair and deactivated the brake. As my wheels were skating along the ground, I looked up and saw that Dorian was moving through the fog from Detroit's sewers.

I kept looking as he rounded the corner and made his way into the Detroit winter. It was harder to see Dorian as he walked further away between the blustering white snow and coiling grey fumes. When he approached the corner, I gulped and felt a lump form in my throat. I watched him fade from view again.

"It's going to be okay, Martin," Ali promised.

"You're going to get better," Mom chimed in.

They made their way to the side of the car.

"On three, we lift him," Ali insisted.

"One. Two. *Three,*" Mom counted.

They lifted me into the backseat. When I felt the feeble *wheezing* of the car heater, I expected to feel safe again. But I didn't. I looked up and saw my family was waiting for me to say something.

"Thanks, everyone," I attempted.

"Let's get you home," Dad smiled.

Dad activated the engine of our Ford.

VROOM!

I looked back to where Dorian disappeared.

I refused to let this be the last time I would see him.

NINETEEN

NEWCOMER

"How are things going with your girlfriend?" Ali asked.

It was the first question she had asked since we had built our combination workshop. With Dorian gone from the Silk Slipper, we decided to make it our own space. The days got longer without him, and we both could have used the company. Even with the Silk Slipper empty, it somehow felt safer than wandering around outside.

"That's personal," I objected.

I rolled my right arm, and no pain came from my side anymore. Mom's Saving Grace really was an impressive spell.

"Don't get all touchy," Ali said. "I was just asking a question."

"They're going well."

"Hand me that mortar and pestle, will you?"

"Sure. If you keep the prying to a minimum."

"I heard you may actually have a date for the Winter Dance."

"Don't you have one?" I asked.

"Between my botany and social awkwardness, that doesn't leave me much time to do anything else."

"The boys must be devastated."

Ali smiled at me.

"What are you planning on wearing, anyway?"

"This?" I offered.

"Martin, that's jeans and a Led Zeppelin t-shirt."

"It never goes out of style."

"You're going to... hold on."

"What?" I asked.

Ali reached behind my shoulder, and examined an ivy plant growing on top of a bookshelf.

"These plants have a mind of their own. Maybe I've been giving them too much manna."

"Is that so?" I asked.

"Yes, actually. I've been doing some reading, too."

"On plants?"

"Artifacts," Ali answered. "There's still a lot of books on magic here. Hidden in a couple of places. The place is practically a library, if you know where to look."

"What have you learned?" I attempted.

"If you give enough manna to something, it can take on a life of its own. Got me thinking about what Dorian said."

Silence.

We didn't look at each other for a moment. Saying his name was more painful than either of us expected. But Ali wasn't one to let awkward silences last.

"Look, Martin. I miss him too."

I looked up to Ali and knew we were sharing the same pain.

"I shouldn't have brought it up," she admitted.

"No, it's important we talk about it. Even with someone new coming, we still need to get that book before anyone else gets hurt."

CRANK!

The doors of the Silk Slipper opened, and I shot up from my chair. We saw a man with short dark hair and a trench coat march into the abandoned motel. I felt my heart sink, knowing this wasn't Dorian.

"You must be the Blackbriars," the man began.

He had a Greek accent and a serious expression. He was also wearing a set of round, ebony glasses that rounded tightly over his eyes. The flat, reflective lenses cast a shadowy reflection of everything he saw. As he turned, there was a faint gleam of silver, and I saw that these glasses came with blinders that made it impossible to see his eyes from any angle.

"That's us," Ali offered.

"Allow me to put your anxieties to rest. You are safe, now that you're in my care," he offered.

"We were safe before," I objected.

"Hardly. One man failed to keep two children safe."

"You don't have to point out what went wrong," Ali protested.

"I'm simply stating the facts, Ms. Blackbriar."

"You must be Ash," I loathed.

"I am. Clearly, we're getting off on the wrong foot. I have spent a great deal of time looking over your case. Your progress so far is impressive. To say the least."

"That doesn't mean we're any safer with you," Alciel protested.

"Addiction Demons have been known to take down some of the most skilled mages in the city," Ash continued. "But they're also throwing in some civilians."

"You're suggesting that whoever is using the Necronomicon is trying to cover up the pattern," Ali added.

"Very perceptive. They started taking down old people, young people, then druggies. It seemed experimental at first, but now it looks like they're pushing the limits of what that book can do. I'd commend them for their boldness if what they were doing wasn't so depraved."

The Gorgon crossed over to the abandoned front desk, where all my potions were laid out.

"Toward the beginning, Proctor had you tending to all manner of victims," Ash said. "You likely had every cot filled. Am I right?"

"Sometimes," Ali confirmed.

"Then it started to change. People started to show up less frequently, but when they were found, they were showing signs of mutation."

"Mutation," I repeated. "I suppose that's one way to put it."

"Their eyes and teeth underwent significant redness and deformity. The cops ruled it as hitting the crack pipe too hard. But clearly, someone is getting bolder and knows how to taunt us. Not just hide from us," Ash concluded.

Ash reached for an emerald marker on the desk and immediately added to Dorian's extensive collection of violet markings on the map of Detroit.

"We wouldn't have come this far if it wasn't for Dorian risking his life," I defended.

"True. But Proctor's gambit came at a price. Whoever has the book is an incredibly powerful mage. And they knew they were being followed. All thanks to his slip up."

Ash put down the marker and took a step back. I saw a large

circle placed where I had gotten hit by the car, right outside of *Belvedere Tea*. Just looking at the street brought back that horrible winter chill and the deeper cold of blood loss.

"It wasn't a slip up. It was a risk all of us were taking," I corrected.

"There's taking a risk for the greater good, and there's needlessly putting the lives of others in danger," Ash answered.

Silence.

"You mean the car crash that came for Martin," Ali started.

"Was no accident," Ash answered.

He pointed to a mark that was further south, toward downtown Detroit. A trail of overdoses acted as a trail of breadcrumbs, and my eyes grew wider as I realized where we'd be going. Almost three miles away from where I was hit by that car, there was a name that made everything come into focus. It was a massive circle beset by dozens of smaller circles. Some were emerald. Some were purple. Together, they revealed the next viper's nest we'd have to visit.

"You kids know about the Stryker Motel?" Ash asked.

"Sure. It's where all the junkies go to get their fix," Ali confirmed.

"I hope neither of you has ever been to this place."

"You hear about it a lot when you go to our school," I corrected.

"There's been more overdoses here than most anywhere in Detroit. And it's within spitting distance of where Martin got hit by a car."

"But Addiction Demons cause drunken car accidents all the time," Alciel pointed out.

"The one that attacked me had a binding rune on its chest.

I'm sure of it," I added.

"It was a car accident where the Wizard was hospitalized, and the driver was dead and afflicted with demonic influence. And all while we're searching for an artifact that controls these types of creatures. Unless you think that's just a coincidence."

"We never said it was," Ali corrected.

"We can't afford to ignore these signs anymore," Ash continued.

"If things have gotten so out of hand, how are you going to fix them?" I asked.

"We don't know for certain what the intent of our target is. Once they get the Necronomicon pried open, they may be going after powerful mages. Or they'll hand the book off to someone more powerful than them. We'll have to keep things quiet for the moment and hit them where it hurts. Otherwise, they'll scatter."

"How?" Ali asked. "We don't even know who *they* are. Just that they have the book."

"Proctor made a mess of things, but at least he kept records of it," Ash added. "We know that someone out there is desperate. They've been taking the risk of using demons, and they're probably just starting to lose control. They'll slip up. And, when they do, we'll be there to catch them."

"These creatures feed on people's suffering," Alciel reminded. "Trying to shoot them or exorcise them in the open would cause more damage."

"That's why we're going to have to accelerate your training a little bit further. Normally, Watchmen wouldn't teach their students any of these things until they were further along. But we're pressed for time."

Ali's eyes lit up, even if she wouldn't have let Ash see it. She crossed her arms, and she steeled herself. She didn't want Ash to read too much into her reaction.

"What are you suggesting?" I asked.

"We're going to have to sneak into the one place where all of the victims have something in common. I can guarantee you that if the last twenty people to have a fatal overdose came from the same place, there's an Addiction Demon lurking around there somewhere. And maybe our culprit will be there calling the shots."

"How are we going to do that?" Ali insisted.

"As luck would have it, the Spectrum gave Martin a demon. One that is infamous for his ability to use Selective Presence."

Twenty.

Unseen

The shutters were closed, and the candles were lit. It was getting colder, and every breath we took seemed to light up in a faint neon glow as we steadied ourselves. It was an unspoken rule that we would commence our training once our breath was steady and tempered.

But something felt off as we looked into the chill streams our breath was making. We weren't sure if it was the new magic we were learning, the new candlelight color that blended with our breath, or that a new set of eyes were looking down on us as we trained.

When we made three steady breaths, Ash began his lesson.

"Most Watchmen try to form a bond with a demonic Familiar," Ash began. "If they choose a Familiar at all."

"Is that their way of fighting fire with fire?" I asked.

"In a manner of speaking, yes. Addiction runs rampant in big cities like rot through a dying animal. There's nobody more qualified to sniff out where these creatures are hiding."

"And that's why we're walking straight into their midst?" Alciel asked. "I'm all for recovering the Necronomicon, but this is more of a risk than we need to take."

"Every day we wait, the Addiction Demons get stronger and the more powerful targets they'll be able to take down. A drunk driver will be the least of our worries inside of a month."

I felt my teeth clench at the thought of being hit by a car again.

"What do we have to do?" I asked.

"You're going to have to take your connection with Alciel a step further. More than just sharing your manna, you're going to have to share spells."

"Share spells? How does that work?" Ali asked.

"Simple. Martin and Alciel will have to use the spell together. If they pull this off, they should be imperceptible by any lookouts they have stationed across the property."

"You mean those skinny bastards with bloodshot eyes that never stop itching their arms?" Ali asked. "Yeah. Real threatening."

"Whether they have magic on their side or not, they're still unstable and dangerous," Ash insisted.

"Then what's the plan when Martin gets inside?" Lyse asked. "He starts rooting around for an Addiction Demon and hopes for the best?"

"We'll be right behind him, and he'll be able to reach out to us if he gets in trouble. We just need to find out where the Addiction Demons are. If they flock around a certain spot, we may find the Necronomicon and be able to snatch it."

Silence.

"It's risky, but the sooner we end this, the better," I concluded.

I turned to Alciel.

"How do you pull off Selective Presence?" I asked.

Alciel's ears twitched.

"For demons, we tend to pull off the spell without an incantation. It's ingrained in our horns and can even be set off by instinct."

"Will that work for me as well?"

"As much as you'd like to regularly disappear from everyone's view, humans don't have that luxury," Alciel smiled.

"What's the Latin phrase we need to use?"

"That would be 'conceal myself from others,'" Alciel confirmed.

"*Dissimulo me de cetera populis,*" I confirmed.

"That's right," Alciel nodded.

Alciel held his claws in front of him, and a golden flame appeared. I performed the same motion, and sapphire flames appeared in mine.

"*Dissimulo me de cetera populis!*" we shouted in unison.

As soon as the phrase left our lips, our manna engulfed us. It was roaring across our arms as though we caught fire. I looked at Alciel, and all he did was smile. As he was halfway consumed by his flame, it turned blue, and the flames ensnaring me turned gold.

It was working.

The terrible hurt turned into an icy chill, and I felt myself close my eyes out of fear. I was sure I had used the incantation properly. But I was left in a state of numbness. I wasn't even sure if I was burned or if I'd lost all of my nerve endings.

I felt the sensation of my eyes opening and breath filling my lungs again. It was clear something had changed. Ali's expression was somewhere between delight and disbelief.

"What happened? Did it work?" I asked.

"Martin? Are you there?" Ali asked.

I looked at my hands, and they were just like they had always been before. No burns, no manna, no transparency.

Alciel chuckled where he stood, and it was clear that some magic was still in effect. His horns and his eyes were glowing both blue and gold.

It occurred to me that the spell *did* work. Selective Presence was meant to fool everyone except for those who had cast it as a spell. We would be able to see each other like always. But it was everyone else that wouldn't be able to see us.

"That was pretty good," Ash said, "for a first try."

"How long will this last?" I asked.

"I'm just guessing here," Alciel estimated. "But I think we can pull off two minutes."

"Two minutes?!" I exclaimed.

"Selective Presence takes a lot of manna. What do you want me to do?"

"The whole point of this was to share our manna and make the spell twice as effective!"

"I've been doing this for centuries. And you had no idea this was even possible a year ago!"

My skull felt like it was about to burst.

"We don't have a lot of manna to work off of, to begin with," I said.

"The more you exert yourself, the more trouble we're going to be in," Alciel warned.

The spell dissipated, and Ali pointed us out.

I felt like I just finished running at full speed.

"There's my favorite troublemakers!" Ali shouted.

"You-you couldn't hear us?" I panted.

"It was pretty muffled. But I'm pretty sure I could throw a rock in your general direction and hit you," Ali smiled.

"You're still giving me a hard time?" I said. "Let me remind you, I'm about to go on a secret mission into a drug den to find a spellbook that's going to kill us."

"I never expected you to go anywhere near Stryker. But searching the place for a book seems oddly fitting for you."

I looked at Ash, and he couldn't help but crack a smile.

"You did a good job hiding your body and your clothes," Ash reasoned. "You should be able to use your phone if you need to get a hold of us."

"And if they see my phone?" I asked.

"The security around the doors may be tight, but once you get inside, you'll be in a room full of junkies. It's not like they'll be bothered. And, if they are, nobody will believe them."

It was hard to refute Ash's reasoning.

"You should probably rest up," Ali insisted. "Get back in shape for your covert op."

"You're right," I agreed.

I threw myself on the ripped-up couch.

"If you can find the Necronomicon, that's the best we could hope for," Ash said. "But if you can't find the book, try and get a layout of the area. The more you gather, the more damage we can do."

"Let's take the fight to *them*," I nodded.

SNEAK

"You sure you're ready for this, kid?" Ash asked.

"You said this place was where it all led back to," I said. "And I checked Dorian's notes on the case that he left behind. It all checks out."

Stryker Motel was just ahead.

There was an eeriness to this place, even when it was covered with a light blanket of snow. Everyone's eyes seemed to dart around with suspicion. And everyone lingered in the corners of the complex with rotten teeth and wiry frames for bodies. A new arrival meant they would all retreat to their dark rooms, and one person would approach them. When we got close enough to see this in action, it was like it was rehearsed. In seconds, everyone was vanishing into the shadows, and it was only a matter of time before we would have a visitor.

"Looks like our presence has already been noted," Ash observed.

"How much time can you give me?" I asked.

"Maybe a few minutes. Everyone here is on the run from something, and they don't take kindly to people that aren't in the market for a hookup. Just look for anything you can find without getting shot at. Books, drugs, demons. Anything that helps move this investigation along."

"What are we supposed to do in the meantime?" Ali asked. "Buy a couple grams of coke while you go skulking?"

"Anything to make the cover more convincing," Ash nodded.

"She was just joking," Lyse interjected. "Please don't buy cocaine."

I looked beyond the dashboard and saw that a skinny punk in a beanie hat was walking toward the car.

"Looks like we've been made," Ash said. "I'll drive up to him. You get out of the side of the car and head into that alleyway."

I readied myself by crouching in my seat.

Ash gave the word when the lookout's view of the alleyway was cut off by his car. My door led straight into it.

"Now!" Ash whispered.

I opened the door so quietly, I didn't even hear it open. I slipped out of the car, and Alciel *skittered* behind me. The door shut fast, and a flare of emerald light shot out behind us.

"We have to do this now, or we'll get caught," I insisted.

"You're right," Alciel agreed.

We held our hands in front of us, and the light appeared.

"What the fuck are you doin' back there?!" a man shouted.

"*Dissimulo me de cetera populis!*"

The flame enveloped Alciel and me like we were soaked in gasoline. The man's eyes darted all across the alleyway. He drew his pistol.

"Let's get moving!" Alciel insisted.

My Companion *skittered* across the courtyard, and everything was exactly as Ash described. There were a handful of people standing outside the doorways. All of them with their bloodshot eyes darting back and forth.

"Where do we even start?" I asked. "They got the whole place locked up."

"We'll think of something," Alciel promised.

I looked ahead for a moment and saw the snow was falling more heavily. But, more than that, there was something else lingering in the air.

"Alciel. What's that?" I asked.

My eyes narrowed. I felt myself straining my manna.

"If you keep pushing that, we're not even going to last our two minutes!" Alciel exclaimed.

The more I looked, the more of them I saw. They were falling down like snowflakes, but they were pitch black. When they got close, you could hear little heartbeats. Each one made them pulse. Mingled in the snowfall was that necrotic pollen that infected the air. Black, sickly, and misshapen pieces of obsidian that knew you were there.

Tiny needles peeked through the black and threatened to stab you if you came close. Like midnight spiders with stainless steel legs. All of them seeking desperate, unsuspecting veins. I now understood why this place always made me shiver. It wasn't the winter cold. It was the dark snow that infected this place and was hiding in plain sight. The Addiction Demons were constantly looking for new humans to claim. New lives to own. And I was walking right into their den.

"No," Alciel whispered.

"What is it?" I asked.

"There are so many Addiction Demons here, they're infecting the atmosphere," Alciel shuddered. "If we get caught, there's no way in Gehenna we'll be able to escape!"

A girl stumbled out of a motel room and into the snow. She was clearly coming down from something. But looking at her terrified eyes, I wasn't sure whether it was narcotics or narrowly escaping from her life. She was covered in bruises, and she looked like she hadn't slept in a week. Her Radcliffe Academy jacket was torn and stained. With what resolve she had left, she picked herself up and ran off into the snow. She wept as she struggled to get on her feet.

Just behind her, I felt the same horrible presence that came from Woodrow Wilson. It was a deep rouge that radiated from the inside. This went well beyond anything we had felt in our first encounter with a demon. And it was more sinister than the demons we had in captivity at the Silk Slipper. There were more of them behind that single door, and they were all dangerous.

"Get out of here!" a pale man shouted.

He spat in the woman's direction. She got up sluggishly and ran away.

He was clearly in charge of whatever was waiting behind that door. But it wasn't just his hostility that got my attention. I looked at the extensive tattoos on his head, arms, and hands. Among the gangland ink, I saw magic runes.

"Kids from that school are supposed to come here with money."

Another gang member appeared. He was considerably larger than his predecessor, and must have weighed three hundred pounds. He had tattoos just like his associate.

"That bitch giving you trouble?" the large gang member asked.

"If people come by here looking for a free hit, we might find some."

"First, that scruffy muthafucka comes looking for trouble, and now you're getting pushed around by kids? Ya losing ya touch, Piper."

The skinny gangster threw himself against the wall and was clearly annoyed. When he turned his head, I saw he had purple bruises on his throat.

I saw an Addiction Demon taking its leave from the room Piper was meant to be guarding, and Piper shivered uncontrollably for a moment. The shade of the Addiction Demon disguising itself as the winter's chill.

"Damn, it's cold," Piper complained.

"Put some meat on your bones," the big gangster jabbed. "Or take some of that money you're making and buy a damn coat."

"Let's follow that demon," Alciel whispered.

We made our tracks in the snow, and I quickly realized that I would be putting us in danger if I kept on this careless path.

I reached down and scooped Alciel out of the snow. I could feel myself getting tired, and I knew that we were running out of time.

I rushed to the concrete that was untouched by snow. For a moment, I thought we were safe. But the Addiction Demon's form was silhouetted against the wall and was creeping toward a shadowy corner in the distance. A set of fluorescent lights were shattered in the direction it was heading. Clearly, this was a path frequented by these creatures long before we arrived.

"Martin, we're running out of time," Alciel insisted. "We

should look for Ash and try to flag him down."

"In a minute," I whispered. "If we leave now, this will all have been for nothing!"

I rushed in the direction the silhouette was fleeing, and I saw there was a door hidden in the shadows.

"Thirteen," I whispered, looking at the number on the door.

This room had an almost volcanic presence behind it. The Addiction Demon let out a slight scream as it passed through the edges of the door and passed inside.

"Martin, you're crazy!" Alciel whispered.

I looked carefully at the door and noticed there were runes scrawled all over it.

"*Hide, binding, magnet.* There's nothing here that will harm me. At least not in the runework," I reasoned.

CREEEEEEEEEAK!

"Who's there?!" a man shouted.

I quickly pushed the door open, and Alciel jumped with me to get inside. We threw the door shut, and we were completely enveloped in darkness.

"They're going to be all over us," I lamented.

"Maybe don't throw the door shut next time," Alciel hissed.

With that, I felt my feet catching fire again. It looked like our time of Selective Presence was up. The flames flashed between blue and gold, and the entire room was illuminated as they rode up our bodies.

The illusion gave way, and I saw that the dark corners of the room were hiding a terrible secret. People were lying all across this room, where they couldn't be seen. All of them had needles in their arms, pale faces, and eyes that stared up with a blank expression. I wasn't sure if they were dead or high.

Even from the floor, this room was terrifying. It was stained a deep black. Scorch marks sprawled all over the ground and somehow reacted to the light we were casting. As the flames rose up, there was a makeshift lab, a wall covered with faces with giant exes through them, and a stand where you would expect a book to be placed. There were burn marks all across the desk, except for a neat rectangle that reminded me of a book being opened.

This was it!

The Necronomicon must have been here.

I thought we were close to achieving our goal until I felt a terrible cold just behind us. I turned around fast and saw the room had changed in the few seconds I had turned my back on it. The pulsing pollen we saw outside was now floating in the air and giving off a series of pulses, like fireflies.

With each pulse, there seemed to be a call for help. One that was answered by the stirring of the bodies that lay in the corner. There was no reaction. The bodies didn't even blink as a dark, gangly figure sprouted from the mass of death and decay.

An Addiction Demon looked our way, and its head violently shook in place for a moment, as if it were vibrating. A putrid crack formed a broken smile where its mouth would be, and a series of hypodermic needles slid into place, giving it teeth. Each of them was coated in a layer of bile and blood.

As it raised its fingers, I saw each one of them was a cigarette lighter, and the violent smog it used as a weapon was forming at its fingertips. Each of them burning with a quelled *scream*.

As it crept closer, the belts wrapped around its arms tightened. It was barely restrained by the rough leather, and its hypodermic smile grew wider. More needles appeared. Like a predator growing more teeth for an impending hunt.

My strength was fading. Alciel and I had already pushed ourselves well beyond our limits. Our magic was almost gone. My bones felt like lead, and my blood felt like kerosene. We were easy prey.

"Fuck," I cursed.

TWENTY TWO

SWITCH

"We better think of something fast, Martin," Alciel warned.

I reached for the door, but the demon glided in front of it to block my path. Only the faint *flickering* of lights already broken by the demon's presence was there to guide me.

"He's smarter than the last one," I said.

"Probably tired of scraps," Alciel reasoned.

Alciel moved closer to me, and I knew magic was no longer an option like we were using before.

"Come on, think!" I whispered.

I looked up and saw the demon floating toward me. Its smile had grown so wide, I thought its head was going to break in two.

It reached out its slender, lighter fingers toward me, and I saw faint hazes form all around the room. Storm clouds of black smog and red lightning had been conjured. The numerous pictures were brought back to the walls.

My eyes darted all across the room. Whenever this creature

got closer to me, the more I was able to see.

"Keep it distracted," I insisted. "I have an idea."

"Hope it's a good one!" Alciel shouted.

My Companion darted around the room like a crazed cat, and, for a moment, the obsidian terror who loomed over us was trying to figure out which one to go after first. Finally, he settled on me.

I reached for my phone, and I took pictures as quickly as I could.

Click. Click. Click.

I didn't even bother to check the camera roll, I just kept the pattern going.

Click. Click. Click.

I wanted to cover every corner of this room, but Alciel was already running himself ragged. I could tell by his heavy breathing. With my last photo, I noticed he was slowing down.

The needle-toothed monster turned to Alciel, sensing its weakness. And with the same opportunistic instinct of a starving rat, it threw itself at him.

The last picture I took was of the chemistry lab, and it gave me an idea. The smell of sulfur and a small bowl of white crystal salts, just like we had at the Silk Slipper. Someone had taken the time to be prepared if the demons fought back.

I raised my hand and pictured the white salt turning blue. The only thought I had was to see this demon burn.

"*Ignis!*" I commanded.

Spark-spark.

"Martin!" Alciel shouted.

A stream of blue was turning the salt to azure. But it wasn't enough. I needed the salt to burn this demon down in a single hit. I was already weak, and I thought for a terrible moment that this might be the end.

"No! Work! *Ignis!*" I demanded.

It was bad enough that I did this correctly and burned down the chemistry lab, but now I couldn't do this right when I really needed it.

Spark-spark-spark!

The salts began to take on an even lighter blue than before. And I could hear the horrible sound of flesh *ripping* and Alciel crying out.

If Dorian was here, he would help. But now we were both in danger, and it all fell on me. And I was failing.

"AAAAAAHHHH!!!" Alciel roared.

I closed my eyes and let myself be overwhelmed by despair. Everything went silent for a moment, and I felt myself losing all the strength I had left. But if I didn't do anything, Alciel would die. To hell with all the other times things that went wrong. I had to save him. I was going to save him.

"*Ignis,*" I whispered.

WHARF!

The bowl caught fire, and it was a torch of pure dark blue. I raised it up, and the flames started to burn my palm. But that didn't matter. It was exactly what I needed.

The Addiction Demon turned to me by twisting its head clean around. It suddenly had a worried expression across its face. I raised the bowl and tossed it in his direction. The creature reared back, and a stream of burning salt crystals started to burn across the room. The smell of rot had gotten worse when the flames hit it. But the screams of the Addiction Demon were enough to make up for it.

"SCREEEEEEEEEEE!"

The creature raised its fingertips and seemed to be extinguishing the blue flame with its own smog clouds, but that only made the fire spread faster. The creature was melting into a puddle of decay. I quickly reached for Alciel.

"Come on!" I demanded.

I picked him up and started looking around the room frantically.

Globs of putrid color had pooled at the base of our escape route, and I reached around for everything else I could find. There was a bag in the corner, and I reached for it instantly, starting to throw everything I could inside of it.

"We don't have long, Martin!" Alciel shouted.

The clock was ticking, but I would be damned if we were going to lose this chance. Thankfully, I took pictures of things that would likely have to stay. Heavy objects, massive displays tacked to walls, and items that were affixed to the ground.

I stuffed the bag full, and Alciel reached for the doorknob. Most of the runes on the door had been completely melted away.

A smell of rot pierced my nostrils, but the sound of the door opening left me no choice. I was running out of manna, and this would be my only chance at escape.

CREEEEEEEEEAK!

"*RAAAAAAAAAAH!*" the Addiction Demon hissed.

I reached for the door and shut it fast behind both me and Alciel. That horrible sound emerged again, and we took a moment to catch our breath.

"You're fucking crazy," Alciel whispered.

"I know," I smiled.

Shik-shik!

Two men ran toward us, both of them armed with pistols.

I coughed for a moment and ducked into the narrow passage that led to the street. The smoke was a light blue, and it reeked of sulfur.

We rounded the corner and weren't spotted by the sentinels watching over the rest of Stryker Motel. I felt like I could have lost consciousness at any moment. I was sweating profusely, and my vision started to get blurry.

"Where's Ash's car?" I demanded.

"I'm looking for it," Alciel insisted.

I wondered how hard it could have been to find a 2009 Jaguar XF Supercharged, but then something caught my eye that stopped me dead in my tracks.

I looked up and saw a familiar face lingering at the side of the motel.

It was Dorian.

He didn't see me, but I sure as hell saw him.

He had no weapons drawn, but was lurking around another corner of the Stryker Motel. One that perfectly hid him from the lookouts. It made me wish we had thought of entering through there.

Dorian's amber eyes looked behind him as though he was checking to see if he was being followed. But then he saw me. For a moment, he hesitated. Like he wanted to rush out to me. But he stopped himself after taking one step.

I saw Ash's car speeding down Grand River Avenue. The car had gradually come to a screeching halt. Gunshots were appearing in the direction Dorian was heading. As soon as the chaos ensued on the street, Dorian gave me a somber look and vanished through that shadowy refuge beneath the steps leading inside the compound. Straight into the blue fire I had started.

I looked to where Dorian disappeared. I felt remorse grip me, and it was like I had been suspended in ice. *How could this have happened? Why was it happening?*

BANG! BANG! BANG!

"GET IN!" Ash shouted.

I rushed to the side of the car and shut the door fast behind me.

SLAM!

SCREEEEEEECH!

Ash drove with all the speed his car could muster, and he kept his eyes on the road.

"What happened?" Ash demanded.

"Alciel and I got cornered, and we ran out of manna," I admitted.

"Did anybody see you?"

"An Addiction Demon. But we managed to get away," I defended.

"Where did you get that bag?"

"I found it in some room. They did a good job covering it up, whoever it was. If we didn't use Selective Presence, I doubt we'd even get close to it."

"Let me see that," Ash insisted.

I begrudgingly handed the bag over.

Ash let his eyes flash from the road to the contents of the bag.

When the gunfire had dissipated into a light storm in the background, Ash pulled his car to the side of the road.

Screet.

He rummaged through everything inside and slowed down as he started to appreciate what we'd gathered.

"A couple of pocketbooks of runes. A list of names," Ash began.

"I also took some pictures of what I couldn't take along," I offered.

I handed him my phone.

Click. Click. Click.

Ash held still for a moment.

"It was here. The Necronomicon was here," he breathed.

I chose to say nothing about Dorian.

"These markings…." Ash whispered.

"What about them?" Ali asked.

She leaned forward and examined the phone closely.

"These are the same marks Watchmen use when they're cleaning up demonic magic," Ash examined.

I looked at the red marks left on the map of Detroit. Every mark was made with the same insidious red that formed an X above each deceased target.

Had it not been for the color, it would have looked identical to the map we had stored at the Silk Slipper. Circles for demon sightings, exes for exorcisms, and squares for clusters of erratic amplifications occurred. Woodrow Wilson High, Belvedere Tea, and the Stryker Motel. The Silk Slipper was thankfully missing from the lineup.

I should have felt better. We were that much closer to figuring out who was using the Necronomicon. But my stomach twisted when I realized Dorian had almost beat us to it.

What was he doing there?

CONFESSION

"Ash must've been happy with what we gave him," Ali reasoned. "He hasn't called us back to the Silk Slipper for almost three weeks."

"I don't like it," I responded.

Lyse was cuddling Ali's arm as she was tending to some plants on her desk. Alciel looked at me with a grim expression. I felt I had a similar look on my face.

"What's that all about?" Ali asked.

She looked at both of us like we just confessed to pushing an old lady into traffic.

"Nothing," I lied.

"You both know something," Ali pressed. "What did you see at Stryker? You've been acting weird all week. But this is the first time you've both agreed to be in the same room with me."

I looked to Alciel and knew we had been found out. I could have hidden the truth from Ash because he was looking for his answers in what I gave him. Ali could tell when something was wrong because she was looking for a way to help me.

"You have to promise not to tell anybody," I prefaced.

Ali dropped what she was doing and gave me her full attention.

"I promise. Nobody will know. Not Mom, not Dad, and sure as hell not Ash," she accepted.

I took a moment to center myself. Now I wasn't even sure I actually 100 percent saw him at the motel. With every passing day of trying to keep it hidden, it felt like a delusion.

"I saw Dorian at Stryker," I confessed.

Ali's eyes went wide for a moment, but then she centered herself instantly.

"That explains why you've been acting this way," she reasoned. "You don't want to tell Ash because you're afraid of how it will look."

"And Dorian saw me. I can't be sure, but it was like he wanted to tell me something,"

"But he didn't," Ali concluded.

"I've been racking my brain trying to think of what he was going to tell me. But I have no idea," I whispered.

Silence.

"You think I should tell Ash," I whispered.

"I think it's important that we tell the right person what you saw. And since Ash has taken Dorian's position, this could lead to some serious problems," Ali corrected.

"Then who are we supposed to tell?"

"For now? Nobody else. The four of us can keep it a secret."

"But why was Dorian there?" I asked. "Was he trying to take the case on his own? Was he trying to protect us? Was he... up to something?"

"Like what?" Ali replied. "You think Dorian was involved with the Necronomicon? There's no way."

"How can you be so sure?"

"Dorian's been there every step of the way. And Ash said it himself, whoever made those marks is making them just like a—" Ali paused.

"Watchman. Exactly. It's entirely possible that Dorian's been using the Necronomicon this whole time."

"It doesn't make sense, Martin."

"Why not? It's the perfect setup for whoever has the book."

"Using the Necronomicon this whole time?"

"It makes sense, doesn't it?"

"It doesn't make sense, Martin. That's why I said that."

"If they had someone in charge of the search for the book on their side, they could hide forever. It'd be even better for them if they were the person throwing us off the trail."

"If Dorian wanted us dead, he would have done it already, Martin. But he hasn't. And if what you're saying is even remotely true, then Ash should be a suspect, too."

"I thought about that, also. But I don't even know where to begin. It's been months since all of this started, and we've constantly been in danger."

"This is a dangerous situation," Ali said. "This whole thing has been insane, but we've made it this far. And we've made it this far by trusting Dorian. Look, I'm glad you told me what you saw, but the only way we can make it out of this is by working together."

Ali looked into my eyes, and everything felt better. At least for a moment.

BUZZ.

I felt my phone vibrating in my pocket.

"Beatrice?" Ali asked.

"I hope so. It'd be nice to take my mind off things," I smiled.

"She's been 'taking your mind off things' every night we've been on leave."

Caller ID: Ash.

I opened my phone and saw there was a message.

"*We're close to an answer,*" I read aloud. "*I'm coming to get you both in ten minutes.*"

Ali looked me in the eye.

"That whole thing with Dorian? It never happened. I'll take it to the grave with me. We all will." Ali promised.

"Thanks, Ali," I nodded.

We immediately turned around and started packing our bags.

"The way things are going, we may be able to get some normalcy back in our lives," I smiled.

"We just might. Part of me was getting tired of being on call for life-or-death situations."

I looked out the window and saw that it wasn't snowing yet. But the cold stillness in the air was difficult to look away from, like a moment frozen in time. I wanted to stay here and let everything around us stop. Maybe for a few hours. Maybe a few minutes. But I knew the snow would continue to fall, and our troubles would be far from over when it returned.

"Hey," Ali said with a smile, "we'll always have each other."

I could feel her smile behind me, and I smiled with her. I felt a little better than before. Time resumed around us. Soft tufts of white started to fall onto the window.

I didn't feel alone anymore.

CONNECTION

"I wouldn't have called you two here unless it was of the greatest urgency," Ash began. "But we've been dealing with a mixed bag of results since Stryker."

He walked swiftly through the threshold and made his way to Dorian's board. It had since been dominated by a massive cluster of marks. All of them concentrated in clusters all across Detroit. Some purple, some emerald, and some crimson.

"Looks like you took full advantage of my trip inside Stryker."

"It helped more than you could know," Ash said. "The marks were very telling. Someone was meticulous enough to keep track of everything and didn't drop a single hint as to what happened. Most of the people on my list and Proctor's match up perfectly with the fatalities on the killer's list."

I looked up at the board and realized there were a handful of faces without exes running through them.

"Who are they?" I asked.

"It was too soon to guess before, but it turns out drugs went missing from every target. That's the one thread tying it all together. And since we've got Addiction Demons all over the place, it stands to reason. One junkie overdose and you get a little bit more influence over those floating husks that feed on suffering."

Ali was intent on knowing who was left.

"These guys look like hardcore crooks," Ali observed.

"I don't expect Dorian got to this point in your training, but you should know something about mages," Ash began.

"What's that?" I asked.

"If you ever see a human criminal on the rise, you can usually find a mage helping them behind the scenes."

"Dorian did mention something about Pablo Escobar," I said, "how the shipments coming into Miami carried Addiction Demons along with it."

"Yes, and if we don't act quickly, we may be looking at a similar development here in Detroit. Someone probably captured every Addiction Demon they could find and held them up in Stryker. And now that the Necronomicon has been pried open enough, they may be close to having the ultimate weapon on their side."

"Who are the culprits?" Lyse asked.

"It's pretty easy to pin down. Most of the other suspects ended up dead this last week. A couple of wannabe kingpins, a few established gangsters, and a couple cultists."

I saw there was one face pinned above all the others. He had a mohawk, tattoos running across his face, and a steely look in his eyes. Like he could kill whoever was taking his mugshot just by looking.

"And this is..." I led.

"His name is Cole Sutherland," Ash said. "An up-and-comer in the Detroit underworld. But as far as Warlocks go, he's pretty mediocre. In fact, he's been struggling to find a place to stay this winter. Got picked up by cops right when the snow started falling. But my guess is he showed gangsters his magic and promised to make their drugs twice as addictive. For no cost."

"The Addiction Demons," Alciel reasoned.

"I've never known a drug dealer to turn down a more addictive drug," Ash said.

"So, what's stopping you from finding him?" Ali asked.

"I've been turning over every stone in Detroit. Forest Park. Chaldean Town. Poletown East. Nobody's seen the guy," Ash lamented.

"If we knew anything more about the book, we might be able to track them down," Lyse concluded.

"The book is probably opening up the possibilities of whoever has it. But performing Selective Presence for any length of time is costly. If they were using magic to stay hidden, they'd never be able to keep it up. Martin and I are proof of that," Alciel explained.

"So, it's not magic," I deduced. "They're choosing a clever hiding spot. Somewhere hidden, unsuspected, and where they can get to all of these places with ease."

I looked up and down the map, trying to find a connection. But the more I looked at Dorian, Ash, and our culprit's clusters of marks, I got further away from an answer. So, I decided to take a step back and look at the entire picture. I noticed there was one thing we didn't think of.

"There's a connection here that we're not seeing," I whispered.

"If you've got something to say, we'd love to hear it, Blackbriar," Ash insisted.

"Our focus is on the wrong thing. We've been attacked from all sides, and we're looking for the source. Woodrow Wilson. Stryker. But every time we've been attacked…."

I reached for a nearby blue marker. Then I made my way to the map. The whole of Detroit was laid out on it, with various symbols showing. Each one of them looked like islands. I knew every location so well, I could picture them in my mind.

Circles for demon sightings, exes for exorcisms, and squares for clusters of erratic amplifications occurred. Woodrow Wilson High, the Silk Slipper, Belvedere Tea, and the Stryker Motel.

"There's been something connecting them all," I pondered.

"The Watchmen have looked over Proctor's records," Ash said. "And we've conducted a thorough investigation of our own. There is no magic connecting them anywhere."

"That's because it's not magic," I answered.

I took a light blue marker and began highlighting the sections implicated with demons appearing. The more I highlighted, the more I saw the connection.

"Woodrow Wilson, Stryker, Belvedere Tea, and… here," I whispered.

I made more connections. Two that were further away.

"Have there been sightings at Gratiot Avenue or Orangelawn Street?" I asked.

Ash's mouth opened slightly.

"There's been some accidents out that way," Ash said. "Drunk drivers. But how could you possibly know that? I received word of them just before I picked you kids up. On the police radio."

I smiled.

"Because every sighting of these demons appears right around an abandoned subway system."

I stepped to the side and let the marks speak for themselves. Wherever the blue of my markings highlighted, there was one of the disparate marks to connect them. It didn't matter if they were purple, emerald, or crimson. They eventually reached my intricate, neglected web of Detroit transportation relics.

"I thought Detroit was sticking to the tram and didn't have a subway," Ash pondered.

Ash stepped up to the board. Even with his eyes fully covered, I knew he was starting to see the big picture.

"They planned on having a massive subway system in 1915. But they scrapped the idea when they lost funding. Some of those tunnels are still there, if you know where to look."

Ash stood up at the board and bit his lip.

"We better check it out. But you all should stay here. I've poured over the notes, and this place is not on anybody's radar," Ash insisted.

Ash turned around to leave.

"The hell we will," Ali objected.

"This is for your own safety," Ash defended. "This isn't some pack of junkies. They might be hiding the actual Necronomicon down there."

"You've been sent here to protect us, and we've shown you we're capable," Ali protested. "In that time, we've helped Dorian with his case, expanded on yours, and we always came out okay. Besides, we're seeing this through to the end."

Ali reached out from behind her and produced a Louisville Slugger baseball bat. Ash looked at everyone in the room and took a deep breath.

"Come on," Ash submitted.

He removed his hands from his pockets and started walking. We followed close behind, and I noticed he only had half of the tattoos that Dorian did on his hands.

"Access to the closest tunnel should be up the street, just past the stop sign," Ali said. "Let's go head-to-head with these psychos again."

"The sooner this is over with, the better," I said.

We were pierced by the cold Detroit air, and our breath formed clouds as Ash reached for the back of his Jaguar. He produced a Walther PPK pistol and a 12-gauge shotgun.

Shik-shik.

"Nice guns," Ali commented.

"Thanks," Ash offered.

"Think that's really necessary?" Ali added.

"It never hurts to be prepared. If Martin is onto something, we should be geared up for anything."

"Do Gorgons have the ability to turn people to stone, or is that just a myth?" Ali asked.

"We can turn people to stone," Ash confirmed, "but the Order wants that book recovered. And they want whoever is using it to be taken alive. With as few complications as possible."

"And turning him to stone happens instantly?"

"It takes some time. But showing someone my eyes could put you all in danger," Ash explained. "It's going to be dark down there. And if you even catch a glimpse of my eyes, the damage will be irreversible. And hard to avoid. My eyes glow when the manna for petrification activates."

Ash continued walking and didn't seem to mind us.

"Do you think we'll get Dorian back after all this?" I asked Ali.

"You really miss him," Ali pointed out.

"He was always there for us. Even though we didn't make it easy."

"And now we're going to be there for him. We'll see him again, somehow. I promise."

Ali looked at me, and I knew that everything was going to work out.

We stopped at the abandoned subway tunnel. It was boarded up, just like any of the buildings on the block. And it was tagged with multiple layers of graffiti.

"I take the lead," Ash insisted.

"How do you expect to see in the dark?" Ali asked. "I'm assuming that throwing up a light could make us a target down there."

"I have better hearing than most people. If they breathe, I'll know where they are."

Ash raised his foot and kicked down the wooden barricade that blocked our path.

KINK-KINK-KRUNK!

A cloud of dust shot out from the hole Ash had made. Once it cleared, we saw a swarm of trash, cigarette butts, and vermin lingering in the bowels of the abandoned Detroit subway station. The smell of oil and rot pierced our noses.

"Everyone stays close. We'll be back before you know it."

Ash began his descent into darkness. We followed.

"*Lux,*" I breathed.

I held my hand out as though I was holding a baseball. And as I breathed that word, I felt the manna *simmering* in the center of my palm, forming a light that filled my hand.

I could see clearly as we were enveloped by darkness. A

dome of light embraced us, letting us see ten feet in every direction. But just beyond that, there was pure darkness. Like the world was being made as we walked forward, and it was being destroyed as we left it behind.

The tunnels had been infected by something. An entity that subsisted on the filth of these forgotten parts of Detroit. The crushing darkness, bitter air, and abundance of vermin made it inhospitable to anyone. I knew we were getting closer, as there was a presence just ahead. One that made my teeth feel like they were vibrating.

The tunnels felt alive like they were reacting to my sudden spike in panic. I tried to keep myself from shaking, but that only made the cold worse. And with my fear, the light started to *flicker* in my hand. Whatever was ahead was waiting for the light to go out. It wanted to let us be absorbed by the shadows, so it could satisfy its hunger.

"Keep it together, Martin," Ali insisted. "We need light."

I remembered that Ali was beside me, and the light came back. She put a hand on my shoulder, and the *flickering* stopped. With a few taps on my shoulder, the light was brighter than it had been before.

"Thanks," I nodded.

Ash looked to the ground.

"We're getting close," he confirmed.

A terrible, bloody red glow appeared along a set of tracks. The archaic letters were identical to the ones I had picked up from Dorian's book and all the training we'd endured.

"Are all of these… runes?" Ali asked.

"*Pull, dark, wild,* and I don't know this one," I recounted.

"*Summon,*" Ali added. "This entire system has been used

to make a giant ritual. Looks like you were on the right track."

"Dorian was on the right track," I whispered.

I wasn't sure if I was feeling better or worse after I said that. I tensed and hoped Ash wouldn't read into what I just said.

Silence.

"They're being magnetized to this city from beneath the surface. And with no one coming to do maintenance on these tunnels, they can get away with it. Even if anyone did see it, they'd just dismiss it as vandalism," Alciel surmised.

SKIT-SKIT.

I raised my torch to the air and prepared my free hand for an exorcism. Ash kept his gun pointed forward.

"We're not alone down here," Ash cautioned.

We all inched forward, my pulse becoming more violent with every moment.

Ash stopped.

"More light, Martin," he demanded.

"*Luminare maius!*" I ordered.

The darkness at the center of the room was so intense, the light from my palm caused it all to *rip* through the air, until there was a ritual exactly like the one we had at the Silk Slipper. Twelve Addiction Demons linked together in a circle, swaying to the tune of a soundless melody. All of them were branded with those harrowing symbols on their torsos. Three rings interlocked.

"They don't know we're here," Ali whispered. "They've been drained and bound to this place, just like Dorian did for us."

I looked up and saw the ashen sentinels of his room were looming over a colossal pile of narcotics. It was a cube of narcotics six feet tall and six feet wide.

"This is enough drugs to keep them here forever," Ali added.

"What?" I asked.

"Every dying junkie has had no drugs on their person. Just like Ash said. Most people probably assume it was stolen from them at their favorite places to shoot up. But now, it looks like this has been drawing the Addiction Demons in the first place. Away from view before they went on a hunt."

"And now we're going to end it," Alciel insisted.

I could feel the hot rush of yellow manna coursing through my arm.

"We have to wait," Ash insisted.

"What? We'll cut them off at the knees if we do this now!" I pointed out.

"But then we'll lose track of the book, and they'll just start all over again," Ash whispered. "If we wait a little longer, we can catch them."

Click. Click. Click.

We heard the sound of footsteps approaching, and we all held our breath.

"They're here," Ali whispered.

"There's plenty of demonic presence here," Alciel said, "I should be able to keep us hidden, no problem."

"Do it," I insisted.

"*Dissimulo me de cetera populis,*" Alciel whispered.

His horns began to glow a deep gold, and the entire world was silent. The light that surrounded us was intense, but it was only for a split second. Gold and blue dominated my vision and then vanished again.

We looked out and saw a figure emerge from the north tunnel. I felt my heart stop. To my surprise, there was no mask. There was a dark-haired man of about twenty years of age. One with a mohawk, tattoos, and a steely look in his eyes. He walked through the tunnel carrying orange light. Just as I had carried blue in a torch. But the light was afflicted with red impurities.

It was Cole Sutherland. Mohawk, tattoos, death stare and all.

He walked to the center of the ritual and let his manna jet into the center with him, affecting the Addiction Demons in his circle. It burned with orange flame and red bursts.

SCREEEEEEEE!

Cole removed the crossover bag he was carrying and unzipped it. A strange feeling of new dread permeated the room as he did so.

Ash charged forward, breaking the cover. The darkness soon filled the room, leaving us in a state of perpetual midnight.

"You move, you die!" Ash warned.

HUMMMMMMMMM!

Crimson eyes looked at us from every direction.

"Close your eyes," Alciel insisted.

I did so. It was as though nothing had changed. Yet, somehow, I felt safer.

HRRRRRRRM-CSSSSSSSSH.

"GAH!" Cole shouted.

Debris crumbled from all around us, and an intense heat emerged. It was like the subway was emitting volcanic fumes.

My eyes opened and adjusted to the infernal haze. The center of the room had gone up in flames. Cole and Ash were running through the North tunnel. Their shadows cast high above us in a haze of crimson and emerald.

I heard the sound of the PPK go off, but I saw flares of emerald go out instead of a typical muzzle flash.

BANG-BANG-BANG!

"Ash!" I shouted.

"Stay back!" Alciel demanded.

I looked up and saw the Addiction Demons were reeling back to form perfect wheels, and that crimson light was erupting from their ashen bodies.

Some reached out to us, but Ali had her bat prepared. She clutched her bat tightly, and red began to course through the splinters. A warmer red than the manna being directed at us.

"*Institue potestem,*" Ali whispered.

The demon rushed at her at high speed, and she let out a final command.

CRACK!

"*Percutio!*" Ali shouted.

The demon reeled back. A bolt of crimson electricity followed by jade sparks hurled it into a nearby wall, crushing it into shards of ash. Two demons came toward me. I held my hands up.

"*Exorcizamus demoni hunc totis virbius!*" I roared.

Blue crests appeared on both of their torsos. I clutched my hands into fists, and they, too, burst into piles of soot. Yellow flames reduced the soot into smoke.

The rest of the demons retreated into the deep tunnels of the east and west of the subway.

I was not certain where they went, but I was certain they would not follow us.

"We have to help him!" Ali called out.

We both nodded and rushed to the north tunnel. Alciel's horns were doused, and the darkness engulfed us. With every step, blue and red flashed to light our way. The more we fought, the more we could see.

"*Lux!*" I conjured.

A fainter light appeared in my hand, but we started running. The sounds of our footsteps reverberated off the walls. And the sound of gunshots made us run faster.

BANG! BANG! BANG!

An emerald light shot out each time. It trailed the bullet for a few inches before vanishing into pure darkness.

“GAH!!!” Cole shouted.

We both stopped for a moment and then sprinted with all our strength until we finally came across Ash.

He had a wound glowing orange on his left side. But in his hand, we saw a black book. It was adorned with a skull. At his feet was a man with three gunshot wounds on his side. The wounds were glowing bright green. As Cole looked up to us, his eyes were corrupted with demonic magic. They were desperate and orange.

We looked up to Ash.

“We got him,” Ash smiled.

Twenty Five

CHANGE

"You sure we should be bringing Cole back to base?" Ali asked.

"It's the best place we can hold him," Ash assured. "Not to mention he'll be in Wayne County jail in a few hours."

"Wayne County jail?" I asked. "That's where you put drug dealers, not demonic Warlocks."

"Not when you cover them in tattoos. If we put enough suppression runes on his body, he'll never be able to use magic," Ash smiled.

I had my doubts, but it occurred to me that runes preventing magic were possible. I'd read about them in Dorian's book. But to apply them to a person was harrowing to contemplate.

"Every Watchman in Michigan will be here before long. We're going to get everything sorted now that we have the book in hand," Ash grinned.

"Who will it go to?" Ali asked.

"The Order, of course," Ash said. "They have agreed to a

Summit Gathering to collect the book, pass sentence on Cole, and discuss what will happen now that we have things under control."

"How can we be sure that he's really the only culprit? What if he had accomplices?"

"Our suspect had a pretty basic profile. And Cole meets it in spades. Drug addict, an affinity for demonic magic, and connections to crime throughout Detroit. And he had the Necronomicon. Plus, he went to Radcliffe Academy a long time ago, where there's been a lot of unexplained drug activity. But that hardly matters now."

"So... it's over," I breathed.

"The Witch and Wizard were killed the last time the book was lost, but now we've secured you both," Ash said. "Why don't you two just relax for a while? You've earned it."

Falling back on this ripped-up couch didn't even feel real. Nor did the cold in the Silk Slipper. Or the fact that it was all finally over.

"You don't buy it?" Ali asked.

"I want to," I responded. "But I can't quite yet."

"That was some slick thinking to get us to the tunnels," Ali offered.

"Thanks," I grinned.

I stared up at the ceiling and had the unexpected weight of worry still hanging on my chest like my body knew we weren't out of danger yet.

"We got a big win," Ali said. "Why can't you just savor it?"

"Because something still feels off," I contemplated.

"Martin, we've been through a lot. You've been running on all cylinders for the last few months. You got hit by a car, for fuck's sake! How about I treat you to some tea after this?"

Ali smiled.

"That sounds wonderful!" Lyse barked.

She wagged her tail and jumped on the ripped-up couch. She nuzzled her head in my hand, and I smiled too.

"Is it possible you've warmed up to me?" I chuckled.

"I think she has," Ali said. "Just give her a few weeks, and she'll get sick of you and your Orson Welles references."

Ali and I looked at each other and then to our Companions. We were all relishing the idea of some downtime. We could appreciate it in earnest, now that we finally got our culprit.

I looked at the table and saw Dorian had left his books on artifacts behind. If anything, it could have been interesting to read about what we just found.

"Maybe you would make a good demon," Alciel chuckled.

"Because I like to read?" I asked.

"Demons love knowledge," Alciel smiled.

I pulled one of Dorian's books on artifacts and flipped to a bookmarked page.

"What's going to happen to the Necronomicon now that it's in the Order's control?" I asked.

"Watchmen are going to handle it like a human bomb squad would," Alciel explained. "They're going to check it over really well, make sure they don't set it off and get it somewhere safe."

I flipped to the sections on the Necronomicon, as small and cursory as they were.

"*'Artifacts of necromancers and demonic mages have the effect of harming whoever is not supposed to be in possession of them,'*" I read.

"It's extra security," Alciel explained.

"Dorian said even he would be unable to read the content

of the book. Who could possibly be able to read it now?" I asked.

"I'm not sure," Ali said. "What does it say in there?"

I opened another annotated page.

"'*In the event of a mage's death, an artifact's Spell Locks may be overridden. But to do so requires an enormous amount of energy,*'" I recited.

"The demons," Ali concluded.

"We're talking in circles," Alciel complained.

"Then we must be missing something."

"You can't be right every day, Martin," Alciel insisted.

"Intuition is its own magic," I insisted. "Something tells me that there's something wrong about this whole thing."

"Wait," Ali interrupted.

"What?" I asked.

"Who was supposed to get the book if Hive died?" Ali asked.

"I'm assuming that would be Dorian," I said.

"Hmmm," Alciel contemplated.

"Did Hive have any family?" Ali asked.

"No. Hive was notorious among demons. And he was never said to have any family. Believe me, my kind was looking to see if we could exploit that. We found nothing," Alciel lamented.

"How can you be so sure?" I asked. "The best person to ask would be Dorian."

Silence.

I looked at the section on the Necronomicon. I looked at Dorian's board, and I felt a horrible wave of dread start to overcome my mind.

"Martin. What's wrong?" Ali asked.

"We've been running in circles. And we immediately got on the right track once he was gone," I realized.

"Martin, what are you saying?" Ali stood up.

"What if Dorian was just using us to find the book? Or what if he was protecting Cole?" I asked.

Silence.

"Martin. You're overtired, and you're not thinking right," Ali insisted. "There's no way Dorian would do that to us."

Ali looked over her shoulder to see if Ash was within earshot.

"There's just no way," Ali whispered.

"I don't want to believe it either, Ali," I insisted.

"Martin. The only reason we got this far was because of the hard work he put in to protect us. To protect our family," Ali objected.

VROOM! VROOM!

The pale glow of headlights showed through the boarded windows of the Silk Slipper. All of us got up and walked over to the windows to see if it was really the Watchmen. Or the police. Fortunately, there weren't any red or blue lights to accompany them.

Ash walked outside to see who had come by for a visit. But when I didn't see him brandishing his gun, I felt myself breathing more evenly and slowly. Almost as soon as he left our sight, the car engines began to shut down.

"Martin," Ali insisted, "I know you're scared right now, but you can't bring this up when the Watchmen get here."

"But what if we've been wrong to trust Dorian?" I asked.

"Then we'll work something out," she insisted. "Right now, this is probably the safest place in the world we could be."

Ash came back into the lobby.

"The Watchmen got here sooner than expected," Ash smiled. "They're just as eager as you are to see the end of this."

He raised his hand, gesturing for everyone to come inside. A procession of figures in hoods, dark jackets, and those armed with classic firearms came into view.

Some of them appeared human, and others had an expression of severity that made them seem less than human. Some were cold, some were grey-skinned, and they all knew they had come to the right place. These were Watchmen. They all offered a slight bow when they entered.

"We are honored to be here," a Watchman offered.

He approached and stopped to give us space.

"My name is Banner, Watchman of Grand Rapids."

"Nice to meet you," Ali attempted.

"If there is any way we can assist you, please let us know."

"There is one thing," I began.

I looked at Ali, and she gave me a look of caution.

"Ash said that every Watchman in Michigan was going to be here. Does that include Dorian?"

Silence.

"Proctor will be joining us," Banner responded.

I felt a slight weight relieved from my shoulders.

I looked out over the six Watchmen in the lobby and knew that Banner had spoken the truth. But I noticed they seemed excited. Finally, a set of headlights emerged, and I recognized the slight delay of the engine when turning off.

TEAR-OOOM.

Dorian was here.

Step. Step. Step.

Finally, he had returned. I felt a weight on my shoulders dissipate, but I felt my eyes honing in on him. I wasn't sure if it was to make sure this was real or whether his reaction would be more reliable than anybody's word.

A familiar frame peered through the darkness, and Dorian came into view. He had a grave expression on his face, but his eyes were warm when he looked at us.

"It's good to see you again, kids," Dorian smiled.

Dorian looked at me first, like he was hanging on to what I was going to say next. He probably wanted me to stay quiet about his involvement at Stryker.

"It's good to see you too, Dorian," I responded.

"This means it's all over?" Ali asked.

"Hardly," Ash answered.

"What do you mean?" Alciel asked.

Banner looked directly at Alciel.

"The Watchmen have done what they have set out to do. All of us have worked hard to identify the Witch and Wizard and keep them safe," Banner explained. And then we identified the owner of the Necronomicon and confiscated it."

"And that's the end of it," Ali finalized.

"Not quite," Banner continued. "We have gathered extensive evidence so we can bring Cole before the Order."

"Which you got, thanks to Dorian's hard work," I recalled.

I even pointed to Dorian, making sure everyone knew who they had to thank for their victory.

"Because of the hard work of *everyone* in this room," Ash corrected. "And while I can speak on the character of every Watchman that's come here tonight, Dorian is still in question."

"How dare you!" I shouted. "Dorian protected us."

I might have had mixed feelings about Dorian, but someone else suggesting it made something go off in me. Something I didn't know was there.

"Take it easy, kid," Dorian insisted.

"I won't just sit here and listen to you get treated like this!" I shouted.

"Dorian was sitting on top of the conspiracy the entire time, and yet he took the longest to report back," Ash added.

"You can't blame him for being delayed. He was training us *and* hunting down whoever was responsible," Ali objected.

"And while you two were under his care, a demon appeared in Woodrow Wilson High, Martin got hit by a car, and all of his evidence was pointing away from the actual crime scene," Ash said.

Silence.

I looked at Dorian. Suddenly, everything was making sense.

"Blackbriar, Dorian has been leading you astray," Ash continued. "You have been in danger from the moment you were put in his care, and you were only safe after he was gone."

I looked to the ground, desperately trying to see things differently.

"That's impossible," I whispered.

I wasn't sure I convinced anybody. Least of all, myself.

"You may not know this, Martin, but Dorian has been desperately seeking the Necronomicon for years," Ash said. "That's part of the reason he was asked to take on this responsibility. He knows that book and the mages that would want it better than anybody. He used to be hunted by us, you know."

Ali and I looked at Dorian. He didn't deny it. He didn't even try. Looking into his eyes, I knew this was the truth.

"Then why would you let him even watch over us?" Ali demanded.

"Because he was the High Watchman of Detroit. He knew the culprits and that book better than anybody. He was the perfect man to look after you kids. At least, for a time," Ash confirmed.

"If you have something to say, then say it," Alciel demanded.

"Dorian is complicit," Ash said. "He was either behind this or was in on it. At the very least, he was negligent."

I wanted to keep defending Dorian, but it got more challenging the more people told me who Dorian really was. They seemed to know about him more than I ever would.

"He will stand trial before the Order. You can hear everything there."

"You don't mean...." Ali whispered.

"Proctor will stand trial for aiding Cole with stealing the Necronomicon," Banner said. "We're sorry it had to come out this way, but it's better you don't seek Proctor out. His part in this is over."

I looked to Dorian, hoping he would say something to alleviate my doubts.

"I had to come here so you kids would know what was happening," Dorian said. "I'm going to that trial, and I'm going to make my case."

Ash nodded, and Banner began to lead Dorian out.

"I don't accept this," I resisted.

"We're doing this for your own safety," Ash insisted.

"I'll be fine," Dorian smiled.

It felt like a lie, and that only made my nerves worse.

Banner took Dorian by the arm and led him out of the room.

"You're safe now, Blackbriar," Ash assured.

He reached out for me, but I batted his hand away.

SLAP!

"Don't speak to us again," I hissed.

Ash looked at us with a brief flash of rage, but it soon returned to quiet acceptance. I rushed out into the cold winter air and watched Banner load Dorian into his own truck.

Dorian looked back at me, just like I did at the hospital. I heard Ali come up behind me. We both looked on with our Companions.

VA-ROOM!

Dorian's car turned over its engine. Dorian looked at us. His eyes were hard, but he looked at us with regret.

"I don't understand," I whispered. "I don't understand."

TWENTY SIX

DEDUCTION

"It was nice of the owner to give us free tea, huh?" Beatrice asked.

I looked up at her and saw she was wearing a white fur coat.

"Huh?" I asked.

"You're really out of it. We have free chai tea, my English project is on *The Count of Monte Cristo*, and the dance is coming up. I thought you'd be happy about at least two of those three things."

"It's been a rough couple of weeks," I admitted.

"Want to talk about it?" Beatrice asked.

"Not really," I insisted.

"I would say we could play the question game, but I'm just going to ask what's wrong."

"A friend of my family got in some trouble. And I couldn't do anything to help."

"I'm sorry," she offered. She let her eyelids flutter from me to the notes I brought along.

"I don't even know what happened. I just know he's in trouble. And now I don't know...."

"Whether you should trust him or not?" Beatrice asked.

I looked up, perplexed by her accuracy.

"Just like where I'm at in Monte Cristo. Edmond is wrongfully imprisoned, and no one believes he's innocent."

"So, you did read it?"

"Maybe," Beatrice said with a smile.

"Well, you don't need my help then. You clearly understand the story."

"I'm not big into this stuff like you are. And it's fun to watch you talk about what you're passionate about."

"Fine. I guess I see a lot of Edmond in my friend. He's done his best to look out for us, and the deck was stacked against him."

"Really?" Beatrice asked.

"One accusation tore him down. And I don't know how he'll ever recover," I continued.

"Just like Edmond. Will Edmond recover?" Beatrice asked.

"I don't want to spoil it for you," I insisted.

"I think you need to talk about something you love. Screw spoilers. Tell me what happens."

I smiled.

"Edmond spends years in prison and is eventually met by a Mad Priest. He educates him for a few years after and even discovers the truth behind why he is actually in prison."

"How does he do that?" Beatrice asked.

"They catch the inconsistencies in Edmond's story. It's not the story of someone who was a traitor. It's the story of a man who was set up."

"Ooooh. Tell me more."

"Edmond was betrayed by Caderousse, Fernand, Villefort, and Danglars. They all made Edmond the scapegoat so they'd be able to get what they wanted."

"And what happens to Edmond?"

"He escapes the Chateau, discovers a massive fortune, and uses it to track them all down, getting his revenge."

"Interesting. Edmond is someone I should get to know. But how did the priest discover the truth if he never even met these people who wronged Edmond?"

"It's the inconsistencies in the story Edmond tells," I repeated.

"But what were they?" Beatrice insisted.

"The letter Edmond was carrying should have been saved as evidence. But instead of preserving it, the magistrate Villefort burned it. From there, the conspiracy was perfect. All of them were set on ruining Edmond's life to enrich their own."

"That's awful," she whispered.

"It's worse than awful. It's terrifying to see how high people can go just by tearing one person down."

My mind flashed to Dorian.

"I know what you mean," Beatrice said.

"Do you?"

Beatrice seemed caught off guard for a moment.

"It makes sense. Jealousy. It can make people do terrible things," Beatrice recovered.

"You have no idea," I started. "Edmond gets blamed for it all, and no one would even—"

"Even what?" Beatrice asked.

"No one would look him in the eye. Beatrice, you're a genius!" I cheered.

I leaned forward.

KISS.

I left Belvedere in a hurry. There may have been hope for Dorian after all. I rushed out to home, but I saw Ali in the street in front of the tea shop. She was coming toward me.

"Martin? What the hell? I was just coming to find you."

I panted and put my hands on her shoulders.

"I think I have the answer, Ali," I began.

"What?" Ali asked.

"I think I know what happened with Dorian."

Silence.

"Martin, I know you want him to be cleared, but the more I think about it, the more it makes sense what Ash—"

"I know, but what if—"

"He taught us how to use magic, but you wound up getting hurt because of it."

"He was trying to help us learn magic *and* track down the Necronomicon."

"Or he was keeping us busy and slowing everything down. The minute he turned his back, you got hit by a goddamn truck."

"Because he had to stay hidden, and he was protecting our parents."

"Martin, all the signs point to Dorian. I've been trying to see another way around it, but nothing else makes sense. You're twisting everything to fit your theory that he's innocent. But we don't know that."

"Or that's exactly what they want."

"This isn't a conspiracy," Ali insisted.

"Just hear me out. Can you do that, at least?" I asked.

Silence.

"I'll always listen to you, Martin."

Ali stepped aside, and we started walking.

"Let's start from the beginning."

"Dorian picked us up and taught us how to use magic."

"Right," Ali allowed.

"And he chose to do that because he was capable of teaching us, and he had to keep a low profile. If the Watchmen made too big a presence for themselves, they would have been a giant target. Or the thief would have run away and started all over."

"Okay."

"And while we were under his care, a demon came to Woodrow Wilson, another at Belvedere Tea, more at Stryker, and we found the source in the tunnels."

"Martin, there was an entryway to the subway system right next to Silk Slipper. He had to know the truth," Ali pointed out.

"Dorian fought and wrangled demons. And he brought them to the Silk Slipper. But you saw how docile they were when we were inside. With Dorian there and fueling the ritual, we couldn't have been safer. But if Cole was in *league* with Dorian, then he could have lured the demons wherever they went. He could have taken the brunt of it with his own body or the Necronomicon. *That's* the contradiction," I pointed out.

"How is that a contradiction?" Ali demanded.

"If the Necronomicon protects you from the effects of lethal magic, but not demonic influence, they may be looking in the wrong place," I concluded.

Silence.

"Maybe he was already affected. We saw Ash take the Necronomicon up with our own eyes. Cole was dangerous and had been using demonic magic before he even came into contact with it."

"Did we?" I asked.

"We didn't get a chance to look at it fully, but yeah," Ali assured.

"Whoever has been killing with the Necronomicon, we won't see any changes in them," I said. "But suppose there's interaction with demonic magic. In that case, it leaves some kind of a trace that the Necronomicon can't protect against."

Silence.

"What kind of trace?" Ali asked.

"The one place nobody would think to look. On Ash."

Ali pondered it all.

"You don't mean..." she whispered.

"His eyes," I concluded.

"With Dorian out of the way, Ash would be in charge of finding a culprit, and he could let them get away. But he didn't," Ali whispered.

"Dorian was thinking like a Watchman. He was looking for demons and accident sites, not with the maps of the subway systems. At least, not the right way. And what if Ash has something else up his sleeve?"

"We can't be sure of any of this, Martin. It's all a theory. And a wild one at that. If we want Dorian to be freed, we need proof."

Ali paused for a second. She let out a sigh as if she were letting me down lightly.

"Martin, he was in charge of watching us, and he failed multiple times. I don't think the Order will let him go just because we ask. Maybe it's best if we just...."

"I'm not letting him die," I countered.

"We need more. How are we going to get them to see things our way?" Ali asked.

"If we can get the Order to test our theory, then maybe

they'll take Ash into custody. It's like Dorian said, there are probably multiple people working together to unlock the Necronomicon."

"And if this theory holds up, they probably don't even have the real one. It's too risky to hand it to the Order. They'd never get it back, no matter how clever they were."

"I don't know who has it. But getting Ash arrested is a start," I concluded.

"Let's assume Ash is behind all of this. Or that he plays a big role. How are we going to convince people to test our theory?"

"You're right," I pondered. "We'd have to get someone to agree to look into Ash's eyes. And even then, we don't know for certain if the influence would negate a Gorgon's eyes."

I looked at Alciel. He popped his head out of my backpack, right on cue.

"Alciel, can demonic mages hide their markings?" I asked.

"It's pretty common for people to try and hide them," Alciel said. "In the medieval period, people tended to wear hoods to hide their horns, or people pretended to be lepers so they wouldn't be able to see rotting flesh. And their eyes would turn some frenzied yellow or red, depending on how far gone they are."

"But they can't conceal the markings with magic?" Ali asked.

"It would only make the markings worse. Demonic magic is highly infectious to any manna it touches."

"Whoever has a marking will be hiding it in plain sight," Lyse chimed in as she rounded the corner and brushed Ali's leg with her side.

"Martin, if there was anything to see, the Watchmen would have found it," Ali said.

I let the cold air pierce my lungs. It all still felt wrong. There was something we overlooked. I just wanted to look Ash in the eye and get the truth. But I knew that was impossible.

I started running.

"We need to get to the Silk Slipper!" I burst.

"Why?!" Ali demanded.

"Because Ash is a liar! And we're going to catch him ourselves!"

REVEALED

I burst through the doors of the Silk Slipper. It was barely an hour from where we had come to our conclusion, but I had no other place to start.

"Blackbriar. It's good of you to actually show up this time," Ash greeted.

"When is the trial?" I demanded.

"It will take place at the Summit Gathering in a matter of hours."

"And the Order will be present?" I asked.

"Of course."

"We want to go with you."

Silence.

"You had a change of heart?" Ash asked.

Ali came through the doors just behind me.

"We just want to be there to see the truth for ourselves," Ali concluded.

“I would normally ask what has brought about such a change of heart, but it’s a welcome change,” Ash smiled.

“I didn’t say this would be a pleasant experience for any of us,” I said. “But we have to know the truth.”

“I understand,” Ash said. “You have been through quite the ordeal. You want to see it end before you can believe it.”

“But I’m sure it’ll end once it’s all out there in the open,” Alciel smiled.

Headlights began to cut through the windows, and we saw that a series of trucks had emerged. All with familiar drivers.

Some of them were quite human, others quite monstrous. But we knew they were all Watchmen. And they were headed to Dorian.

“It looks like you’ll be getting what you want,” Ash added. “They have come here to ensure everything runs smoothly.”

“Are they expecting Dorian to be a flight risk?” I asked.

“They’re expecting Proctor will fight back.”

“And if he does?” Lyse asked.

“It will result in the same punishment when he is found guilty. Death.”

I looked into Ash’s glasses, and an idea was forming in my mind.

“Where are we going?” Ali demanded.

“We’ll be heading to the Riverwalk,” Ash whispered. “Quite poetic, really.”

“The Riverwalk?” I asked.

“As appealing as an actual courthouse would be. We have to go somewhere more secluded. The Order has already decided on the Riverwalk as the location for the trial,” Ash expanded.

I couldn’t get Ash’s words out of my head.

"Poetic? What do you mean?" I asked.

"That's hardly relevant now. What are you hoping to accomplish, Blackbriar?"

"I wanted to speak on behalf of Dorian. He may be on trial, but he's done a great deal to keep us safe."

"Keep telling yourself that. If he were in charge of your protection any longer, he might have gotten you both killed."

Ash started walking out, and we came fast behind him.

"We want to make a statement. We can't just stand by and let this happen without saying a few words."

"You really don't know when to quit, do you?" Ash asked.

"If we were to quit now, we wouldn't be able to forgive ourselves," Ali added.

Ash opened his car door.

"Get in. The Order has a stiff penalty for being late, as well."

I got in the car, and Ali came in just behind me.

SLAM.

"Are you sure this is going to work?" Ali asked.

"It's the best chance we have at saving Dorian."

I looked out at the other Watchmen cars and realized there were only two of them. Something felt off about that.

"But you're wrong. There's no telling how that will backfire...."

SLAM.

Ash took his seat and looked back at us through the rearview mirror, through those same ebony glasses that I felt certain were hiding a secret. I stared into them, hoping my plan would work.

"I admire your determination. But I don't want to hear another word about this after Dorian's sentence is carried out," Ash warned.

"You won't," I promised.

VA-ROOM!

"You two seem determined. But every Watchman in the state is going to be there. It'll be a good chance to get to know them all," Ash offered.

"I'm sure," I relented.

"How do they feel about all this?" Ali challenged.

I felt a terrible presence come over us as we came closer to the Riverwalk. It was only two miles away now, but I looked in that direction, and I could feel something was there. Something powerful and dangerous. Every instinct I had told me to go another way, but the car was taking us toward it. And my teeth vibrated more intensely with every passing second we were drawing closer.

"It's a difficult time for everyone. The last time we came together was after the last Wizard died. It was a real shock to everyone. But now we have found the culprit behind it."

I felt my knuckles grip tightly.

"Dorian had nothing to do with that," I objected.

Click-click. Click-click.

I saw that Ash was turning left onto St. Aubin street.

"You're going the wrong way to the Riverwalk," Ali insisted.

"No, I'm not," Ash assured.

I could feel my heart pounding in my chest.

"Take us to the Riverwalk," I demanded.

I looked at Ali, and we both shared the same worried expression. We both knew you turned right on this street to get to the Riverwalk. Something was wrong.

"The further you are from Proctor, the better," Ash smiled.

I could feel my teeth cease their shivering. My clenched

fists grew tighter, and my heartbeat picked up even faster.

"We're seeing this through to the end!" Ali demanded. "Take us there!"

"No point," Ash started, "Dorian's probably already dea—"

I didn't even think about what I was doing. I felt my fist rush through the air and strike Ash.

SMACK!

Ash veered off the road.

VEEEEEEOOOOOM!

The sounds of rushing cars roared all around us. At first, they were violent and up-close. Then they were peaceful and distant.

"You fucking brat!" Ash shouted. "You almost killed us!"

Click-click.

Ali aimed a Walther PPK at Ash.

"Take us to the Riverwalk!" Ali demanded.

Ash looked up and saw that Ali wasn't kidding. One false move, and she would shoot him.

He turned back, and we were on the path to Dorian again. All the while, that terrible vibration of my teeth came back, as though all of them were warning us it was too dangerous.

TRIAL

"We're here," Ash growled.

Looking ahead, there was a cluster of shadows that made my stomach churn. The instant I saw them, my teeth stopped quaking. It was so instantaneous, I feared we would not make it out alive. As though no more warnings were going to save us.

"Out of the car, *snake*," Ali threatened.

Ash looked at her with disdain and started to speak.

"I'm sure the Watchmen are going to take it well when the Witch tries to shoot—"

BANG!

Ali shot through the windshield, shattering it.

In seconds, we were surrounded.

Ethereal forms appeared in the darkness and the snow, surrounding all of us. With their guns pointed at everyone in the car.

"Try to run away now," I retorted.

"What's going on here?!" Banner shouted.

"We got your real culprit," I announced.

"I thought you were desperate, but this won't go over well, Blackbriar," Banner retorted.

I kicked the car door open.

TUCK!

"How far are you into Dorian's trial?" Ali demanded.

"It's almost over," Banner insisted.

"Of course, it is," I exasperated.

We got out and saw there was an eclectic assortment of dark figures around us. All of them were armed and showed no amusement in their faces.

Among the assortment was a fanged woman, a walking scarecrow, and a lumbering man who was three times bigger than any man I'd ever seen. Beyond that, there were at least nine other figures. But they had us completely surrounded.

"The Order won't take kindly to their Watchmen being kidnapped," Ash continued.

"You kidnapped *us*!" Ali shouted.

She remembered she was holding a gun at Ash but seemed to shrug off the mild embarrassment.

"Enough!" Banner demanded. "Put your weapons down. And you will make your case before the Order."

Ali let the clip fall out of the gun, and she popped the bullet in the chamber. Banner approached her cautiously. Then she tossed the gun into the frozen Riverwalk with a satisfying toss.

Skit-skit. Goarf.

"Looks like those lessons on gun safety are finally paying off," I attempted.

"This couldn't be more dangerous if we tried, Martin."

"That was uncalled for," Banner complained.

"Take us to Dorian," I demanded.

We made our way across the Riverwalk.

"Nice toss," I praised.

"Even if we get killed, it was worth it," Ali smiled.

"You're really sticking your neck out to help me. And to help Dorian," I observed.

"I'll always help you. But just tell me you know what you're doing," Ali insisted.

"I know what I'm doing," I promised.

We passed the Cullen Family Carousel, and I felt a new sense of dread come over me as I looked at it. Those warm and friendly statues that would gleam with electrified life, when activated, now appeared cold and wary. They seemed to be guarding the procession with a newfound icy resolve.

We entered the bitter cold of the Detroit Riverwalk and followed Ash's footsteps to the Port. We saw a procession had been re-formed with fifteen figures. Three figures dressed in white and six imposing officers dressed in black on either side, boxing Dorian at the center for judgment.

At the center was our friend.

Ash and the rest of us formed a final end of the box, sealing him in. Every breath we took, there was a bitter cloud that marked our anticipation. A handful of Watchmen didn't seem to breathe, no matter how long I looked at them. I wondered if any of them were undead in some way.

I looked at the three figures at the front and knew they were the Order.

One of them was a figure with exquisite, elven features. His ears were slightly pointed, and he was wearing a long white robe. He had silver detailing along the fabric, bell sleeves, and a symbol on the center of his chest. It looked to be two olive branches and a chalice at the center. His hair was white, and his face was stern.

He was ice incarnate.

Just to the left was a tan woman who appeared to be from Arabia. She wore a white hijab that acted as an extension of the white robe she shared with the figure next to her. She gave us a smile with full lips. She was everything her counterpart was not.

She was warmth incarnate.

And finally, there was the figure to the far right, on the other side of the cold man. Of all three of them, this was the most peculiar. Rather than possessing the features of a human, this figure only had the general shape of humanity. A head, two arms, and presumably two legs under the robe.

Protruding from the bell sleeves was an emerald claw that was somewhere between a lizard and a velociraptor. His head was arched, with six points coming out to pull the canvas of its reptilian face. His eyes were yellow, and it was impossible to tell how he felt toward us.

"It's good to meet you at last and in... secure hands, Blackbriars," the reptilian man greeted.

"It's good to finally meet you," I welcomed.

"As you have no doubt deduced, we are the members of the Order. I am Sarcodis, and this is Erestor and Parvana."

The sharp-featured man spoke up.

"As much as we insisted on your presence here, we never thought you'd appear before us so... *brashly*. And I can speak with absolute certainty that there is nowhere on Earth that is safer for you now. You are in the presence of every Watchman in the state and the highest ranks of the Order."

"Unless there are any statements you would like to make now, we will conclude the trial," the woman insisted.

"We do have something to say," I answered.

The Watchmen looked to each other as though it was the first time this offer had ever been accepted.

"And that is?" Erestor responded.

"You have the wrong man," Ali protested.

I looked at my sister and saw that she smiled back at me. She really did have my back. The sharp-featured man smoothed his lips and quickly retreated to a condescending smile.

"You doubt us, Blackbriar?" he asked.

"I doubt this entire trial. And everyone here. Ash told us we'd be able to see the trial, but then he lied to us about when it was starting and drove us further away from it. The opposite direction, in fact."

Erestor turned to Ash.

"Is this true?" Erestor demanded.

"Yes," Ash conceded, "but this boy forgets where he stands."

"I know exactly where I stand," I resisted. "I'm here to defend Dorian."

"In that case, I'd like to hear what the Blackbriars have to say," Parvana said.

"Your evidence is wrong. And I can prove it," I added.

Silence.

Parvana turned to Erestor and nodded.

"Very well," Erestor allowed.

Erestor gave Ash a withering glare, then turned to me with a slight ease of his brow.

I stepped forward and looked up to Dorian.

“Dorian Proctor is innocent. All of the evidence you’ve gathered is being used to condemn him because it’s the *simple* solution. Not the right one.”

“Blackbriar....” Sarcodis hissed.

“Dorian gathered all of this evidence and taught us to protect ourselves,” I continued. I could feel my voice getting stronger. “And while it took time, that’s not proof that he was behind this or even involved. And if he’s really the one who’s behind this, or even an accomplice, he had to be under some form of demonic influence. There has to be a trace of it on him, or he simply cannot be the culprit.”

“Your defense is praiseworthy but obviously flawed,” Sarcodis said. “Dorian had neglected to find where the demons came from.”

“He was helping people who were affected by the damage they caused. And it was only because of *his* work that we were able to find out about the subway tunnels. He was looking at the case like a Watchman. Every step of the way. He saw the supernatural answer, not the whole picture. And that was the only reason for the delay. He wasn’t complicit.”

Silence.

“Impressive as that may be, we don’t have any proof that suggests Dorian wasn’t involved. Ash’s evidence proved that he had engaged in a dangerous ritual without giving you proper training,” Erestor pointed out.

“It was a risk we all agreed to, together,” Ali began, “and we were able to protect each other thanks to his training and his guidance. He might have taken a risk, but it brought us closer to finding the answer. In the end, we proved that whoever was behind this had a trace of demonic influence on them. They had to see through the eyes of a demon to launch the attack against us."

"There were no marks on Dorian's body. And demonic magic always leaves a trace. Always," Ali chimed in.

"Dorian was clearly looking the other way and chasing down demons while the Necronomicon was out of reach," Erestor said. "The moment Dorian was removed from the investigation, Ash assumed his responsibilities and found the Necronomicon with ease. It's because Dorian was operating under your nose. As an expert in demonic magic, he would have known how to instruct someone in this magic."

"But who was it?" I asked. "Dorian was tending to us first, and someone else was lying in wait. Someone was tampering with demonic magic to attack us. And if Dorian's theory holds up, then it was multiple people. But who would be the best person to swoop in and take Dorian's place when he was taken away from the case? Someone who was going to steal the glory."

Everyone held their breath, and the Watchmen began to dart their eyes to and fro, trying to eliminate suspects.

I raised my finger and pointed at the true culprit.

"Ash," I concluded.

There were murmurs among the crowd. It was the first time someone was trying to keep their voices down, and I didn't feel like a target.

"Even if that were true, the culprit was found with the Necronomicon, and Ash confiscated it," Erestor countered. "And there's no evidence Ash had even come into contact with demonic influence. If he was behind this, he'd never give up the real Necronomicon."

"Oh, but Ash does have those marks," I said. "You've just

been looking in the wrong place."

Erestor looked at us like he was going to burn us where we stood.

"That's a severe accusation. I hope you can back it up," Erestor threatened.

"Oh, I can," I accepted.

The Watchmen murmured among each other. But this stopped the moment Parvana raised her hand. It was like she had used a spell to silence them all.

"Blackbriar, I have tolerated your accusations for long enough," Parvana said. "The claims of two children who aren't even fully trained are not enough to condemn one of our High Watchmen. Even if they are the Witch and Wizard."

"And when did Ash become High Watchman?" I asked.

"When Dorian failed to protect you and your sister," Sarcodis explained. "We've clearly grown far too lenient since Adrian Hive was assassinated."

"Seems convenient, doesn't it?" I asked. "A man losing his position, only for Ash to take over. And then you find your culprit?"

"Get to the point, Blackbriar," Sarcodis demanded.

"Ash arranged for the Necronomicon to fall out of Hive's hands, and he's been lying to you ever since. He killed the Wizard, arranged for the Necronomicon to be locked away, and has been practicing demonic magic with it for over a decade. But you'd never be able to tell. Because he was clever enough to hide his markings in the one place you'd never dare to look."

"Prove it," Ash challenged.

"Ash's eyes. That's where the affliction from his demonic magic has been hidden."

Silence.

"What?" Sarcodis inquired.

Silence.

"This is outrageous!" Erestor shouted.

"Is it?" Parvana asked.

"I won't accept this!" Banner shouted. "Ash is a good man! He is a High Watchman, and I refuse to have his name slandered!"

"Then have Ash use his eyes to execute Dorian," I demanded.

"Blackbriar, there's no proof that the use of demonic magic will negate a Gorgon's Stare, even if there is demonic magic," Sarcodis warned.

"Because nobody has ever been willing to risk their life to check. That's why it's so perfect," I pointed out.

The Watchmen and the Justices all looked to one another and realized this was a first. And the more I explained it, the more I was sure I was right. And the more they doubted Ash's innocence.

"Demonic magic is infectious and takes away from whatever it touches. And someone has been using demonic magic to look into our base of operations. Dorian was sure of it," I concluded.

Erestor inhaled deeply through his nose and knew this argument had reached its peak.

"Ash. You will execute Dorian Proctor with your Gorgon's eye," he demanded.

"Lord Justice...." Ash began.

"Do it," Erestor finalized.

"It's no secret that Dorian has long been a thorn in your side," Sarcodis insisted. "It would be a fitting end to the story if you passed the death sentence."

Silence.

"As you wish," Ash hissed.

Ash stepped in front of Dorian.

"I ask you all to avert your eyes," Ash insisted.

I looked up and saw that while Erestor was just behind Ash, those who could even get close to eyeshot were trying to decide. Would they follow his order and look away? Or would they bear witness? In any case, it seemed that I wasn't entirely dismissed.

Ash removed his glasses and slowly unraveled the bandages that were around his eyes. In the end, every eye was looking at Dorian.

His petrification would mean his condemnation. His remaining alive would prove his innocence. I saw Ash's eyes were still closed and how smooth they were in contemplating opening them.

I turned my head away. Seconds passed. No emerald flash could be felt through closed eyes. There was no sound of Dorian calling out in pain.

There was nothing.

I worked up the courage to look again. I was careful to only look at Dorian. He was still producing white puffs with bated breath.

"You bastard," Dorian whispered.

We all turned our gaze toward Ash and saw his eyes were not just demonic yellow, more than that, they had turned into a sickly blood red. His eyes pulsed in his head, and he bared his teeth in fury. They were the eyes of a demonic madman with a wild, needle-sized pupil.

"No," Banner breathed.

"Face us, Ash," Erestor demanded.

Ash's breath went from a crystalline cold to a molten flare

with a series of furious breaths. His nostrils radiated flames as he turned around.

"I can't tell you how long I've wanted to do that," he hissed. "But now I can't."

"Have you anything to say in your defense?" Parvana asked.

"I was only doing what I could as High Watchman," Ash insisted.

"Those are the eyes of a man who has given himself to demonic magic thoroughly. You could only reach that shade of red if you were the one handling the demons in question."

Erestor looked at the Necronomicon.

"What would convince you of the book's authenticity?" Erestor asked.

"The Necronomicon is known to have all manner of safeguards around it," I returned.

"It's also been proven to kill. In a way that the Order has seen countless times," Erestor insisted.

"I'm here to prove that Dorian is innocent, not that the Necronomicon is authentic," I insisted. "We'll get to that later."

"If Ash has been handling the demons and wasn't affected by them, then it's possible the Necronomicon itself is not genuine, either," Dorian insisted. "There's another way to determine if it's genuine."

"And what's that?" Parvana asked.

"Hive warded that book to ensure that it cannot burn. Not even in the presence of Hellfire," Dorian offered.

Everyone looked to Ash.

"I refuse to cast," he answered.

"You don't have a choice in the matter," Erestor responded.

The sounds of guns cocking behind Ash made his eyes

close in defeat.

Click. Click. Glock.

Finally, Ash submitted.

Wharf.

Ash held his hands forward, and an emerald flame with a dark center emerged. Erestor placed the book just into the edge of the flame, and the book burned before it had touched the edges.

Erestor raised his hands and held Ash in a binding just above the ground. He appeared to be paralyzed and on fire.

"Why did you kill all those people?" Dorian demanded.

"You still don't get it," Ash growled.

Ash turned to the Order.

"You have lied before this council, framed a fellow Watchman, and attempted to corrupt the very Order that is sworn to protect our world," Sarcodis announced to the entire gathering. "You will be held in Wayne County Jail by Guardians until you are called to trial. One that is more suitable than the one you attempted to corrupt."

Ali grabbed me and pulled me back.

"And Dorian?" I asked.

"Proctor is cleared of all charges," Parvana insisted.

She snapped her fingers, and Dorian's cuffs came undone.

"As the law states, you may request the counsel of a Ravenshade. Or you may bequeath your possessions," Sarcodis hissed.

Dorian ran over to us and embraced us both. We weren't sure if he was grateful for us saving him or just glad to be at our side again.

"*Mitte maga missilem!*"

The air around Ash soon turned violent and *bubbled* with fury. The grasping force that Erestor had conjured was quickly losing its grip, and every Watchman was prepared to launch spells. They didn't even say what spells were being launched. A swarm of jet black reached forward and was aimed directly at Ash's body.

Thrash!

Everything was white for a split second, and then everything was black. I tried to open my eyes and saw each Watchman searching with a massive flurry of *amplifications*. But if Ash was good at anything, it was hiding in plain sight.

I blinked three times. Once to bring the world into light. Once to make the haze go away. And a third time to see clearly. Ash was right in front of me. He raised his hand, and an emerald flame appeared. I could feel the fear turning my blood into acid.

"*Perd—*" Ash hissed.

Qwelp!

Dorian came from behind Ash and held a silver blade to the demonic Gorgon's throat.

Everyone let out a cry and rushed over to us. They all had their guns pointed at Ash's head.

"If you had any more accomplices, now is the time to confess."

"Nobody else," Ash rejected.

"Last chance," Dorian threatened.

Ash closed his horrible eyes. They were glowing bright red under his eyelids. He disappeared for a split second.

Dorian's blade was pulled back violently and deeply.

A squirt of yellow came out of Ash's throat, and it sprayed in every direction. Ali and I jumped back to avoid the worst of it, and it *hissed* into everything it touched. Ash stumbled to the river, and lost his strength as he did so. He settled on the edge, facing everyone.

The Watchmen all fanned out from circle formation to a wedge facing their culprit. They raised their guns and didn't wait for any commands. They let loose with every shot they had.

A storm of gunshots rang off. A cloud of gunpowder and a hail of bullets. And all of them hit home.

The burst of yellow came from Ash with every shot. He lingered on the railing outside of the Detroit River and a pool of blood collected at his feet. The blood began to burn with an unearthly *hiss*. I wasn't sure what did more damage. The acid burns, or the bullets.

Finally, he looked up at us in pure agony and his failed attempt at Selective Presence was over. There was hardly anything left to hide anyway.

He turned to us, spasmed violently, and fell back into the river behind him.

FELCH!

It was the sound of ice breaking. I ran toward the frozen Riverwalk.

"Martin, what are you doing?" Dorian demanded.

"They're looking for the wrong thing. Again," I pointed out.

I looked around at the snow that coated the Riverwalk. There was a series of long drags spanning the dock, leading to the river, among the violent streaks of the last spell performed by the Watchmen.

I saw a hole in the ice. The hot scent of sulfur came up from the water.

"He got away," I breathed.

"Martin, no one else could have unmasked him," Dorian said. "Let the Watchmen take care of it from here. You found out who was behind it all. Let them do their job."

"Like they're going to do anything right," I growled.

I turned my back to the river and saw the Watchmen huddled around Dorian. The Order kept its eyes intently on us.

Dorian's skin was *hissing*. Ali got close to him and saw the spots on his arm were severe. He had a few drops form along his arm, and all of them had burned clean through. Thankfully, there was no bleeding.

"You okay?" Dorian asked.

"We're fine," I assured.

"Are you?" Ali asked.

Dorian looked relieved.

"I am now that you're both all right," Dorian smiled.

Ali dove into Dorian's good arm and embraced him. I couldn't help myself from doing the same. It must have hurt like hell, but he grasped us both with whatever strength he had left. I could hear him weeping. And I could feel the tears forming in my eyes.

We made it.

We might have saved each other from Ash, but we had all taken a hit from the damage he had wrought. And a terrible churning in my stomach confirmed my suspicions.

This wasn't over.

TWENTY NINE

DANCE

"Martin!" Ali shouted.

"What?" I asked.

"Don't tell me you've been reading all night."

"Maybe I was."

My head was still on my desk, and there were books sprawled all across the floor.

"You're hopeless."

"Thanks."

"You better come back from that dance exhausted and hungover."

"Can you just let me sleep?"

"That's what happens when you don't sleep for 24 hours. Throw this on."

Ali tossed a black bag on the bed.

"What's this?" I asked.

"A little something I got for you at the last minute."

I noticed a hanger at the top.

"Something for the dance?"

"Just put it on."

Ali left the room.

SLAM.

I unzipped the bag and found a black suit with white pinstripes.

"Let's take a look," I smiled.

It was an auspicious moment, coming through so much and finally being able to look forward to something. With Dorian saved and working with us again, no sign of Ash, and the dance just around the corner, everything was finally turning around. But I still felt my stomach twisting into knots, as though something was wrong.

ZIP.

I threw the suit on and checked the mirror. I could hear Ali tapping her foot on the other side of the door.

"Let's see it!" Ali shouted.

"I'm coming!" I assured her.

My mom and sister were waiting as I turned the corner. And they covered their mouths when they saw me.

"That suit looks...." Mom began.

"Good?" I hoped.

"Amazing," Ali concluded.

I remembered how I looked in the mirror, and I supposed they were right.

"Just have a good time, Martin," Ali insisted.

I felt the warm fur of Lyse crossing my leg.

"You deserve it," she agreed.

"Just don't leave any purple fur on me. That'll only raise

questions."

"Fine," Lyse promised, "I'll keep the cuddles to a minimum."

HONK!

I crossed to the window and saw a limo outside.

"I literally just got up. I'm never...."

Ali held out her hand and red electricity shot through my hair. It felt like my hair was being pulled into a side part.

"That's better," Ali concluded.

It felt like I had snakes made of electricity coursing through my scalp. I turned to the nearby window. My hair was perfect.

"I look like Sean Connery," I chuckled.

"Don't forget this," Ali reminded.

Ali produced a flower. A red one.

"From downstairs?"

"Better than a flower shop in the dead of winter."

"Ali, how did you buy this suit?"

"Who said I bought it?"

I rolled my eyes and suddenly felt guilty. But when she put the flower in the suit, everything felt better.

"I went through a lot to get this flower grown and that suit stolen. Have some fun for my sake," Ali demanded.

"I'm condoning your life of crime if nothing else."

KNOCK-KNOCK!

"That must be Beatrice," Mom smiled.

Everyone rushed to the door. I felt my heart start to pound.

"I don't know what to do," I admitted.

"Just look her in the eye, say she looks beautiful, and show her a good time," Ali said. She started to smirk. "Just not *too* good."

"How's that working for you? Being imaginative?"

"It passes the time."

Alciel winked at us both before vanishing into the basement with Lyse.

SLAM.

When the basement door shut, the front door opened.

CREAK.

I turned around and saw a gothic angel. She was dressed in a red Victorian-style dress. One that reminded me of Lydia's dress from *Beetlejuice*. She also wore a black corset to go with it. She was wearing makeup befitting Halloween, but I didn't object to it.

"You look amazing," we said in unison.

Beatrice had a blush form across her nose.

I felt my ears go hot in response to her compliment.

"I take it your mom wants to take a picture?" Beatrice asked.

"Absolutely!" Mom insisted.

She prepared her camera and took a few pictures.

Snap. Snap. Snap.

"You know, to prove that this night actually happened," Ali chuckled.

"Ali," I laughed.

"Or in case you go missing...."

"It's just a dance, Ali."

"Your sister is a real comedian," Beatrice giggled.

"She gets it from my dad."

"And you get your charm from both sides," Beatrice smiled.

Both of my parents gave a warm smile.

"We better get going," I insisted.

I walked Beatrice out into the cold Detroit air. I saw the limo waiting for us in the street.

"Martin Blackbriar and the big scary dance," Beatrice said.

"It's going to be fine. I'm here."

I opened the limo door for her. My family watched from the window, and they all waved to me. If Alciel and Lyse could have been there, I'm sure they would be. And, most of all, Dorian. But since he was given his position of High Watchman back, I doubt I'd see him for some time yet. The search for the real Necronomicon was still a top priority.

I waved and felt the warm air of the limo calling to me. I got in and closed the door behind me.

"Drive on," Beatrice ordered.

VROOM.

"I'm loving the suit," Beatrice smiled.

"My sister got it."

"I'm glad. Maybe she and I can go shopping sometime."

She looked ahead nervously.

"Did everything work out with your friend?" Beatrice asked.

"My friend? Oh. Yeah. He's better now."

"You seem a lot happier than you usually do."

Beatrice looked ahead toward the driver.

"You don't seem as *jubilant* as you usually do," I replied.

Beatrice smiled at my choice of adjective.

"You always know how to make me feel better."

"And you do the same for me," I said. "But what's on your mind?"

"It's nothing," she insisted.

"We both know that's not true."

"Fine. Is it true what they're saying? About you not having to tutor me anymore?"

"I didn't know anything about that."

"Yeah. Apparently, I'm doing good enough on my own."

I smiled at how far she'd come.

"I'm proud of you."

"But I don't want to succeed. Not if it means less time with you."

"I'll make time to be with you. Whether you're succeeding or failing," I promised.

"What do you mean?"

She looked into my eyes, almost scared.

"If you want time with me, just say so."

"Okay," Beatrice smiled.

She looked down at her Jack Skellington bag.

"That wasn't so hard, was it?"

"I didn't know what you'd say," Beatrice smiled.

"You just want me to stick around."

"Yeah," Beatrice confirmed. Her eyes were glossy with tears. She was careful not to let any fall.

"Then I will."

"Promise?"

"Promise."

Beatrice leaped forward and hugged me.

I returned the embrace and felt safe. Beatrice held me even tighter. It was the safest I'd felt in a long time.

"You can let go now," I whispered.

"Maybe I don't want to," Beatrice insisted.

She trembled in my arms. Something didn't feel quite right, but I didn't dare raise the issue. Something told me this was something Beatrice needed to do.

"Why do you always carry that bag around?" I asked.

"It was my grandfather's," Beatrice answered gravely.

"What was he like?" I asked.

"I don't remember him. But my family friends tell me about him. What they knew, anyway. He was really secretive, actually. Nobody knew much about him to tell me. He was just... my grandpa."

"Maybe he had everything he needed. Didn't want to dwell on the past," I smiled.

"At least you have a family. You don't know how lucky you are to have Ali and your parents. I'd kill to have, eh, now I'm just rambling. What happens with your friend now?"

"Oh, um, he got a job, and he's making the most of it. He was thrilled to see Ali and me there to support him."

"I'm glad. I had a feeling that's what happened. You only seem to be as happy as your saddest friend."

"Yeah?"

"And, by the way, I finished *The Count of Monte Cristo*."

"Yeah!? What did you think?"

"I thought it was fitting. How Edmond finally got justice."

"It was."

"Do you think that it had to be Edmond? Or do you think that his enemies would have naturally met justice?"

"That's an unusual question."

"I thought you liked our question game."

"I do."

"Well, what do you think?"

"I think Edmond had the right people enter his life. That was a miracle. And all of the right opportunities came to him, and he took them."

"And that gave him the chance to fight back."

"Where is this coming from?" I asked.

The limo stopped moving.

I looked up and saw we had arrived at Woodrow Wilson. There was a barrage of camera phones around the limos. Almost looked like a Hollywood red carpet premiere.

"Let's just have fun, all right?" Beatrice asked.

"Sure," I smiled.

I wanted to leave all my anxiety of the last few months in this limo. But a terrible feeling came over me like a cloud. An unexpected chill came over me, and I couldn't shake the feeling that something was terribly wrong.

THIRTY

BETRAYAL

"Can you believe the turnout?" Beatrice asked.

"I'm still getting over it myself," I said. "That we're together. That I'm going to a dance. That I'm wearing a pinstripe suit in freezing temperatures. It's a lot to take in."

Beatrice laughed.

"They put a lot of effort into decorations," Beatrice observed.

She looked up at the meticulously crafted paper snowflakes, the plastic Christmas trees, and how it was all offset by the gentle snowfall and the colorful Christmas lights.

"But not enough?" I asked.

"Don't get me wrong," Beatrice began. "It is beautiful. We'll just have to call Henry Selick and put him in charge next year. Give this place a real *Nightmare Before Christmas* design."

"You and that movie," I said. I looked out at the people around us. "Everyone's staring."

"Don't worry about them. This is just about you and me."

She picked up the pace until we got to the dance floor. All the while, students were parting as though Beatrice was Moses crossing the Red Sea.

Then she stopped.

Silence.

A familiar set of piano notes played, and there was that famous Michigan voice. Bob Seger. *Old Time Rock n' Roll*.

I turned around and saw Beatrice in her daring *Beetlejuice* dress. She smiled with all the elegance of an angel. A Tim Burton angel. She began to stride toward me.

She stopped only one foot away and began to dance. The entire school was united in celebration along with us. It had been a favorite song of this school since its release back in 1978.

"Having fun yet?" Beatrice called. She danced expertly in her stiletto heels. I could feel the warmth reach my face before my smile did.

"Yeah! More than I've had in a long time!"

Beatrice giggled, a slight blush forming across her nose.

"Me too!"

Many songs played, but they faded into the background as I moved my feet. Beatrice was right. This was just about the two of us. No one else.

Finally, after so many fast songs, I heard the music change to something much slower.

I Wanna Know What Love is. Foreigner. 1984.

Beatrice drew herself close to me, and we looked into each other's eyes.

"I never want this moment to stop," Beatrice whispered.

"I don't either," I returned.

"Martin, what if we just ran away?"

"From what?" I asked.

"All of it."

"I thought you wanted me to stick around?"

"I do. But if we stay here, we're just going to drift apart."

"I'm not going anywhere," I promised.

"But what if there was something out there that made that choice for us?"

"I promise you, that's not going to happen. I'm tougher than you think," I answered.

"Martin. My life is really complicated, and I don't want you to get caught up in it."

"My life is complicated, too. But you stuck around when things were hard. Now I want to do the same thing for you."

Beatrice's eyes began to form tears.

"Beatrice, what's wrong?" I asked.

"There's so much I want to tell you. But I can't."

"*This is Halloween,*" her phone sang.

Beatrice let a tear fall from her eye, and she looked up at me.

"We need to get out of here," she whispered.

"Beatrice, what's going on?"

"I can't. There's just so much I have to explain."

"Then let's start. It's going to be all right. Who's calling you?"

"A friend," she attempted.

"People don't cry when their friends call them."

"Martin, please."

"Who is this friend?"

"I can't tell you his name."

"Ok. What can you tell me?"

"That I'm in trouble."

I pulled Beatrice to the side of the hall and held her still.

"I can't help you if you don't talk to me."

"Martin, if I tried to explain everything to you right now, you'd think I was crazy. I just need you to trust me for a few more minutes."

"Fine," I allowed.

Beatrice hiked up her dress and started running as fast as she could down the hall. I ran with her. The music refused to stop playing, no matter how far we ran. Finally, we stopped at our lockers.

She stopped and turned around to look at me. Her eyes were smeared with mascara, and she gripped her Jack Skellington bag like a child with a teddy bear. She refused to look me directly in the eye. She started to shiver.

"Tell me what's wrong," I insisted.

I walked toward Beatrice, my heart pounding louder the closer I got.

"If I tried to explain what was wrong, you just wouldn't believe me. In fact, you would probably hate—"

"What?" I asked.

I got closer.

"I could never hate you," I assured.

"Then could we just take this chance? We have to get out of here, Martin."

"Where would we go?" I asked.

"I don't know. Out of state. Out of the country. Away from here."

"Beatrice."

"I need to tell you something. But I can't," Beatrice wept.

Silence.

"What is it?" I pleaded.

"I've been lying to you since we met," She confessed.

I hesitated.

"Beatrice. You're scaring me."

"My name isn't Beatrice Hawkins. It's Beatrice Hive."

I looked into Beatrice's eyes.

She wasn't lying.

"What?"

THWACK!

I felt something heavy strike my head. My vision became blurry, and I fell to my knees. I felt lighter, and my vision was going away.

I turned around and let my head fall to the ground. But I tried to keep my eyes focused. I could only see a man in black. One with deep crimson eyes and a hateful growl.

"Ash," I whispered.

I saw a black shape rise up from the ground. I saw the bottom of a boot before...

SMACK.

THIRTY ONE

KIDNAPPED

"You're awake," Ash growled.

"Where are you?" I asked.

My vision came back slowly. I felt that we were moving quickly in the limo, but Beatrice wasn't here with me.

Instead, I looked out and saw Ash. His eyes were glowing as we came to the darkness of an overpass, out of the warm glow of a streetlight.

His collar was open. The cut that Dorian gave him formed a grin as devious as the one he was wearing on his face. There was hardly anything left of him in the tuxedo he was wearing. The state of his hands told me the rest. He was missing two fingers on one hand and one on the right. The rest of him likely had pieces missing.

"What do you want?" I demanded.

"It took some time, but I managed to evade the Watchmen. All to get to you."

"How could you possibly escape?" I asked.

"I've worked alongside those fools since I was a child. Of course, I knew how to get away."

"Where's Beatrice?!" I demanded.

"Oh, she's perfectly safe," he assured me.

"Your word means nothing," I answered.

"Maybe. But before long, we'll get exactly what we want."

I tried to get up, but my hands had been cuffed.

Rattle. Rattle.

"Spell Locked? What could you possibly get out of all this?" I asked.

"This isn't one of your books, kid. People don't tell you their plans in the real world if you keep them talking. You can't talk your way out of this."

"Oh yeah? My talking was enough to expose you to the Order and the other Watchmen."

Ash reared back and struck me.

SMACK!

I could feel the burn from his charred, claw hand long after the strike.

Ash bared his teeth.

HISSSSSSSSSS.

"You're a little worse for wear, aren't you?" I said in a mocking tone. "I'll bet you really want to kill me right now."

"You have no idea," Ash growled.

"But how long do you think you can run from the Order? From Dorian and the other Watchmen?"

"Long enough to finish what I set out to do. And then, when that's over, nothing will stand in our way."

"*Our* way?" I asked. "You mean you and Beatrice?"

"That stupid kid does whatever I tell her to do."

I felt my stomach turn as he insulted her.

"What have you done to her? How much does she know about me?"

"Only what she needs to know. Told her you were a punk and the world wouldn't miss you. She has no idea you and her grandfather are connected."

"She should hear the truth," I insisted.

"I told her what she needed to know. She had to choose between her loving grandfather and some punk she started dating a few months ago. It wasn't hard."

"How could you do this to her?"

"I've been looking after her since she was little. I taught her everything she knows about magic."

"But why go to these lengths? What do you want?"

"You tell me," Ash challenged.

"You're having her kill for you, but she'll get caught one day. One day soon, if you kill me."

Ash's eyebrows raised.

"And when she was caught, you were going to claim that you were the first on the scene," I said. "A lot of good that'll do now."

"There was no way I could have lost," Ash replied.

"Clearly, you were wrong."

"But I've recently had renewed hope for that plan. The last page of the book will work in my favor."

"Why's that?"

"You'll see," Ash promised.

I looked at the floor of the limo. I had no idea how to get out of this.

SHRUSH!

The car was parked. Someone got out of the driver's seat.

SLAM!

"You know, one thing I never understood?" Ash started. "Why did the Spectrum choose a kid as pathetic as you to be the next Wizard? It's not going to ma—"

Ash's eyes went from their bloody red to demonic yellow. They flashed a form of bright green and then turned milky. He took a moment to gasp at the loss of eyesight.

Then his entire suit was stained dark red. His body got thinner, and his suit got heavier. Soaked with blood. Human blood.

The door opened beside Ash. The cold was enough to make us both shiver.

BANG!

A lightning flash from a gun rang out, and a storm of blood splattered the inside of the limo.

"FUCK!" I shouted.

"Finally," Beatrice shuddered.

She opened the door, and Ash fell into the snow.

Sharf.

"Beatrice! Thank God, you're all right."

I trailed off when I looked into Beatrice's eyes. They were the deep crimson of a demonic Sorcerer's eyes.

"No, no, no," I whispered.

"I was hoping you'd be asleep for this," Beatrice said, "but he's insisting you be awake for the ritual."

I tried to keep myself awake, but I could feel myself falling into shock.

The back of my head was throbbing from being struck at the dance. With every passing beat, I could feel splinters of anguish spreading to the rest of my skull. My mind was racing toward darkness as I tried to think my way out of this.

But the faster I thought, the more everything faded away.

THIRTY TWO

RITUAL

"You don't have to do this," I whispered.

Beatrice's hand stopped over the Necronomicon, and she closed it. The magic lingered in the room, but it stopped advancing to the various runes scrawled on the ground.

"I wish I didn't have to," Beatrice whispered, "but I'm the only one who can."

"Ash never told you the truth of who I am. Not the whole truth, anyway," I pleaded.

"He told me what I needed to know," she insisted. "A Wizard's essence was the final thing we needed to bring someone as powerful as my grandfather back. Ash would make sure I had everything else I wanted."

"Did you ever consider why you needed the Wizard's essence?" I whispered.

I struggled in my constraints.

"Don't even try. You're just starting out with magic. There's no way you can cast a spell without free use of your limbs or an artifact by your side."

Beatrice clutched the rose my sister had given me.

"How much do you know about the Wizard?" I asked.

"I know the Wizard is who the Order calls in when you try to use the Necronomicon. Why else do you think I've been using it?"

"Is killing me really going to make your pain go away?"

"You don't know what it's like to lose someone. I'd do anything to get my family back. To have my family still alive like you do. That's why I've done everything I have. That's why I've been hiding here."

I looked around, still unsure of where we were.

"You still don't know? I thought you'd figure it out by now. We're in the Packard Automotive Plant. It's where I found all the Addiction Demons."

"Why here?"

"This place is a husk of what it used to be. Home to any rave party or wandering junkie that wanted to hide. And all that addiction led the demons here."

"What were you thinking? There must have been a whole pack of them waiting here."

Beatrice gripped the Necronomicon.

"There were. They almost killed me, too. What did I know? I just wanted my family back, and I needed a place to do it."

"How did you get out alive?"

"Ash saved me. I thought he cared when he did that. But I guess he just wanted something from me. He wasn't my friend. He didn't care in the end."

"Ash said he could give you your grandpa back," I said,

trying to show Beatrice my sympathy. "But have you ever done it before? Brought someone back?"

"If it's possible, it has to be done with you. And with this book."

Beatrice held the book, and it was shaking in her hands. The tightened hold on the binding made her injured finger bleed more intensely. The ruby drops trickled down her finger and became absorbed by the book's binding.

Beatrice stopped and looked at me.

"It's tearing me apart, Martin. The thought of doing this. But I have to."

"It's not worth it."

"My whole life has been about bringing him back, Martin. Since the moment I lost him. All I knew was that my family was gone, and I had a way to get them back. I was just a baby. It has consumed my every thought. And now I'm going to use this Necronomicon to do it."

"And how are you going to do all this? Addiction Demons and Binding Circles?"

"My grandfather made sure his heir would be able to read this book. I just didn't know how to do it on my own."

"So you got Ash's help? After what he did to you? He was just using you."

"I know that. He was going to betray me the minute this was over. I could feel it."

Beatrice's eyes flashed a deeper shade of crimson.

"If you really were afflicted, how could you keep your eyes hidden?" I asked.

"I could barely keep it hidden with contact lenses," Beatrice explained, "but Ash agreed to help with that as well. But once I wrangled my first couple of demons, I didn't have to worry about that anymore. I have the book to thank for that."

"Why did you let Ash help you at all?"

"He offered to give them back. Ash barely let me enroll in Woodrow Wilson. Like I was some horrible secret he didn't want getting out. And I knew that once my usefulness ended, then I would be done for."

"You can make your own choices now. There has to be something else you want. Why keep doing this? Why not start over?"

"Because I want to know what it's like. To have a family like you do," Beatrice admitted. "And not be treated like something to be hidden away and ashamed of."

"Adrian kept that secret to protect you," I attempted.

"And a lot of good that did to protect our family."

"There's someone else who can help you."

"I'm going to kill Dorian Proctor, too."

Silence.

"The hell you will," I threatened.

"He was supposed to protect my grandpa! He's just as responsible for my family getting killed as whoever pulled the trigger. All he does is tear families apart. That's why I had to put Ash in his place!"

"Dorian saves lives!"

"He let my grandpa die!"

"He loved your grandfather."

"No, he didn't! Not as much as I did! Not as much as I do! And I would never trust him to use *this*!"

She held up the book menacingly.

Silence.

"Now, all that's left is to cut out everything. All the lies and all of the loose ends," Beatrice said.

"How do you plan on doing that? Your Addiction Demons are gone. And the rest of the book is under a Spell Lock."

"After this, I won't need to. There's one spell left. One that is going to give me everything I need."

"What is it?" I asked.

"It's a ritual. A complicated one that allows me to take someone's essence out. The book showed me how to draw it. It's an artifact unto itself. Just as complex as the book I took it from."

"How do you know it won't kill you, too?" I asked.

"Ash might have been a real bastard, but he also taught me everything I know about magic."

I took a deep breath and realized I had one last card to play. One that Ash never planned on using.

"You know why I need to be at the center of this ritual?" I asked. "Why you need my essence? Because your grandfather was the Wizard before me. And because he's still a part of me."

Beatrice stopped.

"The reason Ash let you live was because you could cast this spell. And he would kill you for it. And the Necronomicon would be his."

I didn't even realize it was Ash's plan at first. I was thinking on my feet. Trying to buy time. But I let that revelation play through my head, and I realized it was the truth.

"Bullshit," Beatrice whispered.

Her eyes flashed red and grew deeper in color as she started to absorb what I told her.

"Think about what you're doing. If you kill me, there is no way you'll ever be let go. Ash isn't around to cover your tracks anymore."

"I don't want to kill you, but I *have* to. I need your essence to do this."

"Well, let me warn you. I won't go down without a fight."

"Sure, you will."

Silence.

"Put the book down, and we can talk this over. I can help you get what you want."

"You're lying," Beatrice whispered.

"I would never lie to you."

Beatrice let more tears fall.

"All you've done since the beginning. All you ever do is lie."

"I lied to keep you safe. Clearly, I was wrong."

"Stop pretending like your lies protect me! You don't save someone's life by feeding them lies. Well, that's just what you did to me. In *two* lifetimes! You just kept lying about everything!"

Beatrice's outrage revealed her true feelings. She didn't want to admit Adrian and I might have been the same person. But her outrage was too genuine to ignore.

Silence.

"And you're so much better?!" I challenged her. "You couldn't even tell me your real name!"

"I wasn't going to let you get involved in this! But then I had to."

"I was the person you were hunting!"

"I didn't know that. But now you have to be!"

Silence.

"Martin. I love you. But there's too much at stake for me to turn back now. With the power that you have, I can really get my family back. How many people lose their families the way I did? What if it was your family? Wouldn't you do anything to help get them back?"

I looked at Beatrice. Her eyes were glowing red from the demonic influence. And redder still from tears of heartbreak.

"I know you would," Beatrice sighed, "even if you don't want to admit it now. Because that's what I'm going to do. I'm going to save my family. Once I have your essence, I'll take down the Order, and then I'll carry you with me forever."

"Don't do this," I demanded.

"I'll always love you, Martin," she wept.

"Beatrice!" I started.

"I'm sorry."

"Beatrice!" I yelled.

Beatrice waved her hand over the last page of the book, and the wax markings on the ground began to light up with an otherworldly black light.

The materials Beatrice had gathered were consumed, and I heard snarls sounding all around me. Plumes of sulfur, strange fungi and glowing stones all burst into black flame. It was as though hellhounds were being called from the bowels of Gehenna, and I was their main course.

I felt a terrible, icy shadow begin to crawl up the table and all around my body. I let out a gasp of pain, but then my body was helpless.

The terrible prickling and prodding swam up to my limbs like snakes slithering through my veins. I felt my resistance leave my body piece by piece. My blue aura was suddenly protruding from my chest.

The shadows began to darken around my skin, and I felt an indescribable pain radiate from deep within the center of my heart.

It was not a searing pain. This was far worse. I felt myself leaving my body and entering the outside world. I saw a miraculous beauty escape the confines of my rib cage and begin to float, filling the room with heavenly azure light.

It reminded me of Mom's Saving Grace. I stared at it with what energy I had left, and I became mesmerized by its light.

Beatrice had tears streaming down her face.

"It's so... beautiful," Beatrice cried.

She rose up and reached for it.

No...

For a moment, there was nothing but pure terror. Then I heard the sound.

Krun.

I looked behind Beatrice, and red manna had encased the lock. The door was thrown open violently.

SLAM!

I looked up from beyond my essence and saw Dorian and Ali.

"Step away from my brother, bitch!" Ali shouted.

Ali's wild tufts of hair streamed down her face. She was breathing heavily.

"NO! NO! NO!" Beatrice screamed.

Beatrice clutched my essence.

Bursts of energy shot in every direction, like comets. I could barely feel anything, and my vision became darker. Whenever I honed my vision before, it was like putting on sunglasses. Now I was in pure darkness. The only thing that existed was everyone's essence.

Alciel and Lyse appeared near my feet. They crawled up to the back of the table and began *ripping* the restraints that held me in place. In moments, my arms were free again. Looking down at them, my hands were lifeless shapes that were barely distinguishable from the darkness. Just faint blue *crackles* where circuits used to be.

I had to get my essence back.

It took everything I had, but I reached up and grabbed my essence with both hands. My body illuminated and activated the circuitry I previously could not see. Bolts flew off of every shade of blue I had ever seen, bursting and destroying everything they touched. I could hear the faint cries of everyone around me. Dorian and Ali were struggling against Beatrice.

Ali tried to summon a shield to defend herself, but she was thrown back into the wall, forming a massive dent in the concrete. A faint spot of grey formed at the impact site before it vanished into crushing darkness again.

CRUNNNNN!

Alciel jumped to my side, and his horns began to radiate gold. As his horns were set ablaze, my essence began to take on a darker, golden shade.

I felt my fingers tighten fiercely, and my essence began to pull itself back to me. No command was needed. It was a part of me, and it wanted to come back. I heard Beatrice's fingers *pop* out of their sockets as the essence was returning to me.

"NO!" Beatrice screamed.

Ali raised her bat.

"*Institue potestem,*" she whispered. Then she struck with all the force she could, "*PERCUTIO!*"

CRACK!

Beatrice's head shot down into a cloud of crimson manna, and at the center was the blue and gold essence. I saw a faint silhouette over her lying on the ground, barely able to move. All her strength was trying to hold onto the essence. It was the one thing she'd been hunting for all these months, perhaps years. But in a few short moments, she stopped struggling and released the essence. It shot back into my hands, like a bullet.

WHARF!

My essence retreated into my body slowly, and engulfed me in sapphire and gold flames. I felt like I held the whole world in my hand. Life, magic, power, memories. All of them flooded into me, and I saw another life play out. I saw Adrian's life laid out in front of me.

THIRTY THREE

REMEMBRANCE

"Adrian. You have to put your hands on the goblet," a pale woman demanded.

I could feel myself trembling. I was no longer in the Packard Automotive Plant. And I was no longer in my own body. I wasn't even sure it was the same year. I was plucked from that horrible ritual and dropped into a memory of a day from long ago. A memory that felt more like a nightmare with every passing second.

"I don't want to. Where are my parents?" I asked.

It was a voice that didn't belong to me. But it came from my new mouth. I could feel myself living out a moment that felt so familiar.

Yet, I didn't recognize the home. It was filthy, below street level, and in the throes of some awful winter.

"Just do it, stupid," another boy insisted.

I looked to my side, and a thin, more muscular boy was

sitting next to me. He had black hair and was staring at me with malice.

"Your brother already did it," the pale woman insisted, "and we know he's not the Wizard."

"That doesn't make sense," I said. "Walden's cup had three rings of smoke come up. Doesn't that mean he's the Wizard? He's already so good at magic."

"And you've never had it. Which means you may be the one we're looking for."

"I want to see my parents."

TROAAAAAAAM.

A terrible, metallic drone came over my ears and made me feel like my skull was going to shatter. I tried to cover my ears, but they felt hot and slick.

"NO!" my new voice shouted.

I heard that terrible sound again, but my hands were moving over the gleaming, pewter goblet. They were shaking the entire time, and now they were covered with blood.

Wharf.

I could see an eerie, black flame at the center of the cup. My hands shivered, and I felt the cold for the first time. I looked ahead to the window to try and take my mind off of what was happening.

It was snowing outside. But there was no difference between the cold raging outside and the cold dominating the house. I felt the sting of tears and watched as pitch-black misted from my hands. I was hardly more than a skeleton, covered in bruises, cuts, and cigarette burns. I winced and let the tears flow, just as I let the manna flow.

The goblet started to overflow with purple liquid. Bubbles

formed and began to burst as they met eye level.

Pop. Pop. Pop.

Some released shimmering lights. Others made it feel warmer in the house. Each one seemed like its own little miracle.

For a moment, there was comfort.

But the pale woman's eyes just stared down at the goblet, and starlight appeared at the bottom of the glass. Once the last bubble *popped*, lights had shone on the ceiling. I looked at the woman, and I was terrified. She was mesmerized.

I looked to my side, and the boy was furious.

"Congratulations, Adrian Hive. You are an Alchemist. And you're the Wizard. The one we've been looking for."

***

"Get up!" The pale woman shouted.

We were outside, with the wind whipping in my face. I stood over a mound of snow that was dotted with flecks of crimson. Hardly a day had passed since my previous vision. I was sure of it.

"I'm trying!" I pleaded.

I felt a terrible clawing pain over my eye.

"You're going to stay out here in the cold all night until you get it right!"

"Can I at least put on a jacket? It's freezing."

"You're going to master this spell. Now use your manna to kill this man."

I looked forward and saw that the cold was already close to claiming a man bound to an ancient tree. His body had been melded into the trunk, and he was bleeding profusely.

"I don't care how you kill him. Just use your manna to end his life. His kind will only die that way."

I closed my eyes and desperately tried to think of a way out of this. My hands shook as I tried to think of a way to fight back.

But the cold made my bones shake, and my teeth chatter. I would have done anything to get out of that miserable cold.

I held my hands together just to try and get warm. Looking up at that woman's yellow eyes, I knew there was no way she'd let me out of the snow until I fulfilled her orders.

"*CONTUNDITO!*" I shouted.

My voice carried through the tops of frozen trees.

CRACK!

I looked ahead and saw the face of the man in the tree was malformed. The pale woman with yellow eyes looked ahead and gave the faintest smile.

"Good," she whispered.

***

"I can't keep doing this," I wept.

"She's been working for you for almost two weeks. Just kill whoever she puts in front of you," Walden ordered.

"I can't keep doing this," I cried again.

"You can, and you will. I can't help you against her."

"You always helped me before."

"You need to get yourself out of this. And the people you're killing don't deserve to live anyway. They're less than human."

I closed my eyes and could hear Walden walking out the door.

Creak.

SLAM.

I was alone. I tried to remember my parent's faces, but I couldn't. All that pain I was put through was so terrible, I wasn't even sure I wanted to see them again. For letting this happen to me.

"Don't cry, little one," a woman whispered.

It wasn't cruel and raspy like the pale woman. I looked up and saw a woman in a black vest, black skirt, and white shirt. Her hands were protruding from the darkness, one crossed over the other. But her head was obscured by shadow.

"You've been here for some time, haven't you?" she asked.

"I have."

"I can make it better. We are bound together. Call me Ciershea. I'm your Companion."

***

"Your Companion arrived, and you still can't do it," the pale woman lamented.

"There's clearly nothing you can teach us," Ciershea whispered.

"What did you say, Dullahan?!"

"Adrian is a good boy, and you're just torturing him because you can't be bothered to teach him."

"I was tasked by the Order with expanding his abilities. And you won't stop me."

TROAAAAAAAM.

A silver semblance enveloped Ciershea, and she simply held still.

"This has never happened before," the pale woman whispered.

"Pathetic. Adrian let's break this woman in half," Ciershea whispered.

I felt a swell of fear, and then desire coursed through me.

"Hive. Stand down," the pale woman demanded.

TROAAAAAAAM.

I held my scarred hands up. The pale woman's head began

to shake. She started bleeding from her eyes and nose.

"Ciershea..." I whispered.

"You were told to kill people who outlived their usefulness, Adrian. Now's your chance," the Dullahan whispered.

I focused on this woman who had tortured me for weeks.

"STO—"

QUELCH!

***

"That could have gone better," I lamented.

"Don't worry. The Order has been looking for any reason to get rid of that tiresome woman," Ciershea assured.

"The Order was already hesitant about introducing me to the Witch. They'll never do it now."

"I heard a rumor that she was on her way to Detroit, without the Order's help."

"That's impossible. They wouldn't let the Witch out of their sight. And, if there's any truth to what the Order has told us, she's all the way in Dublin."

"Perhaps. But this one is gifted in turning invisible. It was her first feat after the Alignment. And she's been making great use of it."

"When did you hear these rumors?"

"Nearly a month ago. And I expect she's on her way here. Nobody has seen her in some time."

"What was her name, again?"

"Mila Hollyheart," a sweet voice answered.

I turned around fast and saw that a red-headed elf was sitting in the dead oak tree behind me. She *shimmered* into view, going from invisible to fully visible in seconds. Her legs kicked back and forth like a child without care.

"You're the Witch? How did you get here?" I demanded.

"Evanescent. They were kind enough to give me a one-way trip."

"The company that teleports people? I thought the Order tied up all the loose ends," I pondered.

"Apparently not. Here she is," Ciershea admired.

"That's nothing compared to killing Wilhemina Lovecraft. Did you want your family's book returned?" Mila asked.

"She was torturing me," I corrected.

"Perhaps we should get to know each other. The Spectrum certainly thinks we should."

Mila leaped down from the greying oak tree and landed with a graceful *brush*. She held out her hand, and I took it. It was a firmer grip than I expected. As we shook hands, a white rabbit emerged from behind her skirts.

"Who's that?" I asked.

"My Companion. Flanagan the Puca."

***

"Is this what you want, Adrian?" Ciershea asked.

"I want a chance to have something of my own," I insisted.

I looked down and realized that many years had passed. I was far taller than I was before.

"Dahlia is the best thing that ever happened to me," I whispered.

I looked down at a gorgeous woman. One that looked a great deal like Beatrice. She had porcelain skin, blonde hair, and a slight blush across her nose.

"I want to have a life with her," I insisted.

"What about the life you have with me? I've been your Companion for so long," the Dullahan whispered.

I looked up to the headless woman. She always wore that black vest, white shirt, and pendant.

"You will always be a part of me," I wept.

"But you need somebody to live for. Believe me, I understand," Ciersha insisted.

"Ciershea. You've looked after me all these years. And everything I have is because of the love you have for me. I never would have survived childhood if it wasn't for you."

"You always had your brother. And I took his place as your protector. I know it's selfish to ask for anything more after that."

"I need to find room in my life for you and Dahlia. You're my Companion. She's my wife."

I leaned down and let my scarred hand stroke Dahlia's silky hair.

"Maybe there is a way," Ciershea whispered.

She reached down and gently caressed my hand.

"Love her. And let me protect you."

***

"I'm home!" I called out.

Silence.

I walked through every room in the house, and I desperately tried to find someone. The house had never been this quiet. Ciershea said she would be here before I was. I wasn't sure how I knew that, but I knew it.

Yet, I didn't see any sign of her.

"Ciershea?" I called.

I detected the faint smell of rot. My body froze.

"No. No. No," I whispered.

I rounded the corner and ran to the nursery.

Beatrice was crying. Today was her first birthday. And she

was covered in blood.

"No—" I shuddered.

Pilf. Pilf. Pilf.

The hushed sounds of three silenced gunshots rang out, and I was getting colder. Each shot was followed by green flashes. I fell to my knees. Beatrice was more horrified than I had ever seen anyone.

"I'm sorry," I whispered.

I turned around and saw Ash. He was smiling down on me. I attempted to raise my hands.

"*Consume magicae...*" I whispered.

He stomped my hands down with enough force to break the bones in my fingers.

GELCH. GELCH.

Beatrice screeched.

I felt my coat fly open. Ash started shuffling through my pockets. He slowly removed something.

"Gotcha," Ash whispered.

"No," I whispered.

Beatrice continued screaming.

"You really were a perfect match for this book. It goes with your black heart," Ash whispered.

Ash tried to open the Necronomicon and his gaze flashed from the book to Beatrice.

Ash was silent as Beatrice spent what little strength she had left crying.

"You bastard," Ash started. "You didn't..."

Beatrice was heaving with exhaustion, looking to the ground.

"You made that little girl the rightful owner of this book?"

Ash asked. "I honestly thought you'd give it to Dorian."

Beatrice looked my way, and I felt the life draining out of me.

Ash looked at the book. His face was contorted in defeat. Beatrice continued to look at me with those sweet, blue eyes.

"I'm sorry," I whispered.

My eyes went dark.

***

I looked up with my own eyes. My essence was held in my hand, clutched close to my body, and tufts of gold were shooting out in every direction. I saw Beatrice weeping, only this time with red eyes.

"Grandpa? Martin? Which one are you?" Beatrice asked.

The tears streamed down her face.

"I'm sorry," I whispered.

I raised my essence forward and issued a command. A deeper, more ancient voice following my own.

"*Consume magicae!*" I roared.

Beatrice burst with pink light and was thrown back. The radiated black energy seeping from the runes in the floor reached out and began to tear at Beatrice one at a time.

Her body was not affected, but the ground was absorbing her manna. With each passing blow, she sank to the floor. In seconds, she was unable to even react to the remaining thrashes.

Her pink semblance was almost gone. The roaring fire of her manna reduced to a faint flicker at her center.

A terrible heat took to the floor. Ali rose up and watched in terror as Beatrice lay there, unable to move a muscle. She lay back and was hardly able to stay awake.

Finally, the runes burned away into nothing. There wasn't even a faint outline to capture the general shape of what lay there before.

Just a horrible stain.

My essence retreated back into my hand, and I watched the pitch-black skin of my hand regain life. I could hear the faint *whispers* of a thousand voices as the light came back into my hand. I could hear them more clearly as my senses returned to me. I was finally myself again.

I took a deep breath.

"Martin!" Ali shouted.

"Ali?" I asked.

"Are you all right?"

"Not at all."

I looked at Beatrice.

"Not at all," I repeated.

Thirty Four

Aftermath

"Here's some tea," Dorian offered.

He sat beside me and offered me a small tin cup. I kept looking at the ground. An entire life, Adrian's life, unfolded in front of me, and it wasn't mine. And yet, it was. Even on the ride back to the Silk Slipper, nothing felt real. Sitting there now didn't feel real, either.

I took a sip of the tea without even realizing it.

"It's not Earl Grey," I whispered.

"You sound just like him," Dorian smiled.

I looked up at him.

"Like Adrian," I finished.

"He wouldn't touch it unless it was Earl Grey, either."

"There's a lot you didn't tell us," Ali whispered.

"I didn't know about Beatrice," Dorian admitted.

Silence.

"How could you not know about your mentor's granddaughter?" Ali asked.

"Because Adrian made a point of keeping her secret. He knew that he made some enemies just by being the Wizard, and he wanted to ensure his family was safe. He kept them a secret his whole life. He probably never told them about magic, either."

My mind flashed to when the Necronomicon was stolen. It felt like I kept more secrets than even Dorian could uncover.

"How could he lead a double life like that?" I asked.

I'm one to talk.

"It must have been difficult. I never once heard him mention them. And it was for their own protection. At least that's what the Order gathered when they got to the scene."

"Where was this?" Ali asked.

"It was in Detroit. Where Adrian grew up."

"Did keeping his family a secret really help them?" I asked. "How do we know our parents won't end up dead like that?"

I felt the burn of my eyes trying to form tears. I had just shed enough tears befitting two lifetimes. I couldn't conjure any more.

"No. It made everything worse. And that's why your family is safe."

"Adrian's family died because he was the Wizard," I insisted.

"He lost his family because he didn't tell them the truth. If he told them who he was, the Order would have done everything to protect them. His enemies found out and used that mistake against him. They thought that it would soften him up enough to take him down for good. He must have been vulnerable. Then they killed him."

I remembered that horrible sound and that slight feeling at the back of my head.

Pilf. Pilf. Pilf.

I reached a hand behind my head and felt that it was still intact. The faint *tingle* of reliving that moment still made my hand shake as I reached for it.

"You have no idea how Beatrice managed to survive the attack on Adrian's home?" Ali asked.

"No," Dorian admitted.

"It's because she was taken," I answered.

"You must have experienced *concurrence*," Dorian explained.

"What's that?" I asked.

"It means you saw into the life of another Wizard," Dorian explained.

"But what does it mean? Why did his essence go back?" Ali asked.

"It must have come back to you because the essence was afraid. It had not known anything outside of Martin and wanted to go back. Not to mention it was being rejected by Beatrice. It was drawn to what it knew and repulsed by who desired to harm it," Dorian explained.

Silence.

"Dorian. There was something else. I remembered there was some kind of noise coming from inside my essence. But I don't remember that happening with anyone else that I detected. It sounded like people were calling out to me."

Silence.

"Adrian was not the only Wizard. Both of you reincarnate when you die."

"But I thought Witches and Wizards could extend their lifespan?" Ali started.

"They make a lot of enemies. And it passes on to all manner

of magical species. It's extremely rare for a Witch and Wizard to last much longer than their usual lifespan because someone or *something* usually gets to them."

I thought of Ash.

"I saw myself pass away. While I was holding onto the essence. Ash killed Adrian, stole the Necronomicon, and kidnapped Beatrice."

"But why her?" Dorian asked.

"Because she was meant to inherit the Necronomicon," I explained.

Silence.

"And Beatrice wanted to revive her grandfather. Ash must have thought that if Beatrice unlocked the rest of the book, he'd be able to use it as a weapon."

"But who would go to these lengths to make Beatrice take up this mantle?" Ali asked. "It couldn't just be Ash."

"The Order is already doing some digging," Dorian said. "They want to meet with you at another Summit gathering to discuss what's happened."

I looked to the ground, knowing there was one more thing I had to do.

"Is she all right?" I asked.

"She tried to rip your essence out, and you want to see if she's okay?" Ali asked.

"Yes."

"I'm going in with you."

"Fine. I just want to see her."

Dorian looked at both of us like we were crazy.

"I don't think she's capable of harming anyone. Her body is completely exhausted, and she has no manna to cast spells.

That last spell Martin used really did a number on her."

Dorian got up and led us to the back room. The Silk Slipper was still getting packed up for all the secrets it had hidden inside. I also saw that every Watchman who had come here to condemn Dorian at the Riverwalk had returned. This time, they were tearing the operation down.

"Our work is finished here," Dorian assured.

Dorian held up the Necronomicon. In the corner was a crimson fingerprint. Beatrice's fingerprint.

"Are you sure we can trust them? If Ash could get away with it for so long, maybe they're here to harm us," Ali warned.

"Don't worry," Dorian assured, "they're just as shell-shocked by the news as I was. They want to make up for what they've done. And they thought it best to serve you. Even a High Watchman's orders would come in second to your wishes now."

Banner stood in front of the room where Beatrice was being held.

"I'm so sorry for..." he began.

"Out of the way," I demanded.

"Of course," Banner excused.

Banner stood to the side.

Dorian led us to the backroom where Beatrice was being held. The room felt colder as I came inside. There was a solitary heating lamp, but it did little for warmth or illumination. I saw Beatrice lying there on one of the makeshift beds.

She was still beautiful.

"I don't know why you're doing this," Ali whispered.

"Because I have to," I insisted.

Dorian, Ali, and Lyse stood aside.

Alciel perched himself on my shoulder. I walked up to

her, placed a hand on her hair. I knelt down and looked at her.

"I'm sorry this happened to you," I whispered. I was sure this was something both Adrian and I wanted to say.

Alciel clutched my shoulder.

"I'm sorry Adrian couldn't be there when you needed him," I continued. "But I saw you. When I saw through Adrian's eyes, I saw you. And he loved you with everything he was. He just wanted you to live. Even if that meant he was gone."

I didn't expect to finish with that last statement. It came from deep inside me. From deep inside my essence.

I leaned forward. I brushed her hair away and kissed her forehead.

I got up to leave. I knew I would be going home. And Beatrice would be taken to Wayne County jail. Where she'd never be able to get out.

"Martin?" Ali asked.

I didn't answer.

"I'm not going to pretend I know what you're going through, but you can't blame this on yourself," Ali insisted.

"Why not?" I asked. "I could have done something, and she still got hurt."

"There was nothing that you could have done to save her. She trusted the wrong people."

Silence.

"Martin, she loved you. But she also was terrified of people that tried to destroy the Order. And you managed to save them. You saved more people than you know, but you can't save everyone. And it's because she loved you that she didn't tell you a word about what was really going on."

"I don't know why. I just feel like I lost so much."

"That's called surviving. It may not feel like winning. But we made it. Together."

I looked out the window.

It was snowing.

I looked at my sister, and I knew she was right. I embraced Ali and felt her squeeze me tight. She lifted me off the ground. I returned the embrace.

"We've been looking out for each other for a long time. And when you hurt, I hurt."

I closed my eyes and let the tears fall. I knew Ali was doing the same thing. We separated from one another and looked into each other's eyes. Tears were flowing in her eyes as much as they were in mine.

We walked back to Dorian.

"Are you two doing all right?" he asked.

"We just had to talk things over."

"Circumstances have changed," he continued.

"How so?" Ali asked.

"The Order has been trying to come to terms with everything that's happened. Usually, they're able to root out corruption and gather lost artifacts with ease. But whoever is behind all of this is clearly further deep than we could imagine."

"You want us to step in and help?" I asked.

"I want you to. But the Order does not."

"We won't stand back and do nothing," Ali insisted.

"Quite the contrary, there's no denying you were able to see things the rest of us couldn't. No one doubts your talents, which is why we want to accelerate your training."

"Accelerate it? How?" I asked.

"They want you to start traveling."

Silence.

"We can't just uproot our lives."

"It's called the Pilgrimage. Every Witch and Wizard does it," Dorian explained.

"That doesn't mean we want to," I pointed out.

"The Order is going to hold a Summit Gathering in a few weeks, and they want to meet with you to discuss it."

"Do we have a say in the matter?"

"Of course, you do. After what's happened, we have a rare window of opportunity. One where the Order is being forced to listen."

"If we're going to learn about magic, things have to change," I answered.

"And they will," Dorian promised.

"I want to hear it from *them*," I corrected.

THIRTY FIVE

RESOLUTION

"You brought your Nintendo DS to a meeting with the Order?" Ali asked.

"Give me a break. It's been a rough couple of months," I answered.

"You seem like you're in better spirits," Dorian attempted.

"We're still working through it, but we're willing to go to this meeting."

"Good," Dorian added.

"What exactly do they want from us?" Alciel demanded.

"The Order always does this after the first year of the Witch and Wizard being found. The only problem is that it's not usually as... eventful as yours has been. We're doing yours a bit earlier."

"Where exactly are we meeting?" I asked.

"The Detroit Opera House," Dorian admitted.

"At least they know how to make an entrance," Lyse commented.

We were there within ten minutes.

"Just remember to be respectful to them," Dorian warned.

Ali and I got out of the car and saw the majestic theatre was closed for business. But then again, no one comes to see a show at 2:00 am.

Dorian walked up to the door and pulled it slightly by the handle, finding it was locked. He smiled a little at this and placed his hands directly on the door itself.

A purple pulse rang through the entire door, and we could see tumblers and locks illuminated, as if through amplification. They didn't fade as soon as they appeared; they retained their shape and unlocked themselves one at a time.

Finally, the door let out a deep sound.

VOAN.

With that, Dorian opened the door and ushered all of us inside. I walked ahead, and Ali was close behind. Our Companions were sitting on our shoulders. Dorian didn't take a step beyond the threshold.

I stopped.

"This is as far as I go," Dorian answered.

I nodded and continued on. The air was crisp and fresh as we stepped into the main hall. Barren, but curiously beautiful. It was a place that seemed decadent in the darkness. Posters for recent shows were still hanging. Nabucco. Tosca. Don Giovanni.

Ali made her way to the doors first. She never liked opera and didn't even look at the display. She walked straight to the door leading to the main theatre.

I stopped for a moment to look at the red-eyed Don Giovanni on the promotional art just before the last few yards to the door. Those crimson, steely eyes kept staring back at me as if they were the only living thing in this dark palace. In a flash, I thought I saw Beatrice's eyes in the poster.

"You coming?" Ali asked.

Her voice echoed along the halls, and I turned toward her. She looked impatient. I looked back at the poster and saw that the eyes of Don Giovanni were almost comforting now. Sharp, uncompromising, and brutal. Somehow, that was more welcoming than the warm, tender gaze I remembered from Beatrice.

I took a breath and caught up with Ali.

"You okay?" Ali asked.

"I'm fine," I lied.

We opened the doors to a sea of red velvet chairs on the golden coast of the proscenium stage. It was the only room in the entire opera house with lights on.

At its center were the Justices of the Order. Erestor, Parvana, and Sarcodis. All of them dressed in the same robes from the night of Dorian's trial at the Riverwalk. Ali and I looked at each other. We advanced and did not know what to expect.

So, rather than make the first move, we parted to either side of the central chairs and met up at the front seats. The ones that would cost the most had this been a live performance. We sat just before the Order and let them speak first.

"Welcome, Blackbriars," Erestor offered.

"We trust that the journey here was a safe one," Parvana added.

"It has been a heavy burden for both of you, and now is the time to speak," Sarcodis added.

Silence.

"The journey was not safe getting here," I began. "It has been a difficult time for both my sister and me since our Alignment."

"And while we are grateful for the guidance Dorian was able to give us in that time, we have another problem," Ali added.

"And what is that?" Erestor replied.

He interlocked his fingers in front of him as though he was not pleased with our response.

"Dorian believes the people behind the culprit's actions will try to attack us again," Sarcodis remarked. "He relayed his concerns to me right after she was remanded to Wayne County jail."

"Beatrice," I interjected. "Her name...is Beatrice."

Silence.

Parvana looked at me with sympathy. Sarcodis looked impressed at my tone. Erestor looked like he wanted to skin us alive.

"We understand you went through a terrible trauma, Martin," Parvana acknowledged, "but now that the threat of the Necronomicon is removed, we will be able to give you proper instruction in the way of magic. Any discipline you wish. We shall dispatch our finest instructor and move you to a safer location."

"No," we objected.

I looked at my sister, and we knew we agreed before we continued.

"We're not going to take anyone else as a mentor other than Dorian," Ali continued.

"I'm afraid you don't get a choice in the matter," Erestor resisted.

"And I'm afraid you can't force us into learning about this craft the way you want," I added. "Especially not when your actions almost got us *killed*."

Parvana turned to her associates and gently applied pressure between her lips. The tension was getting to her as much as it was to us. She was just much better at hiding it.

"We are starting this meeting poorly," she admitted. "We can't protect you from the rest of the world, but there is more to learn about magic that will help you come into your own and keep you protected. We only have your best interests at heart. And, clearly, we should have consulted you two first before we made our decision."

"Thank you," Ali accepted. "But we have already made our decision."

"And your desire is to be trained by Dorian?" Sarcodis grunted.

"It is," I answered.

"While we admire your tenacity," Sarcodis started, "you must understand that as Witch and Wizard, your duties will take you elsewhere."

Ali and I looked at each other.

"And while we will do our best to balance your duties to your household and your duties to this Order, we will have to work in tandem to achieve that balance."

"We're willing to move around so long as it doesn't rob us of the chance to have a normal life," Ali offered.

"We will learn under Dorian's teachings," I finalized.

The Order looked to one another.

"And that is your final decision?" Erestor asked.

"It is," we concluded.

"Very well. Dorian shall act as your instructor. You are to remain in Detroit, until you are called. And you are to carry out your duties as they arise. You are excused."

The Justices stood and offered slight bows. We returned them.

"And remember," Erestor began, "you are not to use your

abilities to try and exact any petty vendettas. There is no room for personal vengeance within this Order."

Erestor looked at me when he said this.

"We trust you to make the right choice. So, don't challenge us," he added.

I nodded and left.

Ali and I separated and left for the doors on the opposite side of the room. But as soon as we turned our backs to the Order, we heard a faint noise. It was so quiet, we almost missed it.

FOOSH.

We turned around and saw the Order and their chairs were gone. I looked to Ali, and we both knew we had a long way to go. We abandoned the musty darkness of the Detroit Opera house. We returned to the sharp smell of Dorian's cigarettes on Broadway Street.

"Let's get you kids home," Dorian insisted.

We made our way back to Dorian's Ford F-150.

"How did that go?" Dorian asked.

"We insulted them, and we walked out," Ali confirmed.

"I can't believe you defied the Order's order and got away with it," Dorian smiled.

"That's never happened before?" Ali asked.

"It's happened. It just never goes well," Dorian supplied.

"Well, I say we celebrate," Ali continued.

"How about we grab something to eat?" Dorian offered.

Dorian pointed to a crooked sign in the middle of the street.

"O'Conner's? It's closed?" I pointed out.

I pointed to the sign, for good measure.

"This place never closes," Dorian corrected.

Dorian walked up and placed his hand on the door, just

as he had with the opera house. A small tumbler sounded as a common door would. He pushed it open with the slight sound of a bell.

Ring.

To our surprise, a large man was standing behind a bar cleaning glasses.

"It's two o'clock in the morning," I pointed out.

"And Brian never really sleeps," Dorian added.

"Good to see you again, Dorian," Brian answered.

He had the thickest Irish accent I'd ever heard. He looked up and saw the two of us.

"So, these are the two that defied the Order?" he asked.

"That's us!" Ali answered.

She held up her hand, awkwardly, as though she was answering a question in class.

"Anyone who can stand up to them gets a pint!"

The large man reached down and immediately grasped six glass pints and threw them across the table. They landed precisely at each of the barstools.

"That's very impressive," I admitted.

I took a seat at my pint, and we all worked our way across the table.

"Not all that impressive, really. Lookie here."

He lifted the pint with his colossal hand and revealed there was a rune just underneath. A slight shimmer of lime-green made it appear and disappear.

"*Magnet* rune," he smiled.

"Oh, that reminds me," Dorian said. "No need for formalities now that Detroit is sleeping."

"You make a fair point," Brian nodded.

He then began to shake his head as though he was desperate to try and stay awake. Brian's face soon became thicker, and his beard fuller. He gained four arms, had his abdominal muscles replaced with a gut, and his accent got even heavier.

"I love it when I can finally take the uniform off!"

Dorian and Brian shared a laugh.

"Brian's a good shapeshifter," Dorian smiled. "And an even better bartender."

"Which reminds me...." Brian answered.

He took one hand, made a fist, and a shimmer of limelight came from the center of his palm. He tried to contain it, but the stronger he held it in an arm-wrestling stance, the more our drinks began to appear. Our steins filled all the way, leaving a bit of foam at the top.

"Mom's going to kill us when she finds out we've been drinking," I said.

"Then let's not die sober," Ali celebrated.

She quickly pressed her pint into mine and began drinking it without hesitation.

Clink.

Brian chuckled.

"Martin," Dorian added.

"Yeah?" I asked.

Dorian's eyes had gone soft. He seemed close to tears.

"Happy birthday," he smiled.

Clink.

We struck our glasses together. All seemed right with the world amid the bitter cold and the warm Christmas lights.

ACKNOWLEDGEMENTS

Some of my earliest memories are of my mother reading to me. It didn't matter what the book was. I just remember pages turning, her smiling, and me falling in love with literature.

While I'm grateful to so many authors, my mother was the one who taught me that true magic comes from literature and reading it to people who need it most.

This passion extended to all my most cherished relationships. My hero, Livi. My beloved, Denae. My ally, Taylor. And my illustrator, B. Jung.

All of them transformed this book from a story of a troubled past, and turned it into the beginning of a larger world.

ABOUT THE AUTHOR

T.C. Pendragon was born and raised in Michigan. Whenever he isn't writing, he is certainly dreaming of putting pen to paper. This is his first book he's published, but certainly not the first book he's written.

ABOUT THE ILLUSTRATOR

B. Jung has had a passion for all things fantasy ever since she was very young. She has prolific artistic talents, often breathing life into the works of friends. She lives in Illinois.